LONDON ROYAL

NANA MALONE

COPYRIGHT

This is a work of fiction. Names, characters, places, and incidents either are the product of the author's imagination or are used fictitiously, and any resemblance to actual persons living or dead, business establishments, events, or locales, is entirely coincidental.

London Royal

Cover Art by Staci Hart

Edited by Angie Ramey and Michele Ficht

Published in the United States of America

London Soul
Royal Playboy
Playboy's Heart
Big Ben
The Benefactor
For Her Benefit

Present...

Lex...

I didn't care what I had to do; I would protect the woman I loved with my dying breath.

Nothing was going to change. I'd promised her that.

I'd told her I'd love her forever, which was true. I *would* love her forever. I'd told her I would protect her.

But that was a lie.

Now that my mother's cousin had been assassinated, I was a prince. An *official* prince of Nomea. No longer exiled. No longer banished from a home I'd never known. Now the woman I loved would be subject to the court of public opinion.

Just like before.

And whether or not I liked it, people *would* have opinions, and they'd post about them. In the press, on social media, and to anyone who would listen. That was what had happened the last time my family was in the public eye.

Well, they were entitled to their opinions. If need be, I'd step aside to shield her from as much scrutiny as possible. I would step away from the birthright I'd never asked for. For her, I'd give up anything. For her, I'd give up *everything*.

She looked up from the conversation she was having next to one of my favorite pieces of her artwork at the gallery opening. The smile she gave me was brilliant.

She'd done it. She'd opened her own bloody gallery simply known as *Nartey*. She was going to feature some of her work, but mostly works of up-and-coming artists. I couldn't have been more proud of her. She grinned at me, the white of her teeth a perfect contrast to her gleaming brown skin.

God, I loved her.

Even as she chatted animatedly with the woman she was speaking to, she snuck peeks at me. I could tell she wanted to run up to me. She wanted to hold me. Just like I wanted to hold her. I'd planned this surprise for months.

But I had more than one reason for being there. I needed to let her know that everything was about to change.

When she was finally finished, Abena Nartey Chase made no bones about running up and leaping into my arms. The white dress she wore with the thigh high slits helped her achieve her goal.

I didn't give a shit that we were making a scene. She was my wife, and I planted a kiss on her so deep we made the stuffed shirts blush.

When she pulled back, she looped her arms around my neck. "Hello, handsome. I didn't think you'd be here."

"Did you really think you were going to have a gallery opening and I wasn't going to attend?"

"No, but I knew how complicated things in the Winston Isles were."

I nodded slowly. "*Were*. I'm home."

"Well, welcome home. In that case, the celebration is going to be different than I originally planned."

I lifted a brow. "Oh, yeah? Just what did you have planned?"

"Well, originally, I was going to take the other artists out to a simple dinner, toast with champagne, and pay the bill. Or rather, *you* were going to foot the bill."

I sighed. "Remember, my money is your money."

"Yeah, you know how I don't like that."

I rolled my eyes. It was an old argument, but I left that fight alone for now. "So, what's the change of plan?"

She leaned forward, close to my ear. "Well now, there's definitely going to be a deep throat blow job happening."

I pulled back and clutched a hand to my chest as if I was shocked. "Jesus Christ, who's the lucky guy?" She giggled, and I twirled her around. "I love you."

"I love you too, Alexi." When we stopped moving, a frown settled in her expression as she studied my face. "What's the matter?"

I forced my face into an impassive expression. "What do you mean?"

"Stop it. I know when something is wrong. What's the matter? Is Xander okay?"

I knew my brother Xander had rushed to his wife Hermione's side as soon as he'd gotten the news. Neither one of us wanted our wives hearing about this situation before we had the chance to tell them about it ourselves. "Yeah, he's fine. He's with Hermione Aysem."

She frowned. "He couldn't be bothered to come to my opening?"

I laughed and shook my head, wondering about their odd brother-and-sister-like relationship. It never bothered me.

Lies.

Okay fine, Xander's feelings for her *had* bothered me in the beginning. But that had been resolved long ago. I knew my brother was madly in love with his wife, though he and Abbie still fought like cats and dogs most of the time. "Listen babes—"

Her brow lifted. "Babes? You only say that when you have some bad news to tell me."

"Yeah. Listen, um, can we speak somewhere privately?"

I couldn't help but let my gaze skitter to a man near the door. He was long and lean like me. And looked more than ready for a fight to break out.

Matthias Weller had been more than happy to come home to England with his fiancée. He was on loan from Blake Security temporarily until Xander and I could get our own security team in place. I knew under his impeccable suit he was covered in tattoos.

I didn't know him well, but we'd gotten to chat a little bit on the flight over. My cousin, Sebastian Winston, King of the Winston Isles, had insisted we have the best security with us until we could sort out other measures. Abbie was no fool though, and her gaze followed mine in Matthias's direction. "Why does that look like security at the door, sweetheart?"

I cleared my throat. "Listen, something has happened."

She stepped back. "Let me get my things."

I stopped her though. "No, you don't need to hurry off. It's your opening. You need to enjoy it. But Matthias is going to be with us for a while, as is his fiancée."

She frowned. "That guy has a fiancée? He looks just as likely to eat someone as he does to date them."

I glanced over at him. He did have that *I am a fucking badass* look on his face. "Yeah okay, fair enough. But listen, we don't need to talk about this now. Enjoy the opening. I'll talk to you after."

She shook her head. "No. You tell me what's going on now."

I sighed and then tugged her through the main gallery room and into one of the offices. She crossed her arms over her chest, having no idea that all it did was push up her tits and make my brain take a non-escapable detour.

Focus man.

I dragged my gaze back to hers.

"Sweetheart, if you wanted to get some..."

"Ah, I wish that's why we were in here, but it's not." I cleared my throat. "My mother's cousin, the King of Nomea, has been assassinated."

Her jaw unhinged. "Fuck."

I nodded slowly. "We don't know who did it. We don't know why. But that means I need you covered in case there's any kind of retaliation."

"So that guy out there is supposed to cover me?"

I nodded slowly. "Yes, him and his fiancée."

"What's going on, Alexi?"

"I don't know. I honestly don't. All I know is, right now, you are mine to protect. And I would do that with my life."

"So, this makes you a prince now?"

He nodded slowly. "Yeah, since he had no children and he wasn't married, that means my mother is, by default, Queen of Nomea. But he's got followers who, no doubt, will retaliate if they think that my mother's people had anything to do with it."

"Jesus."

"Yeah, I know. But listen, I don't want you to worry about anything. We're going to get a team. You will be protected."

She squeezed my hand. "Alexi, I'm so sorry."

I frowned. "What do you mean?"

"I know this isn't what you wanted."

"Look, I will step down today if it means my title puts you in danger. Besides, I'm only the spare."

"I know how this works. You might be the spare, but you've only ever wanted your freedom. And now, you're going to be under all the scrutiny in the world."

"*We* are."

"I know. And I could take it. I just—I know you didn't want this."

I shrugged. "Look, when you met me, there were all kinds of things I didn't want. There were things I didn't even know I *did* want. One of them was you. So, as long as I have you, I don't care what happens. As long as you're safe, I'll count my lucky stars."

"You and me against the world?"

I pulled her close and tucked my arms around her. "Yup, you and me against the world."

What I wasn't going to remind her of was just what I was willing to do and what I was capable of if it meant keeping her safe. She was mine. *Forever.* And if anyone threatened that, they'd end up the same way the last guy had.

FIVE YEARS EARLIER...

"To my prince of a brother, while it may not yet be your twenty-fifth birthday, we're going to celebrate all bloody year. You are a little prince amongst men, and I couldn't have a better brother."

I laughed at Xander even as I raised my glass. "Thank you for the toast, Xan. Except, I'm *not* a prince."

He chuckled then. "Oh, we both are. Just, you know, we don't actually have the country or the crowns to go with it, but I lay claim to it all the time. Particularly with the fairer sex."

I rolled my eyes as our friends guffawed around us. We were at yet another nameless club. The latest hotspot. For us, the booze flowed freely, and the women came easily. I loved my brother and my mates, but lately when we went out, I wondered exactly what the purpose was. Maybe I'd enjoyed more than was my fair share of the parties and I was bored stiff.

All around us, there were girls. Tall ones, short ones, beautiful ones. Everyone was stunning in their own way. Most were wearing next to nothing and offering to blow us for access to the

VIP area. They knew who we were, and we preferred *not* to know who they were.

If you're so bored, why do you keep coming out?

That was a good question. The number of nights that I'd been tempted to just beg off and stay home was plenty. But still, the truth of it was that it was better to be with people than alone in my own box. That wasn't ideal. So, I went out.

All around me, my friends were drinking and having a good time. At one point, Jasper crash-landed on my lap. "Come on, give us a kiss, birthday boy."

The scent of alcohol oozed out of his pores, and I shoved his face away. "No. God, how much have you had, mate?"

Jasper chuckled, splashing whatever clear liquid that was in his glass onto his hand. "Why are you asking such questions? We were pre-gaming for your birthday party."

"Jas, it's not my birthday yet. I've got over a month left."

"Yeah, mate, I know. But luckily your brother is a party connoisseur, like myself, and believes that we should party at least three months in advance. Which I can get behind."

"Of course, you can. You realize we basically do this every weekend anyway, right?"

He grinned at me sloppily. "Did you have a point, mate?"

I shook my head. "No. No point. Having fun?"

He grinned and slapped me on the chest several times. "Yup. Having a blast. I'm going to go find a very pretty blonde and have her sit on my lap instead of me sitting on yours. You're not as pretty, sorry."

Bullshit. I was fucking pretty. "No offense taken."

He tried to climb up on his own, but eventually, I had to shove him up off of me. My brother leaned over the back of the couch I was sitting on. "Are you having fun, baby brother?"

"Yeah, are you?" I tried not to slide my gaze to his drink. But it was difficult.

You don't have to take care of him anymore.

It's not like it would help. But Xander was different now, no longer trying to numb his pain with pills and booze. A year ago, I had been chasing after him, worrying about him, trying to get the booze out of his hands and keep the drugs out of his nose.

But he'd gotten a handle on things. He'd stopped with the drugs and seriously pulled back on the alcohol. I didn't even think he liked the drugs. They'd just been something to do, and then eventually they'd become something he needed to function. But when I'd managed to get a camera back into his hands, he'd quit.

The drinking now was more of the social variety. But still, the memory of that time, trying to keep him from killing himself, was stamped fresh on my frontal lobe, and I couldn't shake it.

He caught my gaze then lifted his glass toward me. "Just the one. It's *your* birthday. *You* get to celebrate."

I shook my head. "Nah, mate. I'm just not in a celebratory mood yet. Got a lot on my mind."

He nodded. "Dear old dad?"

"Ah, it's like you've met him. He's a right downer, isn't he?"

"Yeah. That's his job, being a total arse. But try and enjoy this. Birthdays come only once a year."

"This coming from the bloke who insists I celebrate all year? Who celebrates their birthday like that?"

"We do. We're the Chase brothers, and we can do whatever the fuck we want. So if you want to celebrate your birthday all goddamn year, we can. After all, we are royalty, aren't we?"

I snorted. "Forgotten princes of a forgotten land."

He clinked his glass with mine, "Uh, don't forget *exiled* and forgotten princes. Ahh, imagine what it would be like if our dear old ancestors hadn't been ousted. How different do you think shit would be?"

I laughed. "Not much different. Except there would probably be more people telling us what to do."

He wrinkled his nose then. "Ugh! Never mind all that then. As you know, I can't stand to be told what to do. I like my freedom."

We clinked glasses again. "Me too, brother, me too."

Sure, I liked money. I liked making it. I just didn't want to make it for the old man. Nor did I want to get into royal politics. Unlike others in my family, I wasn't obsessed with getting our crown back.

Let other men fight for the crown. I didn't want it. Hell, I wasn't even the oldest brother. The crown, or the lack thereof, was of no consequence to me. No, I needed something else to fill the hole in my chest. I didn't know what the hell was wrong with me. I needed some air, some space, something. I pushed out of my seat and tapped Xander on the shoulder. "Mate, I think I'm done."

My brother frowned. "What? We just got here. It's only been a few hours."

I laughed. "Yeah, I know. I'm done. Tell Nick for me, would you?"

He studied me. "Something's up with you Lex. You're not talking to me."

"Nah, I'm good."

He went serious then, and I knew he could sense it. I was off. He and I had always been thick as thieves. We weren't twins, but that sense of when the other was in trouble, we both felt it. That's what happened when you shared the darkness. You knew when the other one was going under.

"I'll come with you."

I shook my head. "Nah, stay. Have fun."

Xander chuckled and then shrugged. "You know, fun for me is waking up at five thirty in the morning and chasing the sunlight. This is not conducive to that."

I rolled my eyes. "Don't you have classes starting soon?"

He nodded. "I have to teach a bunch of runts how to do what I do. But chances are, none of them will be extraordinary, or at most, there will only be one."

"Ah, you're such a cynic."

"No, I'm a realist."

"I hear you. Look, let me find Nick. I'll say goodbye and then I'm just going to head home."

He gave me a nod. "Fine. Call me in the morning, yeah? I'll pick you up and we'll go for a run."

I grinned at him. "You're going to let me kick your ass again?"

"You never kick my ass." He gave me his trademark smirk.

"Oh, yes, I do."

"In that case, you're on. I should probably stop drinking then."

"You realize I can still kick your ass hungover, right?"

The raised brow and the self-important smirk told me Xander was okay. We clasped palms and gave each other a half hug, and then I wound my way to the VIP section to look for Nick. I headed through the back hallway toward the patio where they let everyone smoke without actually having to leave the club. There was no one on the patio, but when I turned, something caught my gaze. Suddenly, the hairs at the back of my neck stood at attention and I frowned. *What the hell?*

Someone was out there. I narrowed my gaze. And then I felt it, the shadow behind me, and I whirled on the balls of my feet, hands up, ready to defend or attack.

Unfortunately, when I moved, whoever was behind me moved too, so I only caught a brief glimpse before the attack happened.

A fist punched straight to my kidneys, and I howled.

I whipped around and fired off an elbow in the general vicinity of my attacker.

The guy *oomphed*, and I was ready to turn the tables on him. But once I was facing him, ready to go in for the attack, I heard footsteps behind me.

Multiple attackers. Fucking fantastic.

The guy in front of me swept out a leg, trying to sweep me off my feet, but my stance was strong. With a couple of quick jabs, I snapped his head back and moved in for the quick kill. Forearm on his neck, my other arm blocking his free one and attacking. I delivered a couple of knees and then, grabbing onto shirt and skin with my bar arm hand and using my block arm for momentum, I turned his whole body around, so I could see my other attacker. Striking him like this, I could deliver all the blows I needed. I could also keep my eye on whoever else was coming for me.

He was my height. Over six feet, dark hair, thicker build though. My mother used to tell me I was whipcord lean. So, I might not be as big, but I'd learned a long time ago that I needed to be deadly.

When he refused to go down, I adjusted my hold and grabbed his face with both hands, pressing my thumbs into his eye sockets. When he leaned back, trying to save his sight and exposing his throat, I punched him, and down he went.

His partner was coming at me next, and he was also quick on his feet.

I was weaving. I'd had too much to drink for this. But like hell was I going down that easy. I knew what it was like to be helpless and alone. It wasn't going to happen today. "Hey arsehole, you know, we don't have to do this. You can take your girlfriend here and go. I don't want to hurt you."

He smirked and came at me in full-on attack mode.

With his massive frame, he preferred the use of his legs. Taekwondo training was evident. I took some knees. Okay, I'm not going to lie, I took a few punches too. But I gave as good as I got.

I saw someone else coming to the door. *Fuck.* I was losing steam, and I needed to end things quickly.

"What's the matter? Is the little prince tired? We're just going to help you rest. Come with us, and you can rest as long as you like."

Were these my cousin's men? My second cousin was the current king of Nomea. His family had ousted mine from the throne a couple of generations ago.

Why would he be coming after us now? Xander and I hadn't done anything. Just the thought of my brother had me wincing. *Shit.* Xander.

I had to stay alert. What if Xander needed me?

My opening came when the guy delivered a kick to my midsection. I took the brunt of the force, but I also grabbed his leg.

His cocky smirk disappeared quickly as I pulled him off his feet and then launched myself at him. Good old-fashioned ground and pound. Elbows. Punches. I grabbed him by the shirt, and I laid into him. I let the rage take over, the anger; all of it poured out.

Behind me, someone tried to pull me off. And then I could see it, the black bag sliding into my field of vision. I released the guy in front of me, and as he sagged down, I twisted around, determined to avoid the fucking black-bagging.

What the hell was wrong with these people? From my position on the ground, I had nowhere else to go. I didn't really *want* to punch the guy in the nuts, but it was my best line of defense. Elbow backward first, and then I twisted and punched. It didn't take much, and he went down.

Then I was on my feet. The kick I landed sent him several feet back. "Tell my cousin if he wants to come for me, he's going to need more men."

Then I heard a voice from behind me. "Well done. But you really shouldn't play with your food, Alexi."

I released the one on the floor and turned slowly. "Jean Claude?"

My mother's long-time advisor stepped out from the shadows. "You were slow. Lethargic. In the field, that could be dangerous. But you ah..." he glanced around, "recovered quickly. What was this? I taught you a million times, when your cousin comes for you, or anyone looking for ransom for that matter, be efficient, unemotional. This... this was nothing but emotion."

I glowered at my childhood mentor. "This was another test?"

"Of course it was a test. It's all a test, Alexi. At some point, your cousin is going to come for you. He has no children. He will do anything to hold on to his power. You threaten that power, so these scenarios are meant to keep you strong and alive."

I stood and staggered over to the nearest wall, breathing

heavily and deep as two of my assailants groaned and tried to stand. The third wasn't moving at all. I dragged in deep, heavy breaths and watched as his partners went over to him and tried to wake him up. When he finally rolled over, I breathed an extra sigh of relief. I hadn't killed him. "This was for, what? All for a training exercise?"

"Yes," Jean Claude said as he stepped over to me. "And I'm disappointed in how you performed."

I shrugged. "Well, I'm alive. That should be a lesson to you. If you send more assholes after me, I won't be responsible if I kill them. I'm done with your tests. Not long from now, I'll be 25, and you will no longer be my adviser. My father will no longer be in charge of my money, and I won't have to worry about any of this royal bullshit any longer. You've been feeding the same shit to my mom for years that she's going to sit on a throne some-day. Don't you get tired of the false hope? Nomea has a king. And it's never been destined to be me."

"Let's face it. Your brother is unfit. You're the hope. You're the next generation."

I shook him off and headed for the exit. No way was I going to let him see me limp or know that his men had landed one too many good punches. He was trying to prepare me for a future I was never going to have. A future I didn't want. All I wanted was my freedom, and soon it would be mine.

And neither he nor his stupid tests were going to keep me from that.

⸺

Abbie...
Where the hell is it?

I frantically checked the pile of mail. *Bill, bill, advertisement.* Nothing from the University of West London. Worry knotted my stomach. All my other graduate school acceptance and rejection letters had come by now. I'd expected to hear word from them over three weeks ago.

"Hey, Easton, was this all the mail? Was there anything with the packages?" A part of me held on to that last thread of hope.

"Sorry, sweetheart. That's all of it."

My boyfriend, Easton Peters, leaned against the doorjamb between the hallway and the dining room, still dripping from his run, creating little puddles of sweat on the floor. "You have some perfectly good schools to choose from. I don't know why this one is so important to you."

I clenched my teeth and tried not to focus on the fact that, as usual, he didn't support my choice. I also tried not to focus on the tiny puddles. Puddles I'd be expected to clean.

Drip. Drip. Drip.

Instead, I focused on his face. Easton, covered in a sheen of sweat, was still handsome. Perfect, smooth, bronze skin, strong jaw, whiskey-brown eyes. A body that made women salivate. Not to mention, his family was also wealthy enough to sway political turnouts.

My friends liked to remind me how lucky I was to have him. *If only they knew.*

"I know. I need to make a decision, especially if I want to start in August, but I really wanted this program." I inhaled sharply the moment I caught the look of displeasure in his eyes. "But you're right." *No, he's not.* "I'll pick one. If London comes through, I can always pull my acceptance or something."

He frowned, and I braced myself.

Stupid.

Why did I say that? At best, I had a lecture coming. At worst... something else.

Frown lines creased his perfect brow. "Abena, it's bad form to rescind an acceptance. Especially if it's at a school where I pulled strings for you, like Georgetown or George Washington."

I bit the inside of my cheek to keep from snorting at the pulled strings. It wasn't worth the fight. *Keep your cool. Breathe. Don't say anything.* "Of course," I muttered. Ever dutiful. Sometimes I just wanted to scream at myself. Or him...

"Some dreams aren't meant to come true. I mean, let's face it, your photos are okay, but you're not exactly doing gallery openings, are you?"

I bit my tongue. As if I wouldn't have been able to get into those schools on my own. As if his talking to a couple of professors had been the thing that made the admissions boards sit up and take notice. He'd only *just* graduated from law school himself and was an associate with Walters and Logan, a big law firm in town. His family name might have pull, but he, himself, did not. I'd gotten in on my own merit.

But with practiced ease, I kept my thoughts to myself. "I know. I'm sorry. I wouldn't want to do that. I'll think about it carefully."

He snatched up the hem of his sweat-sodden T-shirt and used the material to wipe his brow. The view of his six-pack and strong chest muscles should have had me salivating, should have had me begging to join him in the shower.

Too bad I knew what was under the perfect façade. And it wasn't pretty.

I wanted him to be supportive. I *wanted* him to believe in me. I wanted him to be who he pretended to be. But at the moment, I just wanted him to get into the shower so he would stop dripping on my floor.

"I'm getting in the shower. What's for lunch?"

I swallowed. "I'm making chicken salad."

He sighed, clearly unenthused, but headed off toward the shower anyway.

As much as I hated to admit it, I was deliberately pushing the dates for accepting an offer. Letters of acceptance into law programs from Georgetown, George Washington, John's Hopkins, American University, and University of Maryland all beckoned to me in a neat stack.

But I didn't want to have to think about them. Easton had left them there purposefully, so that every time I walked through our dining room, I'd have to see them. The spiteful part of me yearned to disorder the tiny pile. But I restrained myself.

Petty isn't a good look.

No. It wasn't. And it certainly wasn't becoming of the perfect girlfriend of Easton Peters.

The problem was I didn't *want* to be a lawyer. Sure, it was the natural choice in a family full of them. Both my parents were attorneys. Even my oldest sister, Akosua, was. My middle sister, Ama, had broken the mold to go to medical school, but still, it was a profession the whole family approved of. Not like my passion, photography.

The University of West London had the best MA program in photography in the world. There, I'd have a chance to work with Xander Chase, one of the youngest, most renowned photographers in the world. He'd even exhibited at Hamilton's in London.

Some dreams aren't meant to come true.

Maybe Easton was right. Maybe London was just a pipe dream.

Unless you went on your own.

As quickly as the betraying, insidious thought popped into my head, I shuddered and quashed it. Going on my own wasn't an option. I'd once tried to interview for a job in Los Angeles right out of college. The bruises he'd left on my body had made it very clear that I wasn't going anywhere without him.

I'd been with him since I was sixteen, and he'd come to my school to talk about the benefits of NYU as a college. Even then, everyone had pointed out how lucky I was that a college guy was interested in little ol' me.

That a *Peters* was interested in me.

Then why don't I feel lucky?

Nobody saw what I saw.

He could be sweet. He could be unfailingly kind. We could spend hours talking about nothing. Or debating the merits of superpowers. There were so many happy moments interspersed with the bad that sometimes I wondered if I imagined the bad times.

Like the times when I was afraid or made to feel worthless were phantoms that plagued my mind with lies. Problem was, like phantom limbs, those bad moments sent aches throughout my soul that set like permanent stains.

His sweet moments were like an analgesic that dulled the pain and made me forget it lurked just around a happy corner. His temper was always at the forefront of my mind. But still, despite the fear, there was a part of me that hoped. Hoped he could be different, that I could be.

My phone rang in the kitchen, pulling me out of my reverie.

I raced to grab it, a smile tugging at my lips when I saw who it was on the caller ID. "Hey, Dad."

"Abena, how are you?" My father's baritone voice with its accented English never failed to calm me down.

"Oh, I'm good. Just making some lunch." I stalled, wondering what he was calling about. Neither of us was particularly skilled at small talk. A call from him was not the norm. We always relayed messages through my mother or via text. Nevertheless, I was happy to hear from him. "What's up, Dad?"

He expelled a breath, as if happy to be able to cut to the chase and forego the social niceties of asking what I was making for lunch.

"I need the valuation papers for the condo. I'm trying to up the insurance, given the renovation we just did to the bathroom."

"Sure, I'll grab them." I jogged into the study that Easton had taken over upon moving in and kept an ear out for the sound of the shower turning off. Once Easton was finished, he'd want to eat, so I needed to hurry up with lunch. "One sec, I have no idea what Easton's filing process is."

Quickly, I searched the stack of folders on the desk and found what my father was looking for. As I relayed the information, my gaze landed on the corner of an envelope peeking out from the desk drawer. A Queen Elizabeth stamp was affixed on the thick paper.

"Thank you, sweetheart." My father hesitated. "Are you well? You sound off."

I sighed. His way of asking if I still thought I'd made the right choice by moving in with Easton. My parents had been so against it. After all, in Ghanaian culture, it just wasn't done.

They were so old school. You only moved in with someone after you'd done a traditional engagement ceremony.

The mere thought of marriage made my stomach clench. Not that Easton hadn't hinted it was the next logical step. But every time I thought about it, it felt like someone was tying a noose around my neck.

"I'm fine, Dad," I said as I tried to pull the drawer open. It didn't budge.

"Have you selected a school yet?"

"Uhm..." My voice trailed as I grabbed the letter opener and tried to slide it into the drawer to pop the latch. "I need to. I was hoping to hear from University of West London."

My father harrumphed. "A photography course does not qualify as school."

I could almost see him grumbling and pacing in his office. "Dad, actually, it does. The program is prestigious, and it's at an accredited university."

My father's accented voice pitched lower. "Abena, what do you think you're going to do with a master's in photography? You're *supposed* to go to law school." Of course, to Ghanaian parents, the only appropriate professions and worthwhile educational pursuits included law, medicine, and engineering. I ignored the prick of pain his disappointment caused. I was used to it by now.

"Dad. You already have one daughter who's a lawyer. Besides, with the photography, there's a lot I'm planning to do. With a recommendation from my professor, opportunities in production would open for places like National Geographic and a career in documentary films."

And I was sure a recommendation from Xander Chase *would* open those kinds of doors. But I didn't care about those doors. What I was after was the apprentice position offered to his top student.

"Abena, you can't put all your eggs into one basket. You have to have a backup plan."

"I know. I know. I'll be looking at all the offers tonight, and I'll make a decision by the weekend." I could only hope and pray that the acceptance came before then. I really only had two more days to stall.

The drawer opened with a splintering pop, and for a second I was worried I'd broken it, but it slid smoothly on its grooves. My father mentioned something about my sister, but I had already tuned him out. I pulled out the envelope with its maroon stamp of the queen, and my breath caught. With my blood rushing in my ears, I carefully scanned the return address.

University of West London.

Twice, my brain tried to make my lips cooperate. Twice, it failed. On the third attempt, I managed with a shaky breath, "Listen, Dad, I have to go. Easton's going to want his lunch soon."

I hung up without waiting for a goodbye. Unable to swallow and incapable of breathing, I slowly reached into the already-opened envelope and pulled out the papers contained inside.

My brain short-circuited as my eyes flitted over the cover sheet. *...Great happiness that we offer you a spot... our students... we look forward to hearing...*

Numb with shock, the only coherent thought my brain managed was, *Get lunch ready, otherwise, it's going to get ugly.*

In the kitchen, my body worked on automatic pilot. Chicken salad would not have been my choice of lunch, but Easton hated any Ghanaian food I cooked. I added the mayonnaise and the additional spices I knew Easton liked. I always saved the scallions for last because he liked them fresh but not too big and not too fine like the food processor would have done.

"God, I needed that shower. That run was brutal." Easton's voice was jovial.

I was too numb to answer, as rage battled for dominance with disbelief and sorrow. Instead, I just continued chopping. My mind was unable to form coherent thoughts.

He continued without waiting for a response. "I went down by the library then up Independence. It was pretty. Still spring but with a touch of summer heat in the air."

I smoothed the scallions off the knife into the chicken salad with my finger. While I worked, the bitter scent burned my nostrils. I still didn't speak.

"What's with you?" His tone was cold and held little note of concern.

I knew the moment his eyes landed on the envelope from the school. The air around him shifted subtly, and I braced myself.

His voice was barely above a whisper as he spoke. "Where the hell did you get that?"

Stupid move or not, I wasn't going to let this one go. If there was ever a time to stand up for myself, it was now. I was not the pathetic girl he thought I was. I had been strong once, and I reached deep into the depths of a long-forgotten girl to find a sliver of that strength. "Where the hell you hid it."

I braced for shouting, but nothing happened.

Instead, when Easton spoke, his voice was pleading. "Look, I know I shouldn't have kept it from you, but you have to realize that London isn't going to happen. We won't survive if we don't go together. Law is a more stable profession than photography. I mean, what are you going to do with that anyway? I had your best interest at heart."

My best interest? My best fucking *interest?*

My fingers curled around the knife handle as my anger bubbled to the surface. I forced a deep breath, then another, and peeled my fingers off the hilt. "You lied to me. Every day I asked you, and every day you hid it from me." I searched his handsome face. How had I become this? What had become of the real me?

He waved a dismissive hand. "Look. I did it for you. You needed to make a decision. The *right* decision. And you wouldn't have been able to make it if you'd seen that envelope. Besides, you and I both know that you wouldn't be happy in London."

"Don't!" My body vibrated with fury. "Don't talk to me like I'm a child. You did it for yourself because you wanted me to make the choice that *you* wanted. You're dispica—"

The stinging crack across my cheek snapped my head to the side. A pinball of pain ricocheted in my skull. The burning pain spread from my face to my neck and well into my hairline. I knew from experience now would be a good time to shut the hell up.

But it was as if the stronger woman inside me finally refused to be silenced. I gingerly touched my cheek and glowered at him. "I will not shut up. You lied to me. You *hid* this from me. You made me feel like I wasn't good enough to make this dream happ—"

The next crack was enough to knock me over, and I tasted blood on the tip of my tongue. Desperate to steady myself, I reached up to the counter for purchase, but only managed to bring the diced chicken, mayonnaise, and chopping board down with me.

Easton kneeled in front of me. His tight face registered a barely concealed mask of rage. This was it; I'd done it now. There would be no concealer good enough to hide the bruises he would give me.

And I didn't give a good goddamn. I was tired of cowering.

Instead of lying there, I probed for the cutting board to use as a shield. My fingers wrapped around the knife handle instead. Shaking, I gripped it tight.

Over the years, I'd lost count of the number of times he'd hit me.

Once, I'd even tried to run home. My mother had made it clear, in no uncertain terms, that Easton was the kind of man I needed in my life. And I had better learn how to please him because I wasn't going to do much better than a Peters.

My mother had also pointed out that Easton would be powerful someday and I would benefit from that. She'd called him to pick me up then.

I had learned that day not to go running home with my problems. Once, I considered telling my father. He might have patriarchy infused in his blood, but he would never stand for someone hitting his child.

But even I knew that scenario would end in bloodshed, either with my father dead or in jail for murder. Neither outcome was acceptable, so I kept my mouth shut.

When Easton spoke, his voiced sounded controlled, but I didn't buy it.

"You know better than to provoke me. I don't want to hurt you, but Abbie, you cannot speak to me like that. Are we clear?"

Decision time. I could nod my head and say yes. Or for once, I could stand up to the person who'd hurt me over and over again. The person who'd deliberately tried to keep my dream from me.

With the taste of blood in my mouth and my heart hammering in my chest, I tilted my head to meet his gaze as fury chased away the fear.

Slipping the knife between our bodies, I glared at him. "No. Not clear. You have two minutes to get the hell out of my house, or I swear before God, I will not be the only one bleeding in this kitchen today."

Easton blinked hard, then blinked again, as if he couldn't believe his ears. "Abbie..." His voice held a hint of warning.

My hands shook slightly as hysteria threatened to take over. "Fine, have it your way." The tip of the knife sliced at his T-shirt as I pressed just enough to show him I meant business. The rush of euphoric triumph when the blade carved through skin was hard to ignore.

With a wince, he stumbled backward and fell on his ass. "Abbie, calm the fuck down. Look, I'm sorry. I shouldn't have lost my temper. We can talk this out."

"We won't be talking anything out. You now have sixty seconds to get out." I dug into my back pocket and pulled out my phone. "Or do I have to call the police? Imagine what that will do to a political career not yet started. Probably not much, but think of the scandal. Your poor mother."

His face went ashen. "You know my family has enough money to make any charges go away."

"Maybe, asshole, but the media just loves a smear campaign. Promising young black lawyer fucks it all up. Imagine the head-lines. Just another example of black kids behaving badly."

I knew I'd hit a nerve.

He cleared his throat. "Listen to me, Abbie."

"Thirty seconds." I forced my body into a wide stance, knife held with one hand and pointed in his direction. My phone stayed in the other.

Eyes wide with panic, he pushed himself to his feet and headed for the front door with his back to the exit. "Okay. I'll go, but we're not done talking yet. I'll call you later, and we'll talk this out calmly when you've had a moment to think about things."

"You won't be calling me, because we're done. I will never lay eyes on you again. Ten seconds."

When he reached the front door, he turned and strode through then slammed it shut behind him. Despite the auto locks, I still ran and engaged the deadbolt then the chain. For good measure, I dragged one of the dining room chairs and wedged it against the door.

Adrenaline coursed through my veins, making me shaky as I sank to the floor in the foyer.

Jesus, had I just done that? My body shook. I'd broken up with Easton. Hell, I'd all but threatened to kill him. Now what the hell was I supposed to do?

I laid my head against the door and stared up at the engaged deadbolt. Even though my body shook, my logical thinking functions kicked in. "First things first."

I pulled out my phone and called a locksmith. The call after that was the most important one I'd ever made in my life. I clenched and unclenched my fists as I listened to the double ringing, willing the line to be answered.

"Hiya, my love."

I tried to steady my voice, but it trembled nevertheless. "Faith? It's Abbie. I need a place to stay."

I sat on that floor.

I didn't know how long. Terrified and ashamed, hysterical and... *euphoric*. But I had done it. I had walked away. I had left him. Or made him leave, but that was just semantics.

I picked myself up off the floor, wincing as my shoulder popped. My knee protested, and my head threatened to explode off of my body.

But I was standing. And that was something I hadn't thought I'd ever be able to do. I was on my own two feet. And Easton was out of the house.

Holy shit. Easton was out of the house.

I whipped around and stared at that lock. He still had keys.

You can't stay here.

Right. I had a place to go. My classes wouldn't start for another month, but I would just go to London now. Faith had already said yes, so I had somewhere to go.

Start moving. Passport. Clothes. Go.

My brain sent out the commands, but they all took a moment to process. A much-needed spark of adrenaline was now breaking down to make me sluggish and slow. My head hurt. *Everything* hurt. God, it hurt so bad.

But I had to worry about the pain later. Survival came first.

I didn't waste time. I grabbed the knife from where I'd dropped it. I made sure the chair underneath the doorknob was as secure then went to my closet. I pulled out the largest suitcase I had and started haphazardly shoving clothes into it. I would have loved to take my time and thought through what my future London style would be.

Who are you kidding? What London style will you have? You're a mostly basics kind of girl anyway.

That was true. I did love the basics. Jeans, sweater, some kind of cute top. But none of that mattered because I had survived. And now I was going to live to tell the tale and I was going to London. No one was stopping me from it. I packed the makeup bag, again, with just the basics. I never really learned how to do much more than foundation powder and a subtle highlight. The whole smoky eye thing had bypassed me. A fact that always irritated Easton. He always wanted me to try harder with the makeup.

So I had loads of it, but I had no idea how to use any of it. Not that I needed to anymore, because now I was on my own. Holy cow, I had just broken up with Easton. I'd not only broken up with him, I'd threatened to kill him if he ever touched me again.

Jesus Christ.

I wouldn't let myself think about it. I wouldn't let myself look in the mirror. I wouldn't let the fear that often chased the worry settle in my bones. I'd done it. There was no going back. Not that I'd ever want to.

God, how horrible would it be if, after all of this, I succumbed and went back because I was a coward?

That's easy. Don't be a coward.

Right. When I had enough warm weather clothes shoved in the bag, I ran to get my paperwork. I didn't even have a ticket. *Shit.*

I sat down at my computer, pulled up the Bridge Early site and started to fill in the details. When I got to the portion where they asked for my passport number, I groaned. *Christ, why can't they just let me buy a goddamn ticket?* I ran up to the safe, and my fingers fumbled as I tapped in the code, but when it finally opened, I breathed a sigh of relief and shoved my hand in. I was really going to leave. And better yet, no one would have any idea where I was.

I dug my hand into my identification folder in the safe, looking for that familiar texture of my travel documents, but I didn't find it. I frowned and stuck my head in to a have a good deep look for the passport.

What had I done with it? Easton and I had gone to Costa Rica last year. I went to Ghana every other year, so I was due to go this year anyway. What had I done with my passport?

And then I wondered if Easton had sorted it on his side by accident. Whenever we travelled, he was the one in charge of the documents. He liked to be able to hold on to them. He used to tease me that he didn't want me taking off without him.

But now that joking phrase sent a shiver down my spine. Since we had just the one safe, I didn't have to bother trying to remember his combination. But when I stuck my hand in his identification folder and found his passport, I frowned. There were also little bits of something that felt confetti-size. I pulled out the whole folder and my frown deepened.

Bits of blue plastic fell out. A whole mound of them, enough for two handfuls. When I looked closer, I realized what I was looking at. My passport. He'd shredded it.

Shit.

Had he anticipated this? Had he wondered if, at some point, I would say enough was enough and I would try to go?

I sat back on my heels.

Think. Think. Think. Think. It wasn't the end of the world. I knew how to do this. I could do this. I tried to talk myself through it. Okay, I could get an expedited passport. That would take maybe a little over a week. All I needed was my birth certificate and social security card. The social security card was easy. My mother had that. She'd had mine and my sisters' since we were kids.

I went back to my identification folder and dug around for my birth certificate.

Jesus Christ, again, torn into shreds. Who did that? Who would do that to someone?

I walked back and forth. He'd done this to me. He'd made sure that even if I got the courage to leave, I wouldn't be able to. At least, not right away. He'd made sure that if I ever grew a pair of balls, I would have to wait, that there would be no fast escape for me, and then he'd have a chance at me.

I was so screwed. I couldn't stay there. Sure, I could change the locks. That was all well and good, but he had identification to prove that he lived there, so he could get a locksmith to undo whatever I did.

I couldn't stay here, and I couldn't go to London. At least not yet.

I was going to have to go home.

Lex...

"You tried to have him kidnapped?"

I grinned as I sat back on the couch in my mother's stark white office.

Xander lounged against the floor to ceiling windows as he looked out onto Hyde Park. He looked bored, but I knew him well. He was calculating the light. I could see his fingers moving back and forth as if he was adjusting his angles, adjusting his focus. He was taking pictures. He wasn't even there. Not mentally, anyway.

Jean Claude paced back and forth on the carpet. My mother sat behind her desk, fingers steepled, chestnut hair cascading over her shoulders. Not a gray hair to be found. As always, she looked stunning.

I'd always marvelled how my friends had mums who looked so much older. Not mine though. She seemed somehow perpetually poised somewhere in her early thirties. I didn't know her age for certain, because whenever she had a birthday, she wouldn't tell how old she was. Either way, she looked great... especially when she was on the verge of handing someone their arse.

She wore off-white pants and a casual, pale pink sweater, the only pop of color in the room. Jean Claude stuttered. "L-look, I didn't *really* kidnap him, obviously. He's fine."

"Yes, but you tried?"

"I didn't *try*. I had to keep his skills fresh. Both of their skills fresh. We are on the cusp of something great. Your Majesty—"

She put up her hand. "Jean Claude, I have told you to stop

calling me that. I am not 'Your Majesty.' I no longer have my title, remember?"

He pursed his lips. "But we can change that."

She sighed wearily as if it was an old argument between them. "Jean Claude, my cousin sits on the throne. It's not a throne I have known. It's not even a throne my mother knew. We aren't close to it."

"But you are. There's a lot of talk. People are dissatisfied. They want the old line of monarchy back."

"And that's nice for them. But my cousin has made it clear he has no intention of stepping down, so we have to live in reality."

"Look, you live in reality, and I will act as if the future can change."

She sighed and sat back. "Lex, are you all right?"

I frowned. "You should see the other guys." I was sore, and I had a cut under my eye, which was healing. The scrapes on my knuckles had healed days ago. So I was basically fine. Pissed off, but fine.

But Xander eyed me sceptically. "And when you say we 'should see the other guys,' how many others were there?"

I shrugged. "Three."

Jean Claude rolled his eyes. "Lex, apparently, we need to work on your *restraint*. I suggest you go back to training."

I shrugged. "You can train me all you want, but I will show as much restraint as I feel like at the time."

Jean Claude winced. Xander just smirked. "You took on three guys by yourself?"

"Yeah, where were you, brother? I was worried maybe you'd gotten kidnapped."

"Me? I think the whole world knows better than to fuck with me."

I winced inwardly at his reference. The whole world took him as the dangerous one. The whole world thought he was the one who was out of control. And he *was* out of control or had been for a time there. But it was me, the second son, who was the true menace. But no one knew it.

My mother sat forward. "Jean Claude, this is enough. You've been with the family for a long time, so I let some things slide. But this... you will not put my sons' lives in danger."

Xander raised his hand. "I just want to note that no one has tried to faux kidnap me in a while. Is everyone too scared?"

Jean Claude pursed his lips. "Your Highness, I am more than happy to send men to faux kidnap you. But we all know that you are unsuitable as an heir for your mother, so you won't be an actual target."

I ground my teeth. I hated the way people casually dismissed him. I hated even more that he didn't give a fuck. "Let's be clear, Xander is the oldest. I'm just a spare."

I knew Jean Claude didn't like it. And my mother didn't like me fighting with him. But he wasn't going to treat my brother that way, whether or not Xander gave a shit. "Xander is firstborn."

Jean Claude tugged at his jacket. "He may be the eldest, but given his—history—your mother's other advisers and I think it's best that Xander not be a consideration as the heir. He's undesirable." He slid a glance to Xander along with a shrug that said, *sorry, but true.*

Xander waved him off. "No skin off my nose. I'd make a terrible ruler anyway. Besides, I'm a photographer. That's my life. That's my vocation. That's my dream. I have everything I want. I don't want to be a prince."

I sat forward then. "I don't want to be a prince either."

Jean Claude threw up his hands then. "*You* might not have a choice. And we need a viable heir. So, if both of you forfeit your chances, we'll be stuck with your cousin Derrick from the Winston Isles."

I wrinkled my nose at that. I loathed Derrick. "Let him have it. I'm telling you now, I'd make a shitty prince."

My mother slapped her desk. "Everybody be quiet. There's nothing to worry about. My cousin is still sitting on the throne. So tomorrow, we're going to wake up as normal and do the same thing we did today. Live our lives. My grandparents and my mother were consumed with getting back on the throne. I never chose to live that way. I live with the truth in front of me. And the truth is I am not queen, so I'm not going to live my life as if I were. And I should point out to you, Jean Claude, that if I were to become queen by some fluke, *both* my sons are my heirs, *both* are eligible. You will follow them because I say so."

Jean Claude sighed. "Fair enough, my lady, but how do we know? It'd be a whole lot easier if they looked and acted the part."

Well, I thought, good luck there. Because even though they didn't know it, I knew I was no kind of prince. And if any of this shit should ever come to fruition, the first thing I would do is step down and hand my cousin the crown. Royalty or not, all I ever wanted was my freedom.

I THRASHED as the darkness threatened to overtake me. "No. Please. We'll be good. Please... Don't hurt him."

Wet, cloying cold wracked my body with shivers. Distantly, I saw a figure silhouetted by light, and I reached for it. Desperate for help and companionship, I twisted to try to reach it, but the silhouette remained forever out of range. When the darkness overtook, burning pain seared through my body.

With a cough and a silent, strangled cry, I bolted upright in bed, panting for air. Sweat clung to my skin, and my sheets were twisted around my legs.

Like many nights before this one, I freed myself and dragged my now-wet T-shirt over my head and tossed it toward the hamper. It used to be months and months between nightmares; now it was days. Any first-year psychology student could tell me it was stress. My birthday was coming up, and with it, the anniversary of the one night I never wanted to remember.

I wasn't an idiot though, the dreams started again this week under the stress of the sale. My subconscious was out to torture me.

With everything adding to the pressure cooker, the one beacon of light was the impending sale of my small software company. Even with this new royal bullshit, it meant freedom. Not just financially, but from the oppressive disappointment of my father. And it meant if I walked away from my mother's apparent legacy, I'd be okay.

I knew why I was having the dreams. I understood it exactly, so I wasn't going to spin out, though what I wouldn't give for a week of dreamless nights.

Throwing off the sheets, I climbed out of bed and stalked to the dresser. As I dragged on a new T-shirt, I noticed the light coming from underneath the door. I padded into the living room to find the television still on and a lithe brunette huddled in the corner of my couch with a quilted throw slung around her shoulders. "Gemma, what are you still doing up?"

She turned wide eyes toward me. "I got caught up watching horror movies, and then I couldn't sleep."

"Yeah, well, that makes two of us." I shrugged.

She narrowed her gaze and studied me. "Another nightmare?"

I stiffened. I didn't like her knowing about my demons. "No big deal. I'm going to get some water and head back to bed." I glanced at the clock over the television. It was only one thirty. I'd only managed an hour and a half of sleep so far. "I assume you're staying the night?"

Gemma nodded. "Yeah. I'm knackered. No point driving back to the house just to go crash in bed at home when I can sleep here."

I only nodded. Gemma crashing at my place was nothing new. "Should I bother telling you that the guest-room is all made up, or are you planning on sleeping on the couch?"

She grinned sheepishly. "I could fib and tell you I'm going to bed, but we both know I'm just going to pass out right here."

I shook my head. Since Uni, we'd spent too many nights like this. Neither of us wanting to go home or be alone. To the outside world, we were the perfect couple. No one would believe it if they knew the truth behind the veil. That for years I'd been protecting her, pretending to be her boyfriend. Given the day, it was such bullshit. But her family was old gentry. And stupid. If anyone found out she was into girls, she'd lose everything, and I wasn't going to let that happen.

"Your dad at home?"

She nodded but didn't meet my gaze. "Yeah, so I figured it best to avoid him as much as possible while he's here. It's only for a week, then back to normal."

Gemma didn't have to explain avoiding her father to me. The old man traveled on business most of the time and only came home for a week out of the month. While home, he generally made Gemma's life hell with his bigoted views. No one should have to endure some of the things he said in her presence. "Stay as long as you like."

"Thanks." She scratched her nose. "Um, Lex?"

"Yeah, Gem?"

"You're a really good friend to let me crash and stuff."

I crossed my arms over my chest. I knew where the meandering path she was taking would lead, and I was in no mood for sharing. "Stop. It's what you would do for me."

"Yeah. I suppose. Just, you know, after everything we've been through and everything you've done for me, you never let me be there for you."

I forced a casual smile. "That's because I don't need anything. When I do, you'll be the first person I call." In another life, if things had been different, maybe Gemma and I would have been the perfect couple we portrayed.

"Lex, I notice, you know. The nightmares. The fact that you talk, sometimes shout, in your sleep. I notice."

Fuck. What dark and slithering secret had my brain released when I'd been too out of it to control myself?

"What do I say in my sleep?" I cocked my head and tried for a look that was humored and indifferent. "Am I calling out Gigi Hadid's name? Because that's entirely possible."

Gemma flattened her lips. "You never really say anything I can understand, but that's not the point. I love you, so I worry." She slid her gaze away. "Maybe you can talk to Xander."

I gritted my teeth. I was *not* going to call my brother. He was the last person I could talk to about any of this shit. I worked hard to school my expression. "I appreciate the concern. Honestly, I do. But you have nothing to worry about. Now get some sleep."

Instead of heading for the kitchen, I headed back to the bedroom—I didn't want her watching me too closely. She thought she wanted to know my secrets, but the darkness inside me would change how she looked at me forever.

I was unlovable. That much I knew to be fact.

———

Lex...

In the morning, I was still foggy from lack of sleep, but that didn't mean I didn't have work to do.

"Are you two sure you want to sell this company? With venture capital funding, you can expand the lifestyle brand of

Take Back the Night." Annabelle Smith, our solicitor, asked Nick and I carefully.

We glanced at each other briefly before we both nodded.

I spoke first. "Nick and I have given this a good deal of thought. We want to eventually *become* the venture capitalists for small scrappy companies like ours and prepare them either for sale, like we're doing, or help take them public. A lot of people out there have great ideas but don't know how to follow through. We've figured out how. We might do another small company again and sell that to make sure our feet are well and properly sodden, but we're selling."

Nick added, "We want to strike while the iron's hot. Before someone else comes and tries to copy it with something subpar. First to market is key."

She nodded. "And Toshino, Inc. is banking on that with their purchase. But their team has asked again if you won't both stay on to run it and lend your names to increase the value."

"That's a nonstarter," I said.

Nick agreed. "Look, Annabelle, we've both worked hard to distance ourselves from our pasts. My name might tarnish the brand. While this is meant to be an app for the want-to-be jetsetter, Take Back the Night is still aiming for the elite kind of clientele. That's the whole point. If you start attaching the name Wexler to it, you'll get every low-level sleaze ball from here to Dubai who wants to party with the big boys. Our business clients bank on the exclusivity and class. They won't be thrilled with riffraff joining up. And unfortunately, the Wexler name comes with riffraff."

She sighed and swished her red hair over her shoulder. "Any way to change your mind, Lex? The Chase name screams luxury. Hell, even royalty. We've already taken the steps to protect you from your father's corporate raiding."

I might have different reasons than Nick for keeping my anonymity, but I was still not lending my name. "Sorry, Annabelle, no can do. Even if we do manage to keep the sale quiet until it's final, when my father does find out, he's going to make attempts to block it. To try to claim it for Chase Enterprises. I want to be as separate from him as humanly possible."

She shook her head, no doubt lamenting the loss of additional commission if she could garner us a bigger deal. "Very well. Toshino, Inc. is presenting this as their offer." She slid the paperwork in our direction. "It's understandably smaller because of the lack of brand recognition, but it should make the two of you happy."

The offer was in the ballpark of what I had expected. And it meant I could tell my father to shove it. "That's fair."

"That's a lot of fucking zeros," Nick mumbled.

"Well, you fronted the initial capital, so you should know the valuation," I said.

Nick's eyes bugged. "Yeah, mate, but it's one thing to know theoretically what it's worth. It's another thing entirely to see that number written down in front of you." He scrubbed a hand over his face. "To be honest, Lex, I thought you were full of bollocks."

I laughed. "So you sunk your money into something you thought was bullshit?"

"More like I sunk it because you told me to. I have faith in *you*, but I couldn't see what you could see. But fuck, mate. I see it now."

I wasn't sure if I should laugh or punch him. "Well, thank

you for the glowing endorsement." I turned my attention to Annabelle. "Are they still insisting I sit as CEO?"

She nodded. "Yes, you'll see it in line four, section A. You're to sit as CEO for a term no shorter than six months following the sale of the company. At the end of that term, they will pay you a generous severance." Her smile grew broader. "Between now and then, as long as you two don't receive any undue negative press, you'll be golden."

I barely heard what she said the rest of the meeting. All I knew was that my freedom was so close I could taste it.

IT WASN'T EXACTLY like I ran away from home. But after thirty days of waiting for my new damn passport and enduring my mother's machinations to get me back in Easton's life, as well as Easton's full-blown apology tour, I couldn't be blamed for leaving on a red eye and telling no one I was going.

Seven hundred and twenty hours was more than enough penance for making the mistake of picking Easton in the first place. Hell, that was on top of the years I'd already spent with him.

My mother was a handful. But she was hardly a blip when pitted against my own near-crippling self-doubt. A wash of shame flooded my body for the two times I'd nearly gone back to him.

The first time was three days after I'd locked him out and discovered my shredded passport. The second was just a week ago. My mother's personal nonstop TET Offensive was wearing me down. And Easton was pushing from the other end. He'd gone to my parent's house every single day without fail. I saw to it that we were never alone, but he'd put that full Peters' charm on display.

And I'd almost submitted. He'd even taken full responsibility for our split to my parents. Even my father had believed him, and so had I. He'd promised to go to anger management. Promised to never put his hands on me in anger again. Suggested we go to therapy.

All the things that sounded oh so good.

But then my passport arrived, and I remembered exactly why I was leaving. So I chose my moment and made my escape. No one saw me off. No one wished me luck.

I knew I had to do it for *me*, or I'd be weak and accept a fate I wanted nothing to do with. Once I landed, I made the necessary arrangements. The condo he and I shared was in my name, and I wanted Easton out. I left 'I'm safe' messages for my family but didn't contact Easton, mainly because I wasn't certain I wouldn't cave in to him.

I burrowed deeper under the covers. Packing up all my things and leaving DC behind for London was the right move. Wasn't it?

My phone buzzed on the nightstand, and I dragged the duvet over my head. Maybe if I blocked out the sound, along with the rare English sunlight, my nightmares would all go away and I could return to my happy dream state.

The phone buzzed again, insistent that I look at it.

No.

It could be my mother, one of my sisters, or maybe my father. Worse, it could be Easton. My stomach rolled at the memory of the last time I'd let him hurt me. The way he'd looked at me. What I'd done.

My phone buzzed again.

"Damn it." I snaked a hand out from under my duvet, and chilly air greeted my flesh. I fumbled around for the side table, eventually banging my wrist on the corner. *Ouch.* If that wasn't an omen, I didn't know what was.

When my fingers closed around the phone, I dragged it under the covers with me. "Okay, world, what the hell do you want from me?" I mumbled.

Three text messages. *Fantastic.*

The first was from my mother.

Mom: *Abena, call me immediately. I want to make sure you're safe. Make sure you call me.*

I rolled my eyes. I'd already called my mother *and* left her a voicemail. But my mother had a way of ignoring things that didn't specifically fit what she wanted. And Helen Nartey didn't want a voicemail. She wanted a live convo so she could try to berate me into coming back to DC.

The next message was from my sister Akos, the lawyer.

Akosua: *Abbie, we need to discuss your arrangements with the condo. I served Easton with documents stating he has to vacate so you can sublet the place. You need to call me to review details.*

Crap. That was the last thing I wanted to deal with.

The third message was from Easton.

Easton: *Call me, we need to talk. Your sister wants me out of our place. I need some time to find somewhere else to go. Where are you? I called your sister, and she said you weren't there but wouldn't tell me where you'd gone. Call me!!*

I waited for the slice of pain. But nothing came. Just gray numbness. I felt free to go ahead and delete his message.

The phone buzzed in my hand again, causing it to tingle.

God. Maybe I should have left the stupid thing back home. Started fresh.

The last text was from my sister Ama.

Ama: *I think you're brave.*

I smiled. Of course, Ama would support me, silently though, not out loud to the rest of the family. But still, she supported me. And that was why I loved her.

I tried to close my eyes again to catch another sliver of elusive sleep, but it was no use. Thanks to my family's *reach out and touch someone* campaign, I was awake now. And the sounds from the kitchen told me that Faith, my best friend from college and new flatmate, was awake. Good old Faith. When I called her, frantic and blubbering a few weeks ago, she told me to get my Yank ass on a plane and insisted I stay with her.

I dragged my feet out of bed, and my toes immediately cursed my decision to move to London and not a warmer, more tropical locale. Nevertheless, I rummaged in my suitcase for thicker socks. *Note to self, must unpack.*

My phone buzzed again. *Second note to self—get a different phone or at least a new chip.* One that prevented my family from following me around and demanding all my time.

I shuffled into the living room and kitchen area to assess the damage Faith was doing to breakfast.

"Ah, good morning, love. How'd you sleep? I worried you'd be jetlagged. Then I realized, belatedly, that the room has no drapes. Normally it's not a problem with the weather and all, but today it was sunny of all things, so of course, the sun was going to disturb your sleep and..."

That was Faith. She had a tendency to ramble and speak at the speed of light. Due to her thick Manchester twang, I missed part of what she said, but I got the gist.

Faith bustled around the kitchen, yammering at a hundred miles an hour as I walked over to her. She finally paused when I stepped right in front of her and hugged her tight. I wasn't big on hugging. Any kind of touching usually made me uncomfortable. But in instances like this, sometimes a hug was called for. Without even knowing it, Faith had saved my life. She was the reason I could breathe for the first time in years.

Faith wrapped her arms around my waist. "Ah, love. What's with the hugs? Are there going to be waterworks too? If there are, I've got Kleenex in the pantry."

I sniffled. "No. No. I'm just really happy to be here. Really happy to have this. I'm excited too."

Faith smiled, displaying even teeth and dimples in her heart-shaped face. "You should be excited. No one I know has the guts to do what you did. Pack up in a moment's notice and move out of country. Abbie, I swear." Faith let go of me and handed me a mug of tea.

I took the tea, even as I winced. "Well, let's face it, I sort of ran away."

"Don't call it running away. Call it running to a new adventure. I'm so glad you called me."

"I'm so glad you're letting me stay. I know it's a bit of an imposition."

"Shut up. You know that's bullshit. You saved me from having to get a serial-killing random stranger for a flatmate. I've been considering it with Sophie being gone all the time. Maybe she should move in permanently with her boyfriend."

Sophie was the third member of our triumvirate. We'd all shared a dorm room at NYU.

"Let's not suggest that until I've been here for a while, okay? I've been looking forward to the three of us getting some girl time." I wrinkled my nose as it finally occurred to me that it was Monday. "Shit, Faith, am I keeping you from work?"

Faith worked as an assistant coordinator for a PR firm. "No, I'm working from home today. I've got a pile of calendar stuff I need to pitch, and I'll never get anything done with the other girls in and out of my office."

I took another sip of my tea. "So, this is real. I'm really doing this?"

"Looks that way, doesn't it? What's your first move?"

I exhaled. "Step one is get a job. I have some money saved, but I'll be needing equipment and stuff. It'll be easier if I don't have to deal with the parentals to get it. After that, I need to head to campus and do some administrative stuff. I was lucky they still let me into the course since I was so late accepting." What I didn't let on with Faith was how dire my money situation really was. I had just enough to make it through the semester, but that meant no extras.

Faith nodded. "I still can't believe what Easton did. Sophie called it though. She's always hated him." I suppressed a shudder. If only Faith knew what else he'd done to me over the years.

"I wish I'd seen this coming. Maybe I wouldn't have wasted my college years with an asshole." I squared my shoulders. The sooner I got on with my life, the sooner I'd forget what I'd left behind. It was time to take back some of the control Easton had stolen from me. "But I'm here now, and I'm about to start living. Which means I better get ready for class."

⸻

Abbie...

An hour and a half later, I sat in the back of the small auditorium watching as everyone took their seats one by one.

A collective hush fell over the room the moment Xander Chase walked in. I had seen photos, but they were nothing compared to seeing him in the flesh. I'd known he was young, but honestly, he could have been one of the students. And smoking hot didn't even begin to cover the description.

"You can call me Xander. Mr. Chase is my father."

He was tall, at least six foot two, with broad shoulders and playful dark eyes. Shaggy dark hair framed his angled jaw and features. He also had a smile hot enough to make any red-blooded female consider dropping her panties. Self-confidence and sex appeal oozed off of him in waves.

"So, for those of you who don't remember, I'll give you a brief overview. During the course of a week, you'll have one lecture, two advisory sessions, an assignment, and a critique."

A legend like him was going to give me critiques and advice. Bile churned as my stomach flipped. Of course, I'd expected that, but still. Theoretically knowing my work was going to be picked apart and actually having it happen were two different things.

Then there was also the small matter of being stuck in a room with a man, *any* man, and only one exit. I wrapped my arms around my middle. I'd better learn to steel myself or I wouldn't survive a day, let alone the whole term. He might be good-looking and in a position of power, but he was not Easton. I'd faced Easton and hadn't died. I could deal with this man.

"Oh, and one other thing to get out of the way. I want to remind the female and male students alike that it's pointless to try to sleep with me. I don't sleep with my students. I promise you it's not going to happen, so save us all some time and don't try it. I'd rather get on with teaching you."

Wow.

Okay. Way to put it all out there. I snuck a look around the room and instantly understood why he'd laid out his cards. Every single girl—and at least a quarter of the guys— appraised him. I had to wonder if anyone would make the attempt. There were only fifty students in the program, and of that fifty, only twenty of us were female.

A tiny brunette sitting next to me whispered, "Just a tad full of himself, isn't he?"

I giggled and whispered back, "I'd heard British men had a problem with confidence. I see he doesn't suffer from that affliction."

The girl grinned. "I'm Ilani Bruce, by the way."

"Abbie Nartey." I smiled back.

As I listened, energy hummed through my veins. The work would be exciting, though I certainly wasn't going to enjoy the critiques. But then again, who did?

Xander was speaking again, and I dragged my attention back to him.

"Remember, I hand-selected each of you based on your portfolio submissions. I think each and every one of you has a raw talent waiting to come out. I need your commitment to be honest. Don't give me trite and pretty. I want you exposing your-selves and putting yourself in every single image."

We all nodded enthusiastically.

"Okay, first assignment is as follows. Since all of you are so fresh faced and bushy tailed, I want you to photograph joy. In all of its forms. Gritty, serene, blissful—I want it all. Think you all can manage that?"

There was a general murmur of accord. The excitement was palpable as each of us fiddled with our cameras.

"Good. Now go and do your worst. And by worst, I mean better than your best."

As soon as class was over, I headed over to Xander. Unlike the other students who crowded him, I stopped well outside his sphere of personal space. "Excuse me, Xander?" I forced a deep breath and squared my shoulders. I would have to learn to talk to him if I wanted to work for him.

He cocked his head, and his almost-smiling mouth tugged into a glimmer of a real one as he assessed me. "Little Bird. I'd wondered if you'd come and introduce yourself."

Little Bird? He remembered my photo? I flushed. It had taken me three days to find the hummingbird nest and capture the mother feeding her nestlings.

Up close, I realized Xander's eyes weren't dark at all, but rather a slate gray. I forced out my carefully selected words. "I, uh, wanted to say thank you for giving me the opportunity to study with you. It's already changing my life."

He chuckled. "Well, if you think today was life-changing, then wait until I actually start teaching you something." He studied me closely. "I'm glad you accepted. I was starting to worry that you wouldn't when we hadn't heard from you."

My skin prickled with embarrassment. *He* had been waiting on *my* acceptance? "I had no idea you were waiting on me—"

"Like I said, Little Bird, I hand-selected all of you. In the process I became quite attached to your works. To *you*." This time his grin was the slow, cocky, confident smile of someone who was accustomed to women falling at his feet.

It fell flat on me. The longer I stood in his presence, the less nervous I became. Maybe this wouldn't be so hard after all.

"Right. Well, anyway, thank you again. I'm looking forward to learning from you." With a little boost of confidence, I turned to leave.

He called out to me, "Don't you want to know why I selected you for this program?"

I turned but walked backward to keep my momentum. "Nope. You already told me why. And I know what I can do with a camera." I didn't wait for a response as I turned back around and strode out of the lecture hall.

Ilani followed me out of the building, and we made our escape.

"You're a Yank, aren't you?"

I nodded. "Yeah, I guess the accent gives me away."

My new friend grinned. "Only a little. Listen, some of us took Xander for undergrad and used to get together right after crits to drink our sorrows away. You game for a bit of a laugh after the first one?"

"Yeah, sounds good. The critiques sound pretty scary."

Ilani followed me out of the main lobby into the rare British sunshine. "They are. He's usually not satisfied unless at least one person cries."

My eyes widened, and I swallowed hard, resolute not to be the crying student. "Ouch."

"It's his way, I guess." Ilani shrugged. "Anyway. Good to meet you, Abbie. See you next week."

"Yeah you too." I smiled encouragingly, even though my stomach pitched at the thought of those crits.

As I turned, a chill skittered over my spine, but it wasn't cooler air; it was more of a warning. Almost like I could feel a gaze on me.

You're being paranoid, who would be watching you... besides the obvious.

No. I had to stop. Easton was at home in DC. He wasn't in London. That was the fear talking. That was the little part of me that listened to my family, the part of me that had stayed with Easton. It was the part afraid of change, of greatness. The part of my brain that would have done the safe thing and gone to law school.

If I was going to make it here, if I was going to have my dream, I was going to have to get used to kicking that part of my psyche in the nads at every opportunity.

I wasn't going back to fear. Fear had never made me happy. So I took a deep breath, forced my mind to calm down, and made my brain work. Easton was thousands of miles away. I was afraid of failing, but the only way to truly fail was to not try.

So get off your ass and do this.

As I headed down the cobblestone steps of the Ealing campus and made my way to the bus stop, I let my lens be my eyes. The excitement of the new city fueled my blood. The first step to living my dream was already in motion.

I HOVERED outside Dr. Kaufman's office. Easton might be a lot of things, but he did have one smart idea.

In his quest to win me back, or whatever the hell that was, he'd mentioned therapy. And considering that there was still that weak, small part of me that had almost caved and gone back to him, I figured I needed plenty of it.

The problem, now that I was here, was facing the reality of speaking my truth. I was terrified. What if she judged me? Worse, what if she told me that I should go back to Easton? Or that I should work it out and say I was sorry?

You know better than that. No professional is going to tell you to go back.

Okay, maybe not. But she was definitely going to force me to take a look at things I didn't want to look at. While I was in London pursuing my dream, there were parts of me that were still terrified and afraid. I'd left him behind, but I was still scared.

I walked into the reception area and checked myself in before having a seat. A part of me was desperate to pull out my phone, to lose myself in the banalities of my Instagram feed, but I forced myself to sit there. To look around at my surroundings. I wasn't going to numb the feeling.

No. I wanted to do this. Enjoy this. *Be this.* This version of myself that I could actually be proud of. Numbing the pain of being here wasn't going to help me do that.

Five minutes later, I was ushered into Dr. Kaufman's office. I was surprised when I walked in. I expected an old woman that looked like someone's New York grandmother. Short, with kinky curling hair, glasses, slightly frumpy.

But no. Dr. Kaufman was certainly not frumpy. She was elegant in her movements, and she marched up to me and shook my hand. "Abena Nartey? Hello, I'm Dr. Kaufman. Most of my patients just call me Elisa."

I stuttered. "Oh, I, uh... Sorry, yeah, I'm Abena. Most of my friends call me Abbie."

Her smile was soft and kind. "Abbie, welcome."

As she marched back to a small corner of the room, I watched her. Her hair, dark, sleek, and flat-ironed within an inch of its life, swung and bounced as she walked. She was trim, fit. And she looked young. Her face was smoothed and aligned. Not a single grey hair on her head. She could have been me at thirty. When she turned, she asked, "Would you like some water?"

I shook my head. "No, thank you. I'm good."

She nodded and watched me. "Okay then, why don't you tell me why you're here?"

She gestured me to a seat while she took one across from me. And I silently wondered where the couch was. Weren't all therapists supposed to have a couch? "I— I just moved here from DC. And there're some things I want to work on, to make sure I have the fullest London experience. And I know that if I don't talk to someone, I'm always going to be looking back, I guess. Or even worse, making the same kinds of mistakes I've made before."

She nodded. "Okay, why don't you tell me about some of your mistakes?"

The fear rose up inside of me, like bile trying to make an eruptive escape, but I shoved it down. I was doing this. I wasn't running anymore. I wasn't going to swallow the truth. The truth was like vegetables. It was good for you, even if it tasted like shit. "My ex-boyfriend... abused me for years. When I came here, I was basically running away from him. "

I don't know what I expected. Shock. Surprise. Something. Instead there was a somewhat detached empathy, but her eyes were soft, and she nodded encouragingly. She gestured for me to keep talking. So I did. I told her all of it. How we'd met. How I'd felt. How I'd soon come to feel. How I'd stayed, like the coward that I was.

His betrayal, hiding my acceptance letter, shredding my passport, tearing up my birth certificate. How I'd gone home because I couldn't leave and then ran away from my parents in the middle of the night. How I turned up in London ready for a new chapter, a new adventure. But part of me was still afraid. Part of me thought I should go back. A part of me believed the things Easton had told me.

It all poured out of me. It didn't take long, because once I was on a roll, the words wouldn't stop. I was desperate to purge it. Like I'd overindulged on alcohol. Something that was, in essence, poison to me. And it had to come out, one way or the other.

When I finally finished, she sat back. She made a few notes and then watched me closely. "Can I ask you a question, Abbie?"

"Yeah, I guess."

"Do you love, Easton?"

"Of course, I love him. I mean, that's what got me into this whole mess, I think."

She cocked her head. "Okay, well, what does love mean to you?"

I frowned at that. I had no idea how to answer. "Um, I don't know, that feeling where you know you belong to someone and how they make you feel, and like you could do anything. It's hard to quantify that. It's not even about sex, or about you doing anything to be near that person."

I paused and thought it through. None of those feelings described how I felt about Easton. Maybe in the early days, but lately? No. I'd mostly stayed to keep the peace. To stay *safe*.

She smiled at me then. "You're thinking it through now, aren't you?"

I nodded. "Um, I guess. Once I heard myself say it out loud, I guess that's not love." The shame was quick to follow, punching me in the gut, making me want to bend over at the waist and ride out the pain. "I don't think I've loved him for a long time."

"And why don't you think you loved him?"

The answer was quick. It jumped right off my tongue as if I've been holding on to it like the sour taste of lemons in my mouth for far too long. "Because he betrayed me the first time he put his hands on me."

She nodded. "And that's fair. He betrayed you again and again, didn't he?"

I nodded. "I didn't even think of it as bad at the time. I don't know what's wrong with me that I believed everything he said like it was my fault and that I was responsible."

Her smile was soft. "Well, there's a part of you that held yourself responsible."

"But I didn't ask for that," I whispered.

She nodded, but more in an encouraging way. And I kept talking. When I finally tripped over the answer she was looking for, she put her pen down. "Tell me Abbie, why do you feel responsible?"

Something tickled my cheek, and I swiped at it before I realized that it was a tear. I was crying. In a stranger's office. *Fanfucking-tastic.* "Because I stayed. Because I didn't tell anyone. After that first time, I should have *told* someone. I should have run fast."

She nodded. "So, you and I are going to work on you not feeling like that. You and I are going to work on the things that led you to that position, to that moment where someone hurt you and betrayed your trust, and you blamed yourself. And we're going to figure out all the reasons why."

"God, I'm to blame."

She sat forward and put her hand over mine. "No, you are not. That's not how this works. Here, inside these doors, we tell the truth, and we put the blame where it belongs. When you met him, you were a kid. But I suspect there is a very strong woman in there who's been battling her way out, who's been propping you up. She's the woman who walked out on him. She's the woman who walked out on your parents. She's the woman who flew halfway around the world for a chance to be amazing. Without anything encumbering her, she made it happen, so I want you to focus on that part of you."

I nodded. "I'm scared. I'm not going to lie. I'm scared that he's going to come here and find me. I am scared that I'll be weak and go back. I'm scared of maybe meeting someone and not being able to have a normal relationship because he'll move too quickly. I'm young. I should meet *lots* of someones. I shouldn't have to be afraid of my own shadow."

"I think you should be meeting lots of someones. If you'd walked in here and you told me you were still in love with him, that you were still heartbroken, I'd feel differently. But I think you haven't been in love with him for a long time."

She was right. But the truth of that burned like acid. So if I hadn't been in love with him, I'd let him hurt me for no good reason?

"I can see your wheels turning right now. Angry that if it wasn't love, then why did you put up with all that?"

I nodded and fresh tears started to fall. The rack of tissues arrived at my side as if by magic.

"You'd be amazed at the things the human mind will do to validate our choices. On paper, Easton seemed like the man you *should* want. The one who would get your parents' approval. But you're an adult now. You need to think about the one that gets *your* approval. And I'm going to encourage you to do that. This is a clean slate. I'm not suggesting you fall in love with the next man you meet, but you're young. I encourage you to meet people. Learn to discern the differences in how they treat you and what you're looking for, because I don't think you know yet. And where most women would be figuring that out, you know, when they were teenagers and young adults at the university, you were with Easton, trying to follow a specific path. And that didn't make you happy. You're in graduate school now, and it's as good a time as any."

"But what if someone hurts me?"

She shook her head. "Look, life isn't about getting hurt. Because why would we even live it if that was the whole purpose? We would all stay in our boxes and ordering food and be agoraphobic crazy."

I chuckled. "Are you supposed to say crazy?"

She shrugged. "I'm a little unconventional. Life isn't meant to be sanitized. But I want you to be able to recognize the difference between someone who will hurt you and someone who won't. You don't even have to go on a date to figure that out. There's an intuition that women in particular have. We know. It's instinct. I want you to start to do that, to explore, to do the things that you've always wanted to do, the things that you automatically said no to because Easton or your parents wouldn't allow it. If it fascinates you and you want to do it, I encourage you. In the meantime, you and I will talk weekly. We'll explore your thoughts, what you're thinking, and how you're feeling. Get your brain to start making good choices through things that enrich you and make you happy instead of things you feel like you *should* do."

I nodded slowly. "This isn't going to be easy, is it?"

She laughed. "No, not easy at all. But you're going to take your time. Have a little fun. I mean, after all, isn't that why you're in London?"

I nodded. "Yeah, you would be right about that."

⊏⊐

Abbie...

As luck would have it, the earlier sunshine was a fluke. The skies darkened to a blackened gray, and fat raindrops pelted my arms and battered my umbrella. "Damn it." Sucking in a resolute breath, I marched forward. A little rain wasn't going to ruin my day. I'd come to London knowing the weather pattern. It was just one more thing I'd have to get used to.

Quickly, I checked Faith's scrawled directions to Sophie's boyfriend's place. *1257 Camberwell Road.* I glanced at the numbers on the row houses on my right. 1232, 1234—at least I was moving in the right direction, though I needed to cross the street.

With rain pelting the sleeves of my thick sweater even harder, I trotted to the edge of the sidewalk and checked for oncoming cars. Just as I was about to step onto the road, I heard a revving motor.

From behind, someone shouted, "Look out!"

In one smooth snap of icy talons, fear gripped my spine as strong arms jerked me backward with enough force to knock the wind out of me.

My head swam. In an automatic reply to being grabbed, my body went numb, and my oxygen would only come in short stabbing bursts as my hands flew up in an attempt to protect my face. But then, the tiny voice inside screamed, *You are not helpless.* It was just the motivation I needed.

I fought the stranger's hold and struggled, immediately losing my footing. In the split second my brain registered my downward trajectory, I squealed and tucked my camera into my sweater to protect it as I fell. The arms tightened around me again and turned both our bodies. Nausea swelled as I tried to free myself from the grip of strong hands.

My would-be attacker and I landed ass-first in a grimy puddle with a thud hard enough to make my teeth rattle. I blinked rapidly, my brain trying to register what had happened as a Mini Cooper whizzed by. The driver shouted epithets in my direction.

Unable to calm the panic as adrenaline flooded my veins, I continued to try to free myself and fought for control.

"You're okay. I've got you. Stop struggling. I didn't just save your life so I could hurt you. Just relax for one second and breathe."

The masculine voice crooned low and soft in my ear, working its magic on me inch by inch. In those endless seconds, my brain registered that the strong hands that held me weren't squeezing too tight. They weren't manhandling me. They weren't striking me. In fact, they were only tight enough to have pulled me back. These hands had caused me no harm. *Unlike Easton's.*

I was safe.

Through the thunder of my heart, I heard the splish and splash of heavy raindrops on the pavement and my downed umbrella. My own ragged breathing filtered in next, along with the harsh breathing of my puddle partner.

I yanked my camera out of my sweater and carefully examined it. No cracks to the lens or anything. *Thank God.* I didn't have the money to replace it.

With one arm, I tried to leverage myself up, but I slipped and landed back on my savior's lap... hard.

I whipped my head around to face him, and he stared at me. Raindrops clung to his dark, sooty lashes. His wavy hair was plastered to his head. I tried to make my mouth move, but nothing happened, almost as if the command had gotten lost in the cataloguing of his features.

Wide gray eyes that smoldered. Midnight black hair. Full lips that looked like they were on the verge of smiling. Straight

Roman nose, and a square jaw. He was beautiful. I wanted him on a canvas, just like he was now, his brow lightly furrowed and his eyes concerned. There was something so familiar about him.

"Are you all right?"

I blinked, tried to form the words, and failed. Then I tried again. "Um, yeah. I think so. Th-thank you."

A blond guy stood nearby, holding an umbrella over the two of us. Finally Gray Eyes stood, pulling me with him. His hand was firm and warm, despite the chilly rain. "You have to make sure to look *both* ways okay?"

Again, my brain stuttered as the whiskey-smooth texture of his voice rolled over me. I could listen to him talk forever. Quickly, I tugged my hand free of his. "Um. I—uh." Mortified, I covered my face. "Yeah. Thanks. I'll be careful."

He studied me with a quizzical expression then whispered, "Okay. Cheers."

After quickly checking my camera for damage again, I stepped to the curb once more. Careful to look both ways–twice–I crossed the street to the opposing row houses. As I muttered the numbers to myself, tension slowly ebbed out of me.

I stopped in front of the address Faith had texted. Before I could even knock, Sophie yanked the door open with a squeal.

"Oh, my god, oh my god, oh my god. You're actually here. I can't believe it. Yay!"

The hugging came next. I held my camera away from my body as Sophie wrapped her arms around me and attempted to squeeze the air out of my lungs. Sophie was a big-time hugger. Me, not so much.

"Hey, Sophie, you think you could actually let me in? The back of my pants are soaked."

"Oh, of course. Sorry, babes. I was just so excited." She stopped trying to administer the reverse Heimlich maneuver and dragged me through an elegantly lit foyer with recessed lights and a slate floor. "What happened to you anyway? You look like hell."

A gilded mirror hung in the hallway, and I groaned when I saw my reflection. My braided twist had come undone, and my make-up was now streaked and smudged, giving me the appearance of a wet, bedraggled Koala.

I followed Sophie into the ultra-modern kitchen and tried not to gape. The cabinets were red lacquer and the backsplash was red, orange, and gold glass tile. All the appliances were high-end stainless steel, and the countertops were white marble. This was where Sophie lived? Faith's digs in Chiswick were nice, but this was opulent. "I had a run in with a Mini Cooper and a puddle. Do you have a pair of jeans and a sweatshirt I can borrow? I must look like a drowned rat."

A low voice came from behind me. "I don't know. You look well fit to me."

I jumped and whirled around. I made a quick assessment of him just like I did with all men and filed him into the preliminary category of not-a-threat.

I studied him closer, unsure of what to make of the auburn-haired guy leaning against the counter. He was cute in a quirky way. With his shaggy hair and animated green eyes, I could see how his disarming smile made him even cuter. He had several tattoos on his forearms and one peeking out from the top of his T-shirt. *Fantastic.* His whole aura screamed trouble. But there was something inherently kind about his eyes.

Sophie giggled. "Jasper, behave, would you? This is my friend Abbie from Uni."

Jasper uncoiled his lanky frame and strode over. I wasn't so sure about being in his personal space, but nevertheless, I extended a hand to shake, but instead, he bowed and kissed my knuckles. *Yeah. Charming as fuck.* And he knew it. I tugged my hand back. "Nice to meet you, Jasper."

"I promise you, love, the pleasure is all mine."

I turned to Sophie. "And you know Jasper how?"

"Oh, he's Max's flatmate," Sophie replied.

"Yeah, my room's just at the top of those stairs if you need or *want* anything." He waggled his eyebrows.

I sputtered and laughed. "You're ridiculous, you know that?"

He nodded with unabashed good humor. "I've been told that before."

Faith came from a hallway at the other end of the kitchen and hip-checked Jasper. "Leave her alone, Jas. She's a friend of ours and isn't ready for your flirtation assault."

Jasper rolled his eyes. "Okay, fair enough." He stood directly in front of me, forcing me to take an automatic step back before looking up at him. "But if you come to me, all bets are off." He winked before turning on his heel and jogging up the stairs to his bedroom.

I couldn't help the exasperated chuckle. "Is he for real?"

Both Faith and Sophie shrugged.

"Yeah, that's Jasper," Sophie said.

Faith's phone rang. "You two go ahead. I'll catch up. It's Liam."

Sophie tugged me through an expansive living room into the back hallway that sported two additional bedrooms. "Sophie, this is incredible. Looks expensive."

"Oh this?" She extended her hand and indicated the living room. "This is all Max. I'm just the girlfriend."

Faith had been vague about the details when I had pressed for information about Sophie's man. Maybe if I was lucky, I could meet the mystery guy. "What does he do for a living, and where can I get one of him?"

My friend laughed. "Well, he's a model."

My jaw dropped. "Of course he is." Sophie lived one of those fabulous lifestyles you could only read about in *Us Weekly*.

Quickly, I donned the spare set of jeans and the T-shirt Sophie handed me. I immediately regretted the T-shirt, which had slashes through the sides and was almost completely backless. Sophie usually experimented with designs on her own clothes. "Um, thanks, maybe you have a sweater too?" I asked hopefully.

"Somewhere in the kitchen. I think I left my jumper that goes with those jeans. We'll go look." She continued happily chatting about Max. "Yeah, the modeling jobs pay nicely because he works often, but in addition, he renovates houses and sells them. And he rents out the spare rooms in this place. It's got five bedrooms and a pretty nice garden."

I chewed my lip. That explained a lot.

Sophie shrugged and continued, "You know, he's a bit of a hustler."

"Oh, okay." That was a little vague. But shit, he wasn't my man, so I wouldn't complain as long as Sophie was happy.

Although my overactive imagination kept picturing the beautiful living room tossed and destroyed because of a drug raid. In my mind's eye I could just see the collaged photo, half as it was now and half as it would be after the raid with the mysterious Max sitting in the center of it all. Though somehow as I pictured Max, I interchanged him with the knight in shining armor who'd just saved my life.

Sophie shrugged. "You can call him a bit of an entrepreneur."

Right. "Well, this place is amazing."

"Thanks. We like it."

We heard the front door open downstairs, and Sophie grinned. "That'll be him now."

I turned toward the heavy footsteps and stared.

"You must be Abbie. I'm Max."

I did my best to drag my eyes away from the tall specimen of man that strolled up the stairs from the kitchen with a confident swagger. His dirty blond hair dusted his collar and drifted into his face in thick layers. *Wow.* I knew women who would kill for hair like that.

His green eyes were lively and mischievous and framed by thick lashes. A strong angular jaw and high cheekbones completed the beautiful picture. The only thing that took away from the image of perfection was the bump on the bridge of his nose, but it made him more mysterious. "Nice to meet you."

Instead of taking my proffered hand, he enveloped me in a hug that stunned me for a second. *Great, another hugger.* As quick as it flared, I batted down the irrational fear. I'd really have to remind Sophie that I didn't like to be touched.

He pressed a quick peck to both of my cheeks. "Welcome to London. You're all Sophie's talked about."

"Thank you. I'm excited to be here."

Max pulled Sophie against his side as he asked, "You're coming out with us tonight, right?"

I glanced at Sophie for a little help. "What's happening tonight?"

"Jasper's DJing. You have to come. You can meet Lex and the rest of the gang. Say you'll come," Sophie pleaded.

I hedged. I wanted to get started on some photos and explore a little. But it was also my first night out in London. And it wasn't like I was set up for night shots yet, anyway. I was still waiting on my sister to ship some of my equipment. "Not too late, right? I have work I need to start on in the morning."

Sophie rolled her eyes. "You were always so studious. Sure fine. But we're not taking no for an answer."

When was the last time I'd gone out on a school night? When was the last time I'd been spontaneous? I couldn't remember. I'd locked myself in so tight I'd forgotten to breathe and have a little fun.

Thanks to Easton.

I slammed that thought away into a lock box. It was time to embrace my new life and the new me. The new me who went out on a school night. "Okay, but what the hell am I going to wear?"

CHAPTER 6
LEX...

WHAT THE FUCK WAS THAT?

That girl. I could still feel her soft hand in mine. The zap of electricity. My hand twitched at the phantom feeling.

She'd looked so small and vulnerable with the rain clinging to her long, slim braids.

When her dark almond-shaped gaze had met mine, I felt like I'd been poleaxed. The white jumper she'd been wearing made her ebony skin gleam.

For more than a moment I'd been rendered deaf and dumb. Luckily I'd eventually found my voice and managed to ask if she was okay. I'd probably sounded like a git.

And I knew I really shouldn't be trying to figure out wherever she was going exactly, but I couldn't help it. I angled my head down to the back a little bit. If Nick noticed, I'd just pretend I was making sure she was okay.

Yeah, because that sounds in character.

Where the hell was she?

You're never going to find out because she's a stranger on the street.

I met lots of girls every day. So why is this one different?

You usually don't meet women who you have to rescue. You meet women who want to bone you.

Yeah, good point.

But I didn't get the impression the girl generally needed rescuing. The way she'd protected that camera, like she would have done anything to keep it safe, did I feel that way about anything?

Besides your brother?

When I turned my attention back to my conversation with Nick, he was studying me. "What's wrong with you?"

"What do you mean?"

"I don't know. You were staring at that bird. Do you know her?"

"No." It was true. I didn't know her. I would very much *like* to know her. All about her, actually. Her ins and outs, what she smelled like.

Okay, that was bordering on creepy.

No, just making sure she's okay.

He frowned at me as if to tell me he didn't believe me. Which was fine. "What?"

"I don't know. You're acting weird. Anyway, like I was saying, are you feeling good about the Toshino deal?"

I nodded. "Yeah, it's a good deal and it's a shit ton of money."

"That kind of money will break us both free of our fathers."

I nodded. "Yeah. We can really do what we want."

Nick shrugged. "Not that I don't already, but at least this way I don't have to do the old man's bidding."

While we both had the whole daddy-issue thing in common, Nick's daddy issues were a whole other kettle of fish. His father owned all kinds of night clubs in the city. In all parts of the greater London area, actually. And some up north as well. But the rumors of how he'd gotten there tended to leave a bad taste in the mouth.

Nick wanted nothing to do with him. When it came to partying and such, sure, Nick was more than happy to party on the old man's dime, but if it came down to actually working for him, he had zero interest. He had more interest in venture capital stuff with me than anything of his father's. Plus, I knew for a fact that after his mother died when Nick was ten, he didn't trust the old man one bit. He'd been shipped off to boarding school then, which was where we met. And a part of him had always thought maybe his dad had something to do with it, considering he'd moved in his mistress just a month after his mother's death.

"I mean, it's a fantastic deal. It could give us what we want. There can't be anything bad about it. We've already done the due diligence. It's time to enjoy it, I guess."

He nodded slowly. "You think your dad is going to try and stop it?"

"In a few days, it'll be too late. And then I'll talk to him and he can slink away with his tail between his legs."

"Man, I thought I hated my dad."

I shrugged. "Hate is too strong of a word. I just don't care about him." Years ago, when I needed a father, someone to come and rescue me, I had gone to him. I begged him, frightened, to come and stop what was going on at my mother's house, but he told me I was making it up. My own father. He could have stopped everything. But no, he hadn't come, and my mother had remained blissfully unaware. For years I'd harbored anger against her too. How could she not have known?

How could she not see? Only later did I realize that my

stepfather had kept her on a Xanax and Ambien cocktail to soothe her nerves. She hadn't known. She hadn't been alert enough to save us.

So much of my fury was directed at the old man. He had been alert. He could have saved us, but he'd chosen not to. So nowadays when he asked shit from me, my ready response was, 'Go fuck yourself.'

"I mean, there's still time. Your birthday is not for a few days yet. I know your father is not an idiot."

I shook my head. "No, he's not an idiot. But we've kept this deal under wraps. We got this. Nothing is going to be announced until after my birthday, so it's fine. And once it's all signed, sealed and delivered, I'll be happy to be the one to tell him. Matter of fact, I can't wait."

Nick nodded. "I hear you. We can have a big party when it's all done."

"You know, I think I'm probably done with parties for a bit."

He smirked. "I still can't believe fucking Jean Claude tried to kidnap you."

"The bloke is such a fucking wanker."

"So, he's trying to keep you ready for what, the apocalypse?"

I rolled my eyes. "The royal apocalypse, which is such bullshit. There's no chance in hell my mother sits on that throne."

He was quiet for a moment, and he reached into his coat to pull out a cigarette and a lighter. He offered me one, and I begged off. It didn't matter how many times I had told him. He couldn't seem to remember that I didn't smoke. He lit it, blowing the smoke out from under his umbrella into the misting rain. "But like, legitimately, you could be a prince."

"Technically, I have a title. But it doesn't mean anything

because we're not allowed to go to Nomea. So why use it? Nomea has a king. I'm not it."

Nick laughed. "But you could be it. Imagine, running a whole country. That's the real business."

"It's not real, mate. None of it is real. Jean Claude has just been with my family for a long time. He's one of those true-believer types. He thinks it's absolutely going to happen. And that when it does, my mother needs to be ready."

"I mean, though, what if he's right? What if you could become a prince?"

That would be a nightmare. "I prefer to believe in reality and what's in front of me. Not what could be. Besides, I don't even know if my mother wants to be queen. It's just kind of this thing that a certain group of people expects from her. I don't think anyone has ever asked her if that's what she wants."

He frowned. "If she doesn't, who takes over?"

"I don't know. If something did happen to my cousin, uncle, whatever he is, she's next in line. And if she steps down, it could be Xander, or they could skip from that all together and head for my Uncle Timothy's line. He lives in the Caribbean, the Winston Isles."

"Oh right, the billionaire."

I laughed. "That man has got more money than God."

Nick grinned. "That man is my fucking idol."

"I mean, Nick, how much more do you want? You go where you want. Vacation when you want. The women are all around us all the time. What more could you actually desire?"

Nick grinned. "I don't fucking know, but I know that if I was a billionaire, I'd have it."

I laughed. Unlike me, Nick wasn't the least bit bored. Yeah, he wanted freedom and vengeance for his mother in a way, which is why he was doing what we were doing. But beyond that, he couldn't see the bigger picture. He didn't want anything else. He just wanted his lifestyle without the strings. I worried about him a little. Because if you don't have a goal or any purpose, what was the fucking point?

We crossed over toward Vauxhaul Station. One of Nick's dad's offices was around the corner. He was supposed to pick something up for him, so we'd parked over at Max's before we'd come to run the errand. As Nick went in, I couldn't help but glance back toward where I'd seen that girl.

There was so much more to life. So much more to do and see. And I wanted it all. But to get it, I was going to need to break free first.

Abbie...

"Would you hold still?"

I never listened to Sophie. I squirmed in her arms. "I don't need lashes."

"Everyone needs lashes, Abbie."

I shook my head. "No, I don't. I don't care if you dress me up like a clown."

Sophie pretended to be shocked by gasping and placing a hand on her chest. "Oh, my God, are you insulting how I dressed you?"

I really wasn't. She had me in a pair of leather leggings so tight they made my skinny jeans look loose and a low, backless top that showed off my assets. To help hold up my boobs, she put on some pasty type things that lifted them without the aid of a bra. Not that my boobs were particularly big, but if I ran out there without a bra on, everyone would see how done my chickens really were.

"Look, I don't mind how you dress me. And I don't know what I look like, so I don't know how bad my makeup is. But I'm pretty sure I don't need lashes."

She grabbed my chin. "Hold still before I beat you within an inch of your life."

I couldn't help but laugh at the familiar insulting threat. Growing up Ghanaian, it was common to have your parents often threaten you with corporal punishment. It rarely ever happened.

"Listen, you beat me, and then who will you dress up?"

Faith tsked from the bed. "Hey, no foreign languages. I only speak Irish."

I turned and raised my brow. "I'm not sure Irish is the language you mean. You mean Gaelic?"

She shook her head. "No, I'm fluent with swear words."

We all snorted a laugh.

I finally acquiesced, and Sophie put lashes on me. Because I knew if I didn't give in, she'd just try and tackle me and do it by force. It would be a lot easier if I just let her do it.

She stepped back and studied me. "Hmmm. Suddenly I'm feeling red." She stalked over to the closet and dragged out a slinky red dress. "Put this on."

"I don't suppose I have a choice?"

She merely shook her head, so I did as I was told.

While I changed for the umpteenth time, Faith flipped her magazine on the bed. "Abbie, how's class?"

"You know, I'm actually excited. I think it's going to be awesome."

"And is the prof as hot as we've seen in pictures?"

I groaned. "Hotter."

Sophie chewed on her bottom lip. "What's this about a hot professor?" Her full concentration was on my lashes.

"Just that Faith's obsessed with my new photography professor."

"Well, if he's hot enough to obsess over, maybe you should bring him around."

"What, I'm going to walk up to him and be like, 'Hey, want to come and meet my friends?' That's crazy."

She frowned. "Well, I mean, hasn't he noticed you're hot? We're talking about boning him, right?"

"What is wrong with you two? I will not be shagging my professor. Who are these girls that shag their professors?"

They both just shrugged at me. As if I was the one who needed to get with the times.

I rolled my eyes.

Sophie smacked me for that. "I told you, sit still."

"Ugh, fine."

She got lost in her own little world for a moment. As she worked on the other eye, Sophie broached the subject. "So, Easton? You're done with him, right?"

"Yeah, I'm done with him." I swallowed the churning bile that wanted to make an appearance. Dr. Kaufman was right. I blamed myself. And I hadn't been in love with him for a long time. So it was time to do things that were good for me. Fun for me.

"I mean, I've always hated him, but you knew that. What prompted you to pull the trigger?"

As great as my friends were, it was hard enough to admit to Dr. Kaufman everything that I had been through. I didn't want to go through it with these guys. Inside, I was still trying to make sense of it all. How I'd ended up in that position. Not that it was my fault. She'd helped me see that. But I did tend to make some decisions that weren't in my best interest, and I needed to fix that. I needed to break that cycle of decision-making. "Well, I guess it's been brewing for a while. I've known for way too long that he wasn't the right guy for me. But it's kind of easier to go along to get along, you know?"

Sophie nodded. "You always deserved better than him. You know that, right?"

I sniffed. "Yeah, well, I know that now. And then him hiding my acceptance letter and shredding my passport... That was some next-level crazy. So, I'm here right now."

She shook her head. "I still can't fucking believe he shredded your passport. Who does that?"

From the bed, Faith offered, "Someone crazy?"

"Someone controlling," I added.

Sophie sighed. "Can I ask you something, Abbie?"

"Sure." My stomach flipped and knotted upon itself. Not knowing what to expect.

"I mean, is that why you pulled away from us a little? I'm not saying that you did it on purpose, or whatever. And we weren't upset, but we did notice. Especially after college. We didn't get to see you hardly ever. And all of our conversations were usually cut short by Easton or by you hurrying to do something for him."

A fresh wash of shame splashed on me, just when I thought I'd had enough. There it was, willing to add more. "He didn't like it. He didn't like when I had any other friends, actually. He wanted to isolate me, and it's horrible that I let him. But I'm planning to fix all that. You guys are my best friends. I never should have let anyone come between us."

She sat back and smiled. "No way was he going to come

between us, because when we did see each other, it was just like old times. I just wanted to see you more. And I got the impression you had to *earn* the time with us."

How right she was. "Well, that's all over now. I'm here, and we are going to enjoy every moment of it. I'm recapturing my early 20s."

Both of them laughed. Sophie dusted some powder on my nose and then sat back to admire her work. "You look fantastic."

I turned to blink at Faith. "Do I look like a clown?"

Faith stared at me. "No, you look fucking amazing. Sophie, do me next."

Sophie laughed. "Come on. Come sit your pale ass on this chair and let me see if I can give you some color."

As Faith bounced into the seat I'd just vacated, I stopped in front of the mirror. Jesus Christ, Sophie had given me a vibrant smoky eye with a really pretty gleam. The lashes on my eyes absolutely stood out. Easton really didn't like how I did my makeup, it was never good enough. Never sophisticated enough. I preferred the no-makeup makeup look. He said every politician's significant other should look like she at least tried, so I needed to practice. He also had a lot to say about color and the type of women who wore red lipstick.

But this vibrant pop of color helped me take back my life.

I turned to my friends then. "You guys are absolutely right. No way in hell should I have let him stand between us. Tonight, we party. We have a lot of lost time to make up for."

APPARENTLY, I had never been clubbing properly.

The girls and I headed out with Max and some of the other models to the swank Mayfair neighborhood with its elegant row houses and gorgeous parks. The club had a name I couldn't pronounce and a line out the door that wrapped around the block. And that was the line for women.

Staring mulishly at my borrowed heels, I'd wondered why the hell I'd let Sophie dress me. There was no way I could endure that line in the four-inch stunners. They were beautiful with their red, black, and gold-braided straps, but I'd be ready to cut my feet off at the ankle before I even made it midway through the line.

Then again, when your friend was an up and coming designer, you let her do things like dress you, even at the cost of your comfort. With the flirty red salsa dress, I knew I looked hot. Especially since the damn thing was backless. But the shoes were going to be a problem. I could just picture it. There would be Instagram photos of me running around a London club barefoot, a la Britney Spears pre-conservatorship. I shuddered.

As it turned out, I needn't have worried about the line. Apparently since Jasper was the headliner and Max and one of the other guys were members of the club, all seven of us walked right in as if we owned the place. *This* kind of clubbing I could get used to.

Inside, the club was mostly empty. As if the throngs waiting outside had been nothing but an illusion. I leaned over to Sophie. "If there's no one in here, why the hell do they have everyone waiting outside?"

Sophie laughed. "Image, darling. Only about a quarter of those people will get in because they have the cash to bribe the bouncers. And don't forget, most of those people are coming for the larger club. This area is more exclusive and private."

"But what's the point? Wouldn't they make more money if they just let everyone in?"

Faith and Sophie smiled at me like I was the village idiot. Finally, Faith said, "Honey, this club has members that pay a pretty penny to keep the riffraff out. Besides, it's a hot spot for *OK* magazine darlings and the royals. The princes have partied here, so have the princesses and lesser aristocracy. Princess Alicia was spotted here last week. You can't let the general public in with them. It would be pandemonium."

I blinked. "And Jasper's DJing here? He must be really good."

Sophie shrugged. "He is. He creates beats for some local UK artists too. He's starting to get big." My friend assessed me shrewdly. "You're starting to pay more attention to him now, huh?"

A quick laugh burst out of my lungs. "No. He's lovely, but I don't buy the flirtation for a minute. I won't be spending any time in his, er, DJ booth."

Sophie cackled. "Don't let him hear you say that. You'll only become even more of a challenge."

"Oh, fantastic."

Faith joined us with three shots in her hands. "Okay, ladies, drink up. These are courtesy of Max and the boys at the bar."

I stared at the purple liquid. "What is this?"

Both of them laughed, and Faith just said, "I don't think you want to know." Raising her glass to the two of us, she added, "To Abbie. Welcome to London. And to the three of us, together again!"

"To us," I muttered before tossing back the violet liquid. Surprisingly, it went down smooth and tasted remarkably like grape juice. It wasn't until several seconds later that a warming sensation started in my belly then slowly spread to my extremities, making me instantly relaxed and a little numb. "Jesus, Faith, what was that?"

"They call it a Post Orgasm. Makes you feel loose, huh?"

"Loose is one word for it." I couldn't feel my fingertips.

Sophie grabbed the glasses and deposited them with a barback who moved through the crowd. "Come on, girls, it's time to dance."

Now dancing, I could do.

As we hit the center of the dance floor closest to the DJ booth, I closed my eyes and let the music take over my limbs. Jasper mixed some unfamiliar drum and bass beats along with some mild electronica and infused them into dancehall, rock, and popular rap songs.

The only problem was three women dancing together tended to attract attention... unwanted attention.

It wasn't long before guys started to join us, first dancing on the periphery then eventually sidling up close. Faith and Sophie welcomed the attention. I tried to focus on the music and ignore them. The first guy to slide up behind me had my body stiffening. Immediately, I stepped forward, spun around, and ended up on the other side of our little circle.

The next guy tried a frontal approach. Luckily, I could see him coming and waved him off. Maybe it was time to find Max and the other guys and sit down.

I waved at Jasper, and he frowned but nodded his acknowledgement. Sophie and Faith were too occupied to notice I'd slunk off the dance floor. On the edges where it was darkest, I paused and searched for where the guys had gone.

"I figured I'd try something different and ask you to dance."

I whirled around and let out a small squeak of alarm. The muscles in my lower belly quivered, and my breath caught. My savior from earlier stood in front of me, looking like a cross between an angel of mercy and the devil incarnate. "We have to stop meeting like this," I mumbled.

A smile tugged at the corners of his lips. "Well, there's no rain at the moment, so we should be safe. I trust we were able to save your camera?"

Heat flooded my cheeks. "Yes. Thank you. Honestly that could have been ugly today. I'm indebted."

"How about a dance, and we'll call it even?"

A dance? With him? Pressed up against... "I, uh..."

"Now, I'm not as good as you are, so you'll need to take it easy on me." He outstretched his hand and waited for me to take it. He didn't press or push, just stood there... waiting.

Jasper didn't help me when he switched the track to a dancehall reggae song with a grooving beat.

Butterflies fluttered low in my belly. When was the last time I'd had butterflies? Unfortunately, with those butterflies also came fear. The fact was I didn't know this guy. *But, if he'd wanted to hurt you, he could have already. It's just a dance.*

I glanced down at his hand and placed my palm in his. Determined not to be nervous, I smiled up at him. "Hardly seems fair. You saved my life, and all you get is this dance."

He drew me close, but not too close, keeping his hands at my waist. He waited patiently until I looped my arms around his neck. "It's well worth it to me." The low rumble in his chest as he spoke sent shivers coursing through my body.

As it turned out, he didn't need any help dancing. He moved us easily in time to the seductive beat. I didn't dare look around because I knew what I'd find—couples pressed so close that we might as well be naked and in bed. Dirty dancing was a requisite of dancehall music, but my partner kept a marginally safe distance between us, figuratively if not literally, because with every down swing of the bass, our hips rocked into each other.

I swallowed hard, but then forced my gaze up to meet his. As soon as our eyes met, my heart rate kicked. His slate gray eyes, framed by dark lashes, stayed on mine. Nervously, I licked my lips. He stilled for just a second, causing me to lose my footing and bringing me flush against his body.

I froze, muscles tight. Touching wasn't something I was used to or allowed easily. But with him, I didn't want to be anywhere else. He smelled of mint and something crisp and woodsy, like he'd spent the afternoon outside on the water. I released my strangled breath and let my body relax into his. I felt, rather than heard, the low rumble in his throat as his chest vibrated against mine. His warmth enveloped me, and I could tune out everything but him. As if it were only the two of us on the edge of the dance floor.

There, in the dark, in the arms of a relative stranger, I felt safe.

His hands shifted on my waist as his thumbs traced my hipbones, and I forgot to breathe. Wobbly knees forced me to tighten my hold on him. As if responding to my body's automatic softening, my eyes dipped to his lips.

What the hell am I doing? My brain tried desperately to take control of the situation, but I didn't feel like listening. For the first time in longer than I cared to think about, I liked having someone's hands on me. I wasn't afraid. Instead, I craved it, that connection. My body hummed with vibrant sexual energy. An energy I hadn't felt in six long years. There were nerves, but not from fear or trepidation. It felt good. Better than good. It made me remember how much I needed to be touched. Or rather touched by someone who could make me feel safe.

But just as the last of the tension ebbed out of my body, his thumbs pressed gently against my hipbones, moving me back several inches. He raised his head, and we stood like that for several seconds before I realized Jasper had switched the music. *Oh, God.* I'd been standing there with a total stranger, practically melting into him.

Heat rushed to my face. "I—"

He smiled, and I was too blinded to finish. Gently, his thumbs traced across my hipbones once more, and he let me go. "Thank you for the dance." Then he turned around and walked away.

I spent several seconds staring after him. What the hell had just happened?

"Hey, there you are." Faith's voice broke me out of the fog. "Who was that you were dancing with? I couldn't see clearly."

I stared into the crowd feeling empty. "I have no idea."

Two days later, I stood in front of Xander's office door wishing I hadn't stayed up so late again. I'd need to be careful hanging out with Sophie and crew. I wiped my sweaty palms on my jeans. *Come on. Get it together. You're here to learn.* I couldn't be afraid forever.

Taking one more deep breath to marshal my nerves, I knocked quietly.

"It's open."

"Here goes nothing," I mumbled.

The moment I opened the door to Xander's office, I felt like I'd walked into an episode of *Hoarders*. There were piles everywhere of books and boxes of photo equipment. *Wow.* "Um, is this a good time?"

He grinned as he stood. "Of course. It's your time to use. Here, let me clear you a spot to sit." Quickly, he cleared a stack of coffee table books off a chair and placed them on the floor beside his desk. "There you go. Have a seat, Little Bird."

I flushed. "Why do you keep calling me that?"

He plopped into his seat across from me with a lazy ease.

"What, Little Bird? It's how I see you. I go through every single one of the photos that you all submit for review. Occasionally, one or two stand out. From that point forward, I can't help but look at my students that way, as if that photo encompasses everything they are." He shrugged. "Hence, Little Bird."

There was no way I'd be able to concentrate with him staring at me like that. Like I had his full focus. I tried not to squirm under the scrutiny of his direct gaze. "So, can I ask, what are you looking for in your assistant position?"

His bark of laughter was rich and low. "Right to the point, I see."

I shrugged. "It's why I came to London. I want to work with you."

Something flitted over his expression, but it was gone almost as quickly as it had appeared. "I'm looking for a damn good photographer who can put up with me. Right now, all of you show promise, but I think with some hard work, we can make you shine."

Way to be vague. "I'd just like to know the criteria you're using to measure my work."

His lips tipped up in an oddly familiar smile. "Ahhh, the artist with a type-A streak. I understand. Composition, command of the light around you, the basics but to an expert level. I don't want to be able to tell the difference between your work and an Ansell Adams. But you have to infuse heart into your images. That and confidence. If it's not there, I can't use you."

Heart. Confidence. Considering mine had been ripped out of my chest, and my confidence lay under a pile of shit, I'd have to figure that out. "Okay. I can work on it."

"So, tell me what you're thinking of for your first assignment."

I detailed my plan to photograph the architecture of London and how I hoped to get that gritty urban feel that somehow still managed to convey joy. He listened intently before speaking.

"It's a decent plan. But honestly, I want to push you outside of your comfort zone. I don't want you to take pretty pictures of landscapes. Your portfolio was a little light on portraits. Maybe you can try some this week."

I forced my breathing to even out. Portraits. Absolutely my weakest kind of photos. "I, uh—"

"Hold that thought." He stood and strode to the bookshelf. Xander pulled out a dusty hardcover and handed it to me. Then he got on his hands and knees and searched the lower shelves before finding what he was looking for. "And this."

His fingertips brushed mine, and I jumped. He immediately withdrew his hand and sat on the edge of his desk, giving me plenty of room. *Great.* Now he thought I was nuts.

"I don't understand."

Xander studied me carefully. "You're here to learn, right? And to push your boundaries?"

I nodded.

"Then try something new. Have a look through those two books. Jonathan Frazier is one of my favorite photographers. The first one is a book of his landscapes. The other is of his portraits. Next meeting, tell me which ones moved you the most." He glanced at the clock. "It looks like our time is up for today."

Wow, an hour had gone by that quickly? "Sure. I can do that." I thanked him and picked up my bag to leave.

He stopped me in the doorway. "Abbie." His voice was low

as he leaned forward. "You can't photograph honestly when you're shuttered from the world. You'll have to open yourself and show your vulnerability to hit your true potential."

I tipped my chin up. "I can do that." At least I could try. Landscapes had always been easy for me, but if he wanted to push me, then fine. I'd get some portraits done. Even as I waved goodbye, my brain was already formulating a plan for the kinds of portraits I might be able to do.

Checking my watch again, I hurried out of the media building to meet Ilani for lunch. I'd already hit up most of the campus spots for a potential job before my meeting with Xander. Hopefully, something would come up in the next couple of days.

My friend arrived mere seconds after I did. "So how did your meeting go with Mr. I'd-consider-a threesome-for-you Chase?"

I barked out a laugh as Ilani and I grabbed a seat at the campus café. "Seriously, Ilani?"

The blonde shrugged. "I'm not into girls, but if that man asked me, I'd say hell yes, whatever you want. Come on, he's certainly worth the shag."

"You're ridiculous. Have you had your meeting with him yet?"

Ilani shook her head. "Mine's this afternoon."

I eyed my friend. Ilani had gone for a short corduroy skirt and low-cut fitted sweater. "I see you dressed to impress."

Ilani beamed. "Well, you have to put your best assets on display and see what happens. I mean, he might have said he's not interested, but I know for a fact he's slept with a student before."

Intrigued, I leaned forward. "Really? Who?"

Ilani glanced around surreptitiously. "She was a year ahead of me and in his undergraduate class. Rumor is she made him an offer he couldn't refuse."

"So what happened with her?"

Ilani shrugged. "Well Xander is notorious. Maybe she couldn't keep up."

"Uh-huh."

"Okay, fine, she caught him with some model on a shoot and went ballistic on him."

"Explain ballistic."

"Well, rumor is that their little tryst was all about woman on top. She allegedly grabbed the model by the hair and yanked her clean off Xander, then well, threatened him with bodily harm if you know what I mean." Ilani waggled her eyebrows. "She went completely mental. Screaming and shouting that she was going to end his career. Of course, she's the one who was carted off. He emerged unscathed."

That sounded like something from a soap opera. "Don't you think if all that happened, he'd be a lot less likely to sleep with another student?"

Ilani grinned. "Difference is I only want him for his body. I have no desire for a relationship of any kind. What about you?"

The waitress arrived with water and took our orders.

I shook my head. "Oh, I'm off relationships. I just got out of a bad one, and I'm not eager to repeat the experience."

"Oh no, I meant Xander. What do you want him for?"

"Xander? The only thing I want from him is an excellent job recommendation, if not a job itself, by the end of the year. Other than that, he's all yours."

Ilani studied me. "Are you sure about that?"

I frowned and shifted uncomfortably in my seat. "What do you mean?"

My new friend shrugged. "It means I saw you guys in the hall earlier. It looked like he might kiss you or something."

I blinked. "No. He was *not* going to kiss me. He was busy imparting some knowledge about how I'll need to be more vulnerable. Besides, I'm not interested. I'm staying far away from guys right now. He's all yours."

"If you say so. But from where I was standing, he looked plenty interested in you."

The look of seriousness on Ilani's face was the only thing keeping me from laughing out loud. "I promise you he's not. I'm just a student to him. Besides, with that skirt on, you're sure to catch his attention."

Ilani looked temporarily mollified, but then she added, "Look, all kidding aside, you seem like the kind of girl who could get hurt. I like you, and I don't want to see that happen. Just be careful."

After my chat with Ilani, I decided to take my time and explore the city a little bit more. I'd taken the bus into town, but instead of the familiar spots I'd explored, this time I went toward Notting Hill. I figured if it was good enough for Hugh Grant and Julia Richards, it was good enough for me. What always fascinated me was how friendly people were. Every time I passed someone, I'd get a cheery, "All right?"

I didn't think I was responding correctly though. I would smile and say 'yes, thank you,' but I didn't think that was the right answer because everyone always furrowed their brows and looked at me like I didn't understand what I was doing. I probably didn't. I'd have to ask Sophie or Faith what to say in response. The sun had started to set, and when I looked at my watch, it was already six. Which meant it would be dark soon, and I needed to get back.

On some of the row homes, there had been lanterns strung across the street. My hands weren't steady enough to make that kind of shot work. So I swung the backpack off my shoulder and pulled out my tripod. With a quick setup and a little lighting assist, I captured the kind of shot that I wanted. They were beautiful and whimsical and everything I sort of thought about when I thought about London streets. Cobblestones and lanterns were what I was looking for. That vibe of fun and frivolity. Not exactly what I wanted for a masters, but God, it was what I wanted for life.

Within another thirty minutes, the sun was well and truly making its final stand, and I pulled out my phone to look for a tube stop. I frowned when I discovered the nearest one was over half a mile away. How did I get so far off the beaten track?

I could Uber it. But again, since I didn't exactly have a job yet, I didn't want to spend money I didn't have to. And I had my Oyster card, so might as well use it.

As I marched along, people around me smiled and chattered. People were walking with their dogs as I made a turn on to the high street. It was busier there, and I felt a little less anxious.

But still, I couldn't shake my niggling hyper-awareness of everything that was around me. I made another left and a right. This was the way to the tube stop, right? Shit. I pulled out my phone again and saw the five percent charge warning. I'd left my stupid spare charger at home. Damn it. I pulled out my map and frowned when I realized, yeah, I was indeed off the beaten path. I had to turn around about three more blocks, make a right, another left, and then I'd be back on the high street.

Damn it. I turned around, but there it was again... that warning tripping up my spine and making the hair on my neck stand at attention. What was that? I glanced around, but all I saw were people in their jackets, walking their dogs, smoking cigarettes, carrying their takeout, and basically just enjoying their evening.

Relax. You're freaking yourself out. Just keep moving.

I made my turn, then the next one. But then I heard something behind me. When I turned, my heart beat so fast I thought it was going to explode in my chest. Who was that across the street? Had he been following me the whole time? I couldn't see the guy's face, but he was tallish, a familiar build, athletic. My skin broke out into a sweat. My heart continued to hammer. My brain was sending all the appropriate fear signals. *Run. Run. Danger is coming. You better run.*

I picked up my pace and hoofed it, glad I still had some people on the street with me. Would anyone help me if I screamed?

Or was this like America, where a young black woman might be ignored?

No. The British are unfailingly polite. Someone will stop. Right?

I was nearly running at that point. The booming in my head kept screaming. *Run. Run. Run. Run.*

Oh God, I couldn't breathe. My breathing was short and choppy. And then I turned at just the right moment, and when the light hit his face, the breath caught in my lungs. No.

No. No. No. No. It couldn't be him.

Easton. It was Easton. Easton was chasing me. Easton was coming for me. Fuck.

I broke out into a full-scale run then. I'd been an athlete in high school. It had been a while since I'd run for anything other than exercise, but they weren't kidding when they said the instinct for fight or flight takes over. I took off.

I made my next turn blindly, not even looking. And I banged into a brick wall hard enough to toss me on my ass. Once again, I saved the camera before I saved myself.

I tucked it to me, arms protectively around the lens, then I took the brunt of the fall on my ass and moved back, trying to keep my head up so it didn't slam on the ground. "Fuck!"

"Jesus fucking Christ! Are you all right?"

That voice. Why was that voice familiar?

I laid there, probably far longer than I should have, my jeans getting wet from the puddle I'd landed in. My first concern was that my camera was okay.

My brain gave the command to my hands, and they finally moved as I silently checked my equipment. It was fine.

Fuck.

I rolled up into a sitting position, trying to catch my breath, but the fear was still biting at me, telling me to get up and run. Did I dare look behind me?

I glanced behind me, but I didn't see Easton.

I looked over my other shoulder. Had he crossed the street? Had I missed him?

Shit.

Or, maybe you imagined it.

My head started to pound, and I groaned as I looked up at the person kneeling in front of me, talking to me.

My vision came into focus and I gasped. "Xander?"

"Ms. Nartey?"

"What are you doing here?"

He chuckled low. "Well, considering you're in my neighbourhood, that's my question for you."

"This is your neighborhood? But I left you at school a few hours ago."

He chuckled then. "Yes, and I had some student appointments, and now I'm home. And um, only to find that my students are following me."

I scowled then. "I am not following you. God, you're so full of it." He chuckled again.

"I see you're feeling better. Here, let me help you out."

I had no choice but to take his hand. My backpack and my ass were still in the puddle, and I still wanted to protect the camera. I let him help me up, and I groaned when I assessed the damage. "Jesus, I'm soaked. How awesome."

Standing that close to him, I realized just how much taller than me he was. I wasn't short, but he loomed over me at over six foot two. Bloody fabulous. And he was warm.

I could feel the heat emanating off of him. I had to resist the urge to move closer to him, because first, he was my teacher, and second, that would only serve to make him somehow more pompous. And I wasn't that girl. Faith was kidding when she said I should shag my professor. I wasn't here for that. And I didn't think he'd appreciate it.

Oh crap, he was talking to me. I tried to focus on his words, but the fear had my heart hammering too loud.

"Abbie? Did you hear me?"

I winced. "Sorry. I just—I thought someone was following me. I guess I overreacted."

His brows snapped down. "What do you mean someone was following you?"

"I was trying to find the tube station after taking some pictures and I just, you know, I had a feeling. I'm in a strange city, it's dark, and I'm running around taking pictures. And then I got the feeling someone was following me. I know. It sounds crazy. I'm sorry. I'm going to go. I just need to breathe a minute."

He shook his head. "No, you're coming with me."

I blinked at him. "What?"

"You're coming with me. I'm not going to let you run off to the tube by yourself in the dark after you've already fallen and thought someone was following you."

I tried to shake him off. "No, I'm fine. I'm a big girl. I can take care of myself."

He watched me, looking as though he wanted to reach out, but I deftly avoided his touch.

"I promise I'm fine."

He shook his head slowly. "No, I'm saying you're not fine. Chivalry isn't dead, and besides, my mother would kill me if I didn't at least see to it that you're okay. Why don't we step into this pub, and I'll call you a cab or an Uber?"

I didn't want to pay for the Uber, but I didn't want to tell him that. "Um, right. Okay."

"You're fine. You're perfectly safe in my hands."

I laughed at that. "I don't think a female student has been safe in your hands since you started teaching."

As soon as the words were out, I wanted to bite them back. "Oh my God, I'm so sorry. I just got flipped and basically what you said before, and oh my God, I just—I'm not feeling well, and I can't control my mouth."

He chuckled softly. "Hey, you know what? That's fair. I already opened that door. And you're probably right. I may have dated a student or two, once or twice."

I raised a brow. "Once or twice?"

He laughed as he led me to a booth in the corner and waved at the bartender. When the waitress came over and asked for drink orders, I shook my head. Xander ignored me. "I'd actually like tea for her. And one of your pastries, or anything you have."

"I'm not hungry."

"What if they're for me?"

"It's dinner time. Not tea and coffee time."

"Well, before I put you in a taxi, I'm going to make sure you eat something. And have some tea. Tea always seems to fix everything."

I laughed. "I'm not sure tea will make me not crazy."

He shrugged. "It's worth a shot. So, want to tell me why you think someone is following you?"

"You're not going to let that go, are you?"

He shook his head. "Nope. Are you afraid of someone?"

Oh, hell no. You are not doing this. I was not going to confess everything to my very good-looking male professor, who probably had many panties dropping all over the country because he was stupidly attractive. I didn't know where to look when I gazed at him. And God, he knew how to melt you with a look, but something told me I didn't want to get involved with him beyond a professional level.

Sure, I found him attractive, but I wasn't necessarily attracted to *him*. There was something that drew me to him, some familiarity. But it was off. Not like when I got saved by the other guy a couple days earlier. That instant spark that had me feeling stupid for hours afterward... It wasn't like that. But that was good because he was my professor.

Yeah, dumbass, don't forget that.

"I'm not afraid of anyone."

He cocked his head. "You're not telling me the truth."

"I don't have to tell you the truth."

He nodded. "Fair enough. Maybe you should avoid walking the streets without a friend late at night."

"What kind of world is it that I can't walk around without a chaperone?"

He shrugged. "You can. But I'm just saying you were scared."

"I'm fine. I overreacted."

He shrugged. "If you say so. In the meantime, if you get that scared again, anywhere, like on campus or anything like that, not that we're friends or anything, but you tell me, and I'll make sure that you're not scared anymore."

I frowned. "What are you going to do?"

"Well, for starters, I can get security to walk you to your bus. That's easy enough. And if someone deliberately scares you, not that that's what this was this time, but we can talk to the school administration. Have security posted, that sort of thing. But you were just overreacting, right?"

I met his gaze and nodded slowly. "Yeah, just overreacting."

I'm sure Dr. Kaufman would have a field day with this, but speaking my truth wasn't going to happen with my teacher, no matter how kind he was being. When my tea came, I was actually grateful for it. And the pastry was delicious.

But what I was more grateful for was Xander. He talked to me. Calmed me down. Asked me about home. Not about family, or boyfriends, or anything like that, but about my favorite shooting spots and my favorite subjects and some of the best places that I'd shot and places for great light. As if everything about me from the past that was important was all he was actually interested in, not that superficial stuff. It made me feel more normal and calmed me down.

By the time the Uber arrived, he'd already paid for my pastry and tea, despite my irritation and annoyance about it.

"Come on, I dragged you into this cafe. I pay."

When he opened the door to the Uber, he glanced down at me and gently guided my elbow and helped me inside. "Listen

Abbie, I'm serious. If you should get scared like that again, I do want you to tell me. Because I can make that experience better for you."

Just before he closed the door, while we're still connected, I met his gaze. And there it was... a spark of something. Something a little bit like I felt the other day with that guy who saved me from the Mini Cooper. Now why the hell would I feel the same way?

"You ready for dinner?" I asked Xander as I narrowly avoided stepping on a box of lens filters.

"Yeah, just let me put away the student portfolios," Xander muttered.

I looked around Xander's tiny office. "Just where do you plan on putting them, Xan? It's not like you have a lot of room in here."

"Take the piss all you want, mate. I have a system." He stuck the portfolios on an already overflowing shelf. "Besides, it's not like I have an assistant right now. Most of this stuff will move to my studio anyway. Once that's done, it'll be downright tidy in here."

I just laughed. "Sure. Whatever you say."

Xander studied me as we left his office and took the back hall to the staff parking lot. "So, what's with you?"

I shoved my hands into my pockets and kept my gaze straight ahead. I didn't need Xander probing into the dark recesses of my mind. "Nothing. Why do you ask?"

Xander dropped his camera bag in the boot, then strolled

around to the driver's side of his Pagani Huayra. "Seriously, Alexi? You seem to forget it's my job to study the nuances of human features and emotion then capture those moments."

I wasn't in the mood for Xander's attempts at psychoanalysis. I carefully opened the passenger door of the Huayra. The car was both the fastest and the flashiest of Xander's vehicles. I preferred to run around in something more subtle, but Xander liked the attention. Although, I had to admit the thing was cool.

"I'm not biting, Xander. Let it go."

"I can't. It's written all over your face. The tight set of your mouth. When you smile, it doesn't quite reach your eyes. Your body has a rigidity to it. Especially in your shoulders. Like you're poised and ready to take action on something. Not to mention you're fidgety as hell."

I immediately stopped playing with the hem on my hoodie. "I am not fidgety."

"Come on. Why don't you just tell me what it is? Is it Gemma?"

I was careful to keep my voice neutral. "When did you become an agony aunt? I'm fine."

Xander narrowed his eyes and studied me as we came to the stop sign at the campus exit. "No, it's not Gemma, but it is a woman. Go ahead and tell me I'm wrong."

"You're wrong." I kept my face averted toward the window. Maybe dinner with Xander had been a bad idea.

"You forget I know you better than anyone. Who is she?"

I dropped my head against the headrest. "She's no one. Just a girl. I don't even know her name." But as luck would have it, I'd seen her with Max's girlfriend, which meant if I was so inclined, I could track her down.

Xander shook his head. "See, I've got the skills of a detective. Maybe when this photography thing is over I should join Scotland Yard. Screw that, I'm going big. MI-6 all the way."

Despite myself, I laughed. "You're full of shit."

"Maybe, but I figured out some woman is tying you in knots. Gemma got a clue?"

Xander was the only one who knew the truth behind my relationship with Gemma. And he thought I was insane to go along with it. "There's nothing to tell Gemma. I haven't done anything, and I'm not going to." I said through clenched teeth. I couldn't pursue it. I wanted it too much.

"Yeah right. You've got the look of a man on a tight string." Xander shook his head as he easily navigated the streets of Ealing on his way to the motorway. "Though I have to say, I like this look on you."

I frowned. "What the hell is that supposed to mean?"

"Oh, I dunno. I feel like you've used your relationship with Gemma as an excuse to never get close to anyone. Sure, you have a discrete dalliance here, a hot fling there, but you've never had to be in a real relationship with someone you care about who would actually have to get to know the real you."

"Shut it, Xander."

Xander laughed. "Why? Because I'm telling you the truth? You are avoiding intimacy because you're afraid of what you'll have to show and share. It's classic."

I rolled my eyes. "Oh, I'm the one with love issues? Says the man who goes through women like you've heard they're about to become extinct or something."

Xander grinned. "I do love women. But we weren't talking about me. Besides, I've turned over a new leaf. Women are to be treated with respect. We were talking about *you* and some woman getting under *your* skin. It's a good look for you."

"Wow, Xan, I had no idea you were such a romantic." I eyed him again. "Shit, you're not sleeping with another one of your students, are you?"

Xander's eyes bugged. "No! Hell no. I learned my lesson the first time."

I laughed. "You know they have those rules for a reason."

"I said I'm not fucking sleeping with her."

"Her... so there's a her?"

Xander cursed. "No. I have a student. She's promising, that's it."

"And you want to sleep with her."

"No. Damn it. I want to teach her."

I had to laugh. "Exactly what do you want to teach her, Xan?"

"Shut up, baby brother."

"Yeah, that's what I thought."

Xander was quiet for several moments before he quietly said, "The old man called me. Or rather had Mum call me."

"Fucking fantastic. Whose side are you on, Xander?"

"Yours. Always yours."

I glared at him. "Then why are you pushing his agenda?"

"I'm not. I swear. I personally think you should tell the geezer to fuck off like I did. I just worry he'll pull the trigger on his threat."

"Well, he's welcome to. Very soon, I won't need his money."

"It's more than money you're walking away from, Alexi. It's not always easy to do. I wouldn't think any less of you if you took his deal."

Blood boiled under my skin. "After everything that happened, you think I'd take the easy way out? I don't want anything from him."

"And everything comes back to that."

I ground my teeth. "Of course it comes back to that. We were kids, Xan. He was supposed to love us, and instead he treated us like we'd tarnished his good name."

"Never said he wasn't a prick."

"Well, I want nothing from that prick. I knew that night he didn't give a shit about us."

Xander nodded. "Also true. That night changed everything, but we survived."

Had we? I didn't feel like I'd survived. I felt like a storm-battered buoy most of the time. "It was a hell of a price to pay."

Xander nodded slowly. "Just as long as you understand what that will mean for you."

"Yeah, it will mean my freedom."

DINNER WITH XANDER went infinitely better once we stopped talking about our father. Though, I knew next time I'd have to lay off the Scotch. It had been two days and I still hadn't fully recovered.

My skin buzzed, my brain was foggy, and my focus was shot to hell. But that could easily be because I knew I was about to see my mystery girl again. My blood rushed just thinking of having her in my arms again.

When Max had told me to pop 'round, he mentioned Sophie was having some friends around too. I prayed her friends included the American girl. And just like that, the force of the gravitational pull was too strong to ignore. I knew I had it bad. I didn't even know her name and I was a total sap.

I tried to focus on what the hell Jasper was saying, but my brain could only focus on the sounds of Sophie and her friends as they walked in the door. Sophie bounded in with her usual energy, her friends in tow.

She greeted me with a hug. "Hey, Lex. I want you to meet my friend, Abbie Nartey. And of course, you know Faith."

So, at last I had a name. I forced myself to smile and mutter a greeting to Faith as I kissed her on both cheeks, but I couldn't take my eyes off of Abbie. When I turned my attention to Abbie, I steeled myself for the current of electricity.

She met my gaze with a sheepish smile and said, "Actually, Sophie, we've already met. Sort of."

I cleared my throat. "Abbie, it's nice to meet you, officially." I shouldn't touch her again, but I knew if I didn't, I'd probably regret it the rest of the night. Stepping forward, I took her hand and kissed her twice on the cheek. I took note of her stiff posture again. Yeah, she was definitely not comfortable with touching. I slowly let out a breath before backing away. Her gingery shampoo made my nose tingle. I ached to keep hold of her. I was in trouble. *A shit load of trouble.*

"Earth to Lex, pay attention, mate. This is your birthday, after all. And we've got a week to make it epic," Max muttered.

I rolled my head and tried to massage my neck. "I'm not sure what you need me for. I told you my criteria. I really don't want it to be seedy. No surprises and no strippers. I want to know what's coming."

As Sophie chatted with her friends, my gaze kept wandering in Abbie's direction. The memory of her pressed up against me, melting into my arms, snuck into my frontal lobe. And the memory alone was enough to trigger a kick of lust to my groin.

Jasper, relentless flirt that he was, lost focus on the birthday plans and hit on the girls instead. Specifically, on Abbie. I couldn't help the pang of jealousy as Jasper turned his full-wattage grin on her.

"You're looking beautiful as always, ladies. Especially you, Abbie."

Faith just laughed and shook her head. Abbie blinked at

Jasper once, then twice, then said, "Do these cheap lines really work on girls?"

Jasper frowned. "Yes, usually."

Abbie shook her head. "I'm not sure why. They could use a dose of sincerity."

I grinned. So, she wasn't shy or afraid to call things as she saw them. I liked her even more.

Jasper clutched both hands over his heart and pretended to die. "You wound me. That's okay though. I have thick skin, and I'm not giving up."

There was no way I was letting Jasper hold too much of her attention. I smiled at Abbie and asked, "Did you girls have fun at the club the other night?"

She chewed on her bottom lip and hid a smile. Good, maybe I had her thinking about our dance.

Abbie stuttered, "Y-yeah, it was fun. I had no idea Jasper was such a good DJ."

Fantastic. I'd given her the opening to give Jasper a compliment. *Moron.*

"What's this about no strippers?" Sophie asked.

Max rolled his eyes. "Lex doesn't want strippers at his party. We're trying to convince him he's got to do it."

Abbie met my gaze as she slid into a chair between Faith and Jasper. "Why don't you want strippers? Aren't you supposed to want strippers?"

Nick guffawed. "See, Abbie speaks sense. You're a man. There should be naked women there."

"I prefer any naked women I'm around to be there because they want to be, not because they are allegedly working their way through University or something."

Abbie laughed and the sound filled my head. "What are you

going to have if not strippers?"

Wow, someone who actually cared what I wanted. "Maybe a little poker, some music. Something low key."

Max tossed a pen at me. "No way, no how, Lex. It's your twenty-fifth birthday. It has to be fun. You can be mellow *after* this party, but in the meantime, Jasper and Nick and I will plan it."

"Any chance I'm going to escape it?"

"Nope," Max said with a grin.

"Fine, I give up." Through my peripheral vision, I watched as the girls headed up to one of the bedrooms. Try as I might, I couldn't keep my mind focused on the conversation. Eventually, the guys stopped including me and just talked football.

My phone buzzed in my pocket, and I frowned the moment I pulled it out. Dad had been calling all day. If I didn't answer now, there was no way the old man would stop. "I'll just grab this on the patio."

No one paid me any attention as I headed up the stairs to the living room then out onto the patio. "What's the problem?"

His voice was terse. "Did you speak to your brother?"

Damn it, could I get no fucking peace from the man? My mind went to a point in my life when I'd needed the old man and he hadn't made the time for me. But now, when *he* wanted something, it was all I could do to get away from him.

"Yes, I did. I also thought I made it clear that you'd have a decision after my birthday, not before."

"What is there to think about? It's not as if you'll forgo the money you've gotten so used to. I have a problem I need you to address in Japan in a few days. You'll need—"

"No." I kept my voice controlled, but anger simmered under my skin. I hated how he treated me like a foregone conclusion.

"I'm not going to Japan. I'm not going anywhere until my decision is made." If I told him to shove it up his ass now, the old man would know something was up. His assumption that I wouldn't give up money was right, at least partly. If the old man got wind of the sale, he would move heaven and earth to stop it, and I wasn't going to let that happen.

"You're walking a tightrope. Your birthday is in a few days."

"And you said I had until my birthday to decide, so I'm taking the time." I hung up before my father could say anything else. Even talking to the old man for five minutes was enough to make my temper bubble over.

A voice from my left startled me. "Everything okay?"

Abbie. The anger morphed into something else far more dangerous. "Shit, I didn't know you were out here."

She ducked her head as she stepped out of the shadows. "Yeah, sorry. We both had the same idea." She held up her phone. "I didn't mean to eavesdrop."

I shook my head. "Just family drama."

Her smile was rueful as she spoke. "Tell me about it."

She shifted toward the balcony door, and my mind searched for something else to say to prolong the conversation. "How's the camera?"

Her brows knotted together then rose as she tilted her head.

"Your camera? I figure since I was its knight in shining armor, I should ask after it. After all, I nearly died performing its rescue."

She laughed, and I felt like I'd been lit up from the inside.

"Yeah, it's good. You know, it was a tough ordeal. But with a little therapy and some new filters for medication, she'll be all right."

"Glad to hear it." My fingers itched to touch her again, but I knew better. Even if she'd welcome the touch, I needed to stay very far away from her. A girl like her would tear me up inside. I knew what I was. And once she found out the same, she'd run for the hills. I was better off staying away. "Next you're going to tell me she has a name."

Abbie grinned and took two steps toward me. Hell, if she came any closer, I'd forget about my damned don't-touch-her rule.

"I call her the badass money maker."

I laughed. "Are you serious?"

"Of course. I've taken all my best photos with her. I have another two cameras, but they don't seem to do it the same way she does."

I held up my hands. "Okay, okay. Fair enough. Badass money maker it is." I rubbed my jaw. "My brother's a photographer, and I don't think he names his cameras. His other appendages yeah, but never his cameras." The moment I'd let it slip about Xander I wanted to bite my tongue off. I prayed she didn't ask if she might have seen his work. I didn't need her going all starry-eyed once she knew about the infamous half of the Chase brothers.

Abbie cocked her head. "You can't mock her name. I like it. Besides, your name is Lex. Please tell me your parents had a sick sense of humor and your last name is Luther. That would be perfect."

"A Superman lover, I see." Well, wasn't she full of surprises? "And Mum and Dad do not have a sense of humor, thank God. It's Chase, actually. Alexi Chase."

Abbie frowned "Is Chase a common surname in the UK?"

He inclined his head. "Common enough. I suppose it's like the surname Smith. Why?"

She shook her head. "No reason." She studied me carefully. "Anyway, I like it. Alexi sounds Russian."

"My maternal grandmother was Nomean actually. Grandfather was Greek. Nomea is this little island off the coast of France. Dad's British." I cleared my throat and watched her carefully. She tucked one of her braids behind her ear, and I longed to touch her. Who was I kidding? I couldn't be casual with her, and I couldn't let her get too close and see me for who I really was, so my only option was to stay away from her. I could try to be good.

"I think I prefer Alexi."

"And is Abbie short for Abigail?"

She wrinkled her nose. "No. It's Abena. Abena Nartey."

I cocked my head. "Beautiful, like its owner."

She ducked her head. "Uhm, thanks. I guess I should be grateful I wasn't born on a less attractive sounding day."

I furrowed my brow. "I don't understand."

"Like Sophie, I'm from Ghana. My name means *born on Tuesday*."

I grinned, laying it on thick. "What a coincidence, Tuesday is my favorite day of the week."

She laughed. "You're almost as bad as Jasper now."

"Oh, ouch. I like to think I bring my own flair." I liked her. Enough to ignore the warning bells clanging in my skull. When she was relaxed, she was funny and sarcastic and kept me on my toes. *Want her.*

"Well, if it's any consolation, I think you're probably a better dancer."

"Hell, yes. I can give you another demonstration anytime you like."

Her gaze snapped to mine, and a smile tugged at her lips. "I um, thought I already repaid my debt."

"You did. This dance would just be because it's fun." Maybe I was pushing my luck. Maybe she'd scurry away again at a moment's notice.

But she didn't. I lost track of how long we stayed outside talking about nothing in particular. But I sure as hell didn't plan on leaving before she did.

It wasn't until Faith called her name from somewhere inside the house that she excused herself.

"Duty calls. I guess I'll see you around, Alexi."

Oh, hell.

The way she said my name held me transfixed. Abena Nartey was going to be a problem.

When I opened the door to the barge on the morning before my official birthday, I stood stunned for several seconds.

"Don't look so surprised, it's not like you've never seen me before," Dad said.

I didn't move aside to let him in. "Well, I've just never seen you *here* before. Are you dying?"

He sneered. "You can only wish. Now step aside, and let me in."

I didn't see any way around it. If the old man wanted in, I wouldn't stop him, but I'd sure as hell have exterminators come through afterward and clear out the bad energy. "What's up, Dad? I still have time to tell you my decision."

"I do know it's your birthday shortly. I was there for the big event after all. I'm not totally oblivious."

I frowned. "Considering that you've only been around for a couple of birthdays that I can remember, and given that you usually have your secretary pick my present, I'm pretty sure you're not here because of my birthday."

He squared his shoulders. "Well, you would be wrong. Tomorrow, once you've properly turned twenty-five, I want you in the office. But for today, I'm here to give you something."

I worked hard to keep my expression neutral. "Yeah okay, Dad, but you could have had someone bring whatever it is over." I hovered near the door. "I'm actually late for an appointment."

Dad scoffed. "I think your friends can wait. After all, it's only a party. You're busy talking to your father."

I gnashed my teeth. I didn't have time for this bullshit. If I didn't hurry, I'd be late for my meeting with Toshino. But the hell I was going to tell the old man any of that.

"I really do have an appointment, Dad."

He shoved his hands into his pockets as he shook his head. "Fine, we'll continue with our conversation tomorrow. Do you at least want to see your present?"

No, I didn't. "Sure. What is it?"

He pulled out a set of car keys and tossed them to me. The BMW key fob matched the one I already had for my car. "You bought me a car?"

He nodded. "I asked my secretary to go and pick up something a young man in his twenties would want. She came back with this. A BMW 6 Series convertible. I don't know what you're driving these days, but I'm sure this is better."

No. Not better. Exact replica was more accurate. Was my father that clueless that he didn't even know what I drove or that I'd bought the car for myself? Hurt chased annoyance as I took the keys. "Yeah thanks, Dad." I'd find a charity in the morning to see if they'd come pick up the car. At least I could do something useful with it. "If that's it, I need to get going."

He eyed me up and down once more. I held his gaze

directly and wished I knew why my father had stopped loving me.

I didn't have long to wallow because Mum called as soon as he left. "How is one of my favorite sons?"

"You know that doesn't actually mean anything unless you designate one of us your favorite, right?"

She sniffed. "You know I can't choose. You and Xander are both so dear and darling to me."

"Right. So, what's up?"

"I know your father just left."

Ahh, so the old man had called to complain. "Really, Mum. I don't want to fight about him today."

"And we won't." She placated me. "I was just going to say I have the perfect charity to drop the car off with."

"You can relax, Mum, I'm not even that pissed. It's not a surprise after all. Of course, he wouldn't be paying attention."

She laughed, and it made me smile. Her laugh was one of my favorite things. "Well, that's a change. There was a time not so long ago that you would have both deteriorated into an all-out shouting match."

"Yes, I like to call that period last week." I sniggered.

"My, how you've matured since then."

"Well, having it out with him would have ruined my birthday, and I'm not willing to do that."

She was quiet for a moment. "You sound different."

I had to roll my eyes. She was constantly trying to slink into mother hen mode. "No, I'm not sick. I'm eating, and I'm not working too hard."

"Oh, stop. Let an old woman worry."

"I doubt anyone would have the courage to call you old."

She laughed. "They'd better not. But no." She paused. "It's something else. You sound lighter, somehow. Happy, almost."

Yeah. Almost. "I don't know what you mean." Except I did. I'd be seeing Abbie again tonight. Except tonight, I was going to content myself with seeing her from afar. If I got too close, I'd do something stupid.

"If I didn't know better, I'd say you met someone."

I coughed. "Mum, stop. Have you forgotten, I'm with Gemma?"

She sighed. "No. I haven't forgotten. I'm just saying as much as I adore Gemma, I don't think you're particularly passionate about her. I don't think she inspires this kind of levity in you. Everyone deserves passion, Lex."

"Um, Mum, this is fast becoming a very awkward conversation." I shoved a hand into my pocket as I said a silent prayer that she didn't expound on everyone needing passion.

She sighed. "Fair enough. I mostly just called to wish you a happy early birthday and tell you that your present will be delivered to the Brixton Youth Center tomorrow. I figure you'll want to be on site for it. I've arranged for that basketball player Thai Curry to visit."

I frowned. "Um, do you mean Steph Curry?"

"Oh, yes, that's the one."

I laughed. "Thank you, Mum. That is a brilliant gift. Just send me the details. The kids will be so excited. I can't wait to see their faces."

"I'm glad you like it. After all, what does a mother get for the son who has everything?"

"It's brilliant, Mum. Honest."

"Good. But Lex?"

"Yeah?"

"I meant what I said about passion. I'd hate for you to let the past stop you from finding someone you can really love. No matter who that might be."

"Even if it doesn't look good for the crown?"

"The crown isn't real yet. Don't you dare put your life on hold because of it. Too many before you have put their lives on hold."

IF I WAS GOING to continue hanging out with Sophie, I'd have to get some comfortable shoes and hydrate better.

Bending over, I adjusted the strap of one of the sexy, black, sling-back stilettos she'd put me in. When Sophie had come home to the flat, Faith and I had both been surprised, but Sophie had only been there to grab an outfit and drag me out the door with her. Faith had been smart enough to beg off with the excuse of having to work.

As I stumbled behind my glitterati godmother, I mouthed to Faith, "Save me."

She only laughed and waved me off.

The glitterati life was fun, but I was starting to see it for what it was. The same crowd at different venues, looking vaguely bored and searching for something to entertain them.

A month ago, I never would have dreamed of this place. A few weeks and a transatlantic flight later, *I* was bypassing club lines, hanging out in VIP, and being flirted with by guys who were so beautiful they made me feel inadequate. *Like Easton.*

Nevertheless, I was kidding myself if I thought I was skipping Alexi's birthday. Just the idea of seeing him again made my heart race. I didn't want to examine those feelings too closely. Because then I'd have to think about what that meant.

It's just a crush. A crush is safe. You know better than to look for more.

Besides, I'd made a promise to myself. I was going to live every experience. I was going to find joy in the mundane. For years, I'd been a shell of myself.

True, I knew what happened when I danced too close to a flame because I was enthralled, but... I wasn't going to let that happen again.

As usual, Max and the boys took care of me while Sophie flitted about hugging and air kissing the beautiful people. I had always wondered how she managed it—to be equal parts sincere and fabulous.

Two sake shots and one absinth drink later, I still hadn't seen hide nor hair of the birthday boy. Head buzzing and needing some air, I trudged up the dingy back stairs looking for the roof. Maybe it was for the best that I'd yet to see Alexi.

It didn't matter what he did to my insides; he was first and foremost a guy, so I'd have to be careful. Secondly, he was out of my league. And finally, he was too much like Easton—too handsome, with access to money and power. I'd fallen for the smooth, good-guy image before. I wasn't going to be fooled again. I couldn't afford to be. I already had too many scars from my first encounter.

I shoved open the sticky rooftop door, and the chilled air immediately cleared my alcohol-fogged mind of any Easton thoughts. I wasn't going to think about him or what I'd left behind. Or worse, how I'd let myself be treated. And I was certainly not going to think about *how* I'd left it all behind. I was going to focus entirely on *my* life. This new experience. I would only be able to live in this dream world for so long, and I wanted to enjoy every single aspect of it. Even if it did feel like a fantasy.

The dingy stairs and heavy door were misleading. Instead of the industrial landscape I expected, the club's roof was a lush green garden. A massive trellis obscured most of the view of London nightlife, save one exposed ledge with padded bench seating.

Sucking in the air like it was fresh water after a drought, I escaped to the bench and toppled onto it. I slipped off Sophie's shoes and immediately started rubbing my feet, wondering what kind of hangover I'd have in the morning. Was there a rule against mixing sake and absinthe, like there was for beer and liquor? Hell, back home I barely even drank, save the occasional martini if I was out with Easton.

A couple of weeks with Faith, Sophie, and their rag-tag bunch of model boys, and I was buzzed on a rooftop in London. Maybe this was my *Sex in the City* moment. Though, I doubted Carrie, Miranda, Charlotte, or Samantha would have been up on a rooftop alone.

"So, first you crash my party, and then you crash my sanctuary. We have really got to stop meeting like this. It could be hazardous to your health."

I whirled around to find Lex sitting in a hidden alcove about three feet from me. "In case you didn't know, it's your birthday. I think you're supposed to be at the party."

Alexi shrugged, and I was fascinated by what the action did to his shoulder muscles.

"Well, the most intriguing girl there barely made time to

talk to me. She was occupied by the DJ and a stream of would-be suitors, so I came up here to lament."

A flush crept up my neck. He'd been waiting to talk to me? "Sorry I haven't wished you happy birthday properly yet. Sophie can be Sophie. Apparently, there were lots of people I just *had* to meet."

"Yes, I saw." He cocked his head. "You looked visibly uncomfortable."

I snorted. "You caught that, did you?" I'd have to be careful with him. He was way too observant. "Not real big on hugging or air kissing."

He scooted out of the alcove and sauntered over to join me on the bench. I caught a whiff of cologne as he sat. Something musky, but also crisp and intoxicating.

"So, tell me, how did you end up here? In my sanctuary."

"Well, I didn't see a sign, so sorry to crash your private party. And sorry to crash your actual party. I got enveloped in Sophie's plan, as usual. I heard you guys planning the other day, but I had no idea it was your actual birthday until we got here."

He shook his head. "I was teasing. Any friend of Sophie's..."

I hid a smile. *You don't even know this guy.* Well not true exactly. I knew he had a penchant for rescues, and he had family problems.

And he makes your skin tingle when he touches you. Yeah well, I needed to go ahead and forget that one. *And he makes you feel safe.*

"Well, I had too much sake and chased it with absinthe, so I seriously needed some air."

He chuckled. "Yeah, that'll do it."

"I'm waiting for the hallucinations to kick in any moment now. Will I really see a green fairy?"

He chuckled low, and I wanted nothing more than to melt into that sound.

"I think you're safe from little green fairies. The absinthe they serve these days is missing the wormwood, so you're unlikely to hallucinate."

"What? Then what was the point of all that? The sugar cube and the flame? I thought I was getting something really extraordinary."

"Well, you got the experience at least, if not the buzz."

I sighed and slouched. "Bummer. Not quite the London experience I was expecting."

"Oh, come on, at least you came to a cool party." He winked.

"Yes. There's that." My arm accidentally grazed his, and I sucked in a breath as I shifted away. "But that's not what I meant. I meant the first time doing something out of my norm. Stepping out of the box."

"Ahh." He nodded. "Seems I have a little adventurer on my hands."

"Ha. I'm hardly an adventurer." I shivered.

Lex shrugged out of his jacket and shifted toward me. Unsure of what he meant to do, I stiffened and leaned away from him an inch. His grey eyes met mine, and his smile was soft. Careful not to move too quickly, he slid his jacket around my shoulders. The warmth of his heat cocooned me.

Relax, Abbie, go with the flow. For once, be brave. I closed my eyes, and without thinking, I snuggled into his coat and leaned into him.

The moment my body made contact with his, we both stilled, and I didn't dare breathe. When it finally came to a choice of inhale, or pass out, I dragged in air quickly.

The moment I tried to slide away, he scooted closer and threw an arm around me.

For three long seconds, I forgot how to speak. My brain, unable to command my body to move away, took stock of my emotions. Anxiety level—DEFCON One. Fear level—low. Lust level—skyrocketing.

Minus a deep breath of his own, Alexi seemed completely unaffected by our close proximity. When he spoke again, his voice was mellow, modulated. "So, you don't think you're an adventurer? How did you end up in London, if not?"

If he could be cool, then so could I. "Would you believe it if I told you I ran away from home? Left my life and my apartment and my b—" I halted just short of saying boyfriend. I amended. "I left my family just to prove that I could do something extraordinary, *be* something extraordinary."

And ditched my abusive ex.

He was silent for several beats, but I could tell his eyes were on my profile. My skin tingled under his scrutiny.

"That's brave as hell. You are an adventurer."

"Well, the jury's still out. Everyone back home thinks I'm going to give up and go back if they bug me long enough."

"Well, how long has it been?"

I grinned and forced myself to meet his gaze. "A couple of weeks."

———

Lex...

I held Abbie tighter as she shivered again.

What the hell was I doing? This was not part of the plan.

And there was something about the way she stiffened whenever anyone touched her. It screamed baggage.

But she was relaxed in *my* arms now. I should let her go. But I liked her. *Really* liked her.

All the more reason to let her go, mate.

Because there was something about her that read damaged. Like me. Broken, like a bird.

I didn't do damaged. *Sure, you don't.* I was damaged enough for the two of us. I didn't need to take on anyone else's baggage.

At the same time, there was something so exposed and open about her. Something vulnerable but strong, unlike the girls I usually met. The over-processed, coy, game-playing girls who pretended they had no idea who I was or what I was about. But Abbie didn't seem to know. She seemed real.

I wanted a slice of that reality. Wanted to touch it, if only for a minute. Hell, I was at my birthday party, and only a handful of those people would I call my friends. I would have preferred to be home with a pile of movies.

I smiled at her. "So, after a couple of weeks, what do you think of our little island?"

"Besides having fallen completely, unashamedly in love with the history, and the energy, and the diversity, and the atmosphere?" She shrugged, feigning indifference. "It's okay. If you like that kind of thing. And school has been awesome so far."

"School?" The hairs on my neck stood at attention. *Relax. There are a hundred schools in London.* She could be studying at any one of them.

What's the best one for photography?

No. No way. This didn't mean she was Xander's student. I could have asked, but I didn't want to get into it. Because what if the answer was yes? I wasn't accustomed to the flare of jealousy when it came to my big brother, but I understood the pull he had on women.

Would she be as susceptible as every other woman in London?

"Yeah. I ran away from home to do a Master of the Arts in Fine Art Photography. My parents are beside themselves. It's like I said, 'Hey, Mom and Dad, I want to go be a drug dealer in London.'"

I laughed nervously. My brain kept trying to rationalize all the ways she couldn't be Xander's student. She could go to Camberwell or University of Arts. They were the most competitive with University of West London for fine arts degrees. All I had to do was ask.

Ask dumbass.

But I didn't want that truth glaring at me. This was a complication that I didn't need. So instead, I said, "I get the non-supportive parent thing."

She shrugged. "Yeah. It's no big deal. I don't need their approval."

But the way her shoulders slumped said she cared no matter what she spoke.

"So you're here to become the next Annie Lebowitz?"

She beamed at me. "You know Annie Lebowitz?"

I made a mock wounded face. "I know things. I'm not just a playboy who has fabulous parties, you know."

"I stand corrected."

Her tongue peeked out to moisten her lips, and all I could do was stare.

She gave me a nervous smile. "What are you staring at?"

I nodded absently. "*You.* Your mouth, specifically."

She rolled her lips inward. "Um, why?"

Lit by the moonlight and the lanterns on the roof, she looked incandescent. And I knew I was going to do something stupid. "I'm trying to talk myself out of kissing you."

Abbie shifted away an inch to look at me more fully. "You don't want to kiss me?" Her voice was small when she asked.

It was all I'd wanted to do since I'd saved her from that Mini Cooper. The pull toward her was like the gravitational force of the sun. I could fight it all I wanted, but sooner or later, I'd be sucked into her orbit.

"Because I'm probably not the kind of guy you should get involved with."

Her eyes rounded, and she mouthed, "Oh."

I liked her. And not just because she was that broken-looking girl I'd rescued from a Mini Cooper. But because she was brave and adventurous but didn't know it yet. "But I've been doing a pretty crappy job of staying away from you."

Abbie licked her lips again and I bit back a groan.

"I-uh." She started again. "Alexi, I—"

Alarm bells rang in my head. This was a bad idea. A *very* bad idea. Worst idea I'd ever had. Worse than even dancing with her and getting a vivid picture of how her body would slide against mine in bed. But I didn't care. In the morning, I'd figure out a way to leave her alone. But right now, I just wanted to taste her. Just one taste. I could stop at one.

Reaching out a hand, I cupped her cheek. "I really am going to hell for this."

I dipped my mouth to hers. As soon as our tongues met, electricity coursed through my body. I pulled back in an effort at self-preservation.

Her lashes fluttered open, and she blinked up at me.

I reminded myself of the million reasons why I shouldn't do this. With everything else going on in my life, I didn't need complications. But Abbie briefly placed her fingertips against her mouth, and I forgot about what the prudent thing to do would be. Instead, I dragged her forward and kissed her again. On a shocked breath, she opened for me again. I angled my head to deepen the kiss, and all thoughts of good sense evaporated.

This is stupid.

Stop.

Do you really think you can touch her once and stop?

Barely aware of what I was doing, I cupped her face and rubbed a thumb over her cheek. Unable to stop kissing her, I delved my tongue inside, tasting her. Her unique flavor wove an intoxicating web around me, trapping me like any beautiful predator.

When I touched my tongue to hers, she stilled and backed away, flattening a hand against my chest.

My heart thudded so fast, I worried I'd have a heart attack. Pain radiated center mass as I waited for her response. Her fingers clenched in the lapels of my shirt, but she still held herself back from me. *Shit.* I'd taken it too far. I'd wanted a taste, and I'd taken more than she was prepared to give. "Abbie, I'm sorry. I got—"

She cut me off by tugging me to her and fusing our lips together.

Holy. Shite.

I didn't need further invitation and dragged her onto my lap so she straddled me, her dress shifting up to expose her thighs.

My brain managed a few strangled messages like, *You're literally making out with this girl in public. What if a photogra-*

pher catches you? But the rational messages were drowned out by the pounding need coursing through my veins.

Abbie dipped her tongue into my mouth, and my brain stopped functioning. Sliding my tongue over hers, I tried to decipher every flavor. Mostly, she tasted like something sweet, strawberries—maybe her lip-gloss, maybe the strawberry infused sake.

I sucked on her tongue, and she gasped into my mouth. When I did it again, she responded in kind by doing the same to me. The electric current flowing through my body sent a jolt of electricity straight to my dick.

Holding her tighter, my fingers skimmed her waist and slipped under my jacket to play with the skin on her bare back. She gently rose on her knees, then resettled on my lap, bringing her molten heat more solidly against me. She repeated the action over and over again, and anything rational flew out of my head. I clamped both hands on her hips and rocked mine in a steady rhythm. The more she rode me, the more I groaned.

Alarms rang in my skull, but I couldn't stop. She tasted like heaven. If I wasn't careful, I'd be reaching up under her dress to see just how wet she was. If I wanted to go extra dumb, I'd end up shagging her right here on the roof.

But rational thinking was not my current strong suit. I had one directive; I wanted her slippery wet flesh sliding, soaking, or clamping around me post haste. Hands full of the flesh of her arse, I considered sliding one hand to the promised land, shoving aside whatever flimsy piece of string she was calling panties, and sinking deep. I would feel better if I made her explode around my cock.

Are you sure about that?

Well, it was a hell of a start the way I saw it.

She was the one who tore her lips away. "What the hell are we doing?"

My lips were slow to get the memo. When I couldn't chase her lips, I settled for that soft patch of skin just under her ear. My brain struggled for purchase as Abbie's question filtered into my consciousness. What was I supposed to say? If I said the wrong thing, she'd scramble back downstairs. "I haven't a clue," I muttered between kisses. "But it feels fucking incredible."

I gave her another slow, drugging kiss that made me dizzy. Hell, I knew nothing about this girl except that I could go on kissing her forever.

She moved against me fluidly, and through our clothes, my cock sought out her moist heat. All I could think about was getting her closer and closer and burying myself so deep inside her that I wouldn't remember my own name.

Fuck, the way she moved.

She trembled in my arms as I slid a hand between us and skimmed over her ribcage, pausing only as my thumb grazed the underside of her breast. My erection pulsed painfully against the fly of my jeans.

"Alexi..."

Through the fog of lust, I dragged my lips from hers and finally found my voice. "Y-yeah, Abbie."

Her moan was low and throaty, but instead of pulling me toward her, she gently pushed me away. "I–Um..." She swallowed as I kissed the column of her neck. "We–I can't do this."

My body registered the command my brain gave to stop, and I dragged my eyes open to peer at her. Hers were wide and hazy with desire and something else. Not fear, but trepidation maybe? I immediately released her.

I forced my hands from her body and ran them through my

hair. I cleared my throat and prayed it would help clear my mind too. "I got a little carried away. I apologize." The words sounded like I tore them out one by one.

She blinked rapidly and slowly unfurled her hands from the front of my shirt. "Yeah, me too. That was... uh... intense."

Intense. Sure. That was one word for it. More like we'd both been doused in rocket fuel then lit on fire. "Yeah, I'll say." I prayed for some semblance of control. "C'mon. I'll take you back to the party, and from now on I'll be a perfect gentleman. I promise."

She ducked her head. "Maybe if we could slow down for a minute."

I lifted her off my lap and set her back on the ground before righting myself. She leaned on me for support to slip her towering heels back on. From the corner of my eye, I noticed a shadow in the far corner of the roof. I frowned but wasn't sure what it was until I saw the flash.

Shit.

Right away, I tucked Abbie into my side. "Let's get out of here. It's getting a bit cold anyway." My mind tried to determine if I'd noticed any flashes while we'd been making out like a couple of teenagers. Had that scumbag caught a picture of her? Would I have to tell her who I was before we even got started? The mere thought put a damper on my mood. *Or is she the one who called the paparazzi?* I dismissed the thought almost as soon as it emerged.

I paused as we got to the door and hazarded a glance back toward where I'd seen the flash.

Abbie frowned. "What's the matter?"

I rubbed the end of my nose. "Nothing. Sorry. I was just

thinking. Or rather trying to force the blood to my brain so I could think. It seems you have quite an effect on me."

She ducked her head again, and I deliberately tipped her chin up to face me. I smoothly stepped directly in front of her so anyone watching would only have a view of my back. "C'mon, what's up?"

Abbie averted her gaze. "I—I don't usually do that."

"Enjoy a London evening on a rooftop? I highly recommend it."

"No." She chuckled. "I barely know you. And I just got out of this thing. I'm basically a mess."

I forced my hands into my pockets instead of on her. "It's okay, Abbie. I'm not going to bite. That's not how that was supposed to go at all. I'd been hoping for something a little less... combustible."

Problem was, now that I'd tasted her, I knew I didn't have a prayer in hell of staying away.

I swayed into him. It would be so easy to go back to kissing him. Kissing as well as dry humping him on the bench.

That was... new. What kind of idiot was I? It was one thing to want to be adventurous; it was another to get so caught up. It had to be the alcohol talking, because I did *not* do that.

Hooking up wasn't really my thing. And I wasn't sure why, but it was really important to me for him to know that. "Combustible. Right. I just feel like I need to breathe for a minute. Catch my breath." *Get my brain working.*

His smile was slow, but it reached his eyes. "I can live with that. How about we go dance?"

What? No. Dancing was far worse. Because with dancing I'd be pressed up against him and remember what he tasted like. Maybe if we just talked for a minute longer I could get my bearings. "I was thinking we could stay up here a little longer. You know, talk a little more. Maybe you can tell me why you're really hiding on the night of your birthday party."

I tried to step around him, but he blocked my path. "Maybe we should grab coffee or something for that kind of chat. It's a very boring story. Besides, if we stay up here, I won't be thinking about my life story. I'll be thinking about how you taste. Anyway, I can't really disappear too long from the party. It's only a matter of time until someone comes looking for us."

I flushed. We could have totally been seen. The thought hadn't even entered my mind. I'd been so *consumed*. Actually, no thought had entered my brain. I'd been entirely focused on getting as close to him as humanly possible.

I blinked up at Lex, the chasm between what I wanted to do and what I should do growing ever wider. "You're right. Lead the way to the dance floor. I wore these shoes for a reason. They should get used."

"Ladies first, of course."

As I preceded him down the stairs I wondered, why him? Why this guy? The last thing I wanted to do was get caught up in a guy so hot I didn't dare touch him. Not to mention a spoiled rich kid. He might not be making it rain, but the air of wealth clung to him.

But Lex had a way about him. I could see myself so wrapped up in him that nothing else mattered. One kiss, and I already knew he would consume my life if I let him.

⸺

Lex...

I followed Abbie into the din of the party. Jasper had switched from the dance tracks to Robin Thicke. The mellow and seductive sounds of "Lost Without You" filled the room, and couples gravitated toward each other, holding on tight, some nearly shagging on the dance floor.

I knew it wasn't a good idea. But I wanted to hold her again, just to feel her skin against mine before I had to let her go and put the mask on again.

Her hips swayed with each graceful stride, and I had to work hard to keep my brain from wandering too far down a path I couldn't pursue. Before she melded into the throngs of party guests, I snatched her hand.

Whirling to meet my gaze, she paused just on the edge of the crowd, hanging on the precipice between fantasy and reality. I pulled her in close before leaning in to whisper, "Just one dance before I let you go?"

She blinked up at me before a slow smile spread on her lips. "Which one of us is going to be in debt after this dance?"

I smirked. "I have a feeling it'll be me, but it's a debt I willingly take on."

My brain wrestled with my libido for control of the situation. I didn't kiss her again, but instead, held her to me so her head tucked neatly under my chin and the scent of her shampoo tickled my nose, making me think of somewhere tropical and secluded.

I brushed my fingertips over the soft skin at her lower back. The satiny texture of her flesh teased and sent electrical pulses through my blood.

I glanced quickly around before drawing her further into the dimness where no one would see us. And in the darkened peripheries of my own party, I started to enjoy myself.

I tapped her lower spine in time with the music, wishing the moment could last. When my hands slid further up her back, she inhaled suddenly, and I drew my head back to look down at her. "Are you okay?"

The tip of her tongue peeked out again, taunting me. "Yeah, uh, you sent a shiver down my spine."

"Good shiver or bad shiver?"

Her lashes lowered. "Good." *Too right.*

Thanks to the blood roaring in my head, I couldn't think, couldn't remember all the reasons I should let her go, the reasons I couldn't hold her like this, the reasons to walk away. I repeated the shiver-inducing caress, and she whimpered.

"I wish you wouldn't do that, Abbie."

Her voice was soft. Barely discernible over the music. "Why not?"

"Because it makes me want to misbehave, and we've already misbehaved enough for one party."

Her brows furrowed before she met my gaze again. "You're trouble, you know that?"

"You wouldn't be the first person to tell me that." But she would be the first who mattered. What the hell was wrong with me? I barely knew her, but I was already risking too much just to spend a little more time in her presence. I needed to get a serious grip.

With the song fading in the distance, my brain exerted a final defensive maneuver and won the battle over my libido. Gently, I set her away from me. "Thank you for the dance, Abbie. I'm sorry about the kiss. It won't happen again."

Then I turned around and deliberately walked away.

I STUMBLED several steps before I found my footing. The instant I'd left the warm cocoon of Lex's arms, I felt empty, and that scared me. *And* he wasn't mine to hold onto.

Unable to find my friends with a quick scan, I sidled up to the bar, looking for a good viewing spot. I signaled the bartender and asked for water.

"Hello, Little Bird."

I jumped as the voice whispered over my consciousness. I whirled around. Sure enough, Xander leaned against the wall. Clutching my hand to my chest, I asked, "What are you doing here?"

His smile was wry as the corners of his eyes crinkled. "I could ask you the same thing. Are you here to pilfer my photography gig?"

It was only then that I noticed the camera around his neck. "Oh, you're working." Who was Lex that he could afford a photographer of Xander's caliber just for his birthday? "Not poaching, I swear. I'm here for the party."

He chuckled softly. "You can relax. I'm only having a bit of fun with you." He nodded toward Lex. "I saw you dancing with the birthday boy."

I silently thanked God for the low light in the bar, because it meant that my sudden flush was hidden. "I, uh, yeah."

"You know him well?" His question was almost too soft to be heard over the din of the rap song Jasper played.

I shook my head. "No. Not really. We just met recently."

"Pretty saucy dance for two people who just met."

I frowned. The dragon that was my temper woke from a long slumber and stretched its talons. Though cooler heads prevailed, and I remembered Xander was my teacher. I cleared my throat and searched the crowd for Max or Sophie. "No, not really."

"Not from what I could see at this vantage point. As you know, the camera never lies."

Had he photographed us dancing? What had my face looked like with Lex's hips pressed into mine? If it reflected what I'd been feeling at the time, euphoric desire and a little giddiness, then I was in trouble. "You'll need an artist release to use that." I couldn't put my finger on why, but Xander's being there irked me. His butting in irked me even more. Something else about him bothered me too. Maybe it was his air of overconfidence, but something about him pushed my buttons, and I had to resist the urge to toss my drink at him. That would have been a waste of perfectly good water.

"That I would, if I intended to use it for anything."

Through gritted teeth, I asked, "So how do you know Alexi?"

Xander grinned. "Alexi is it?" He smirked. "I used to throw away his dirty nappies."

Confused, I blinked.

His sudden laugh transformed his face, making him even better looking, but also making him approachable and less cocky. "He's my brother."

Brother? Well that explained the common last name. And Lex had said his brother was a photographer. But I had a feeling he'd deliberately not told me about Xander. Granted, probably many a girl got close to Lex hoping to brush against fame or something.

Now that I looked closely, I wondered how the hell I could have missed it. Alexi cocked his head the same way Xander did. Had the same almost-smiling uptick of his lips. And their bone structure was similar as well. Except Xander's eyes leaned toward dark slate, and Alexi's were a soft silver. "Oh. Small world, I guess."

"Indeed." He continued to study me. But again, his scrutiny wasn't sexual... exactly. At least I didn't think it was.

I stood there, awkwardly shifting from foot to foot to distribute my weight in the killer heels. I wanted to appear nonchalant, but he unsettled me. "What? Why are you staring at me?"

His grin flashed. *Wow.* It should be illegal for him to do that in public. The simple act of smiling made him look angelic and sweet, but he was possessed of the devil's charm.

"Relax. I already told you, I don't sleep with students." He shrugged. "Your face is interesting. I'm trying to figure out the best light to shoot you in."

He thought *my* face was fascinating? *Right.* Didn't mean I was going to let him shoot me though. "I don't think so."

He nodded absently. "Well, if you change your mind, I suppose you know where to find me."

"I suppose I do." I began to wonder exactly how many of his students he'd '*photographed.*'

His next question surprised me.

"What do you want with my brother?"

I wasn't sure I'd heard him right. "Excuse me?"

"My brother—what do you want with him?"

Bewildered, I sputtered. "I—I don't want anything from him. I barely know the guy. It was just a dance."

Xander's eyes were stormy as he leaned into my space. He smelled like Lex. They apparently had the same taste in unique cologne. The scent swirled around me, and I had to shake my head to clear it.

"Bullshit. I can see it on his face. You intrigue him. Let me do you a favor and give you some advice. Steer clear of him."

Heat prickled my arm. "I'm sorry, but as far as I'm concerned, I only need to take your advice in the classroom. Outside of it, I can take care of myself."

He cocked a brow. "Who said I was worried about *you*?"

With open-mouthed shock, I could only stare as Xander sauntered off to join the throngs on the dance floor. He was immediately joined by a blonde and a brunette, each vying for his attention.

Who did he think he was? I had a father, and I didn't need to take love advice from my professor, who looked more like a player than any teacher I'd ever seen. And if he wanted to steer me away from Lex, he'd seriously miscalculated and just done the one thing likely to make me run *toward* his brother.

Be smart.

The problem was I knew what was smart. But the moment Alexi had kissed me, something shifted inside me, and I couldn't go back.

Lex...

I forced my legs to move in the opposite direction of where Abbie stood. I needed to get as far away from her as possible. And I needed to start using my brain, right fucking now. If that fucking paparazzo had gotten a picture of my face, I was royally screwed. Not to mention the shitter I'd just put Gemma in.

I scanned the crowd for her and eventually spotted her chestnut mane by the chocolate fountain. She was deep in conversation with another woman. Even as I battled the crowd to get to my supposed fiancée, I felt her eyes on me. It wouldn't help me keep my head if she kept staring at me like that. "Hey, Gem, can I talk to you for a minute?"

She smiled up at me as I pulled her aside. "Yeah, Sure. Where did you vanish off to? For a minute, I thought you'd left the party, but I noticed Nick was still here."

Unable to meet her gaze, I muttered, "Look, Gem, we have a problem."

She arched a delicate dark brow. "Out with it, Lex."

"I was on the roof. There was a paparazzo up there."

"Are you serious?" She rolled her eyes. "They are such a pain in the ass. I'll go talk to the owner right away. You shouldn't have to deal with that shit on your birthday. Can't they just fucking leave you alone, for once? It's not like you were up there doing lines of coke or anything." She frowned. "Were you?"

I blinked once, then again. "No. Fuck. No. Nothing like that, but, uh, there was a girl."

Gemma blinked at me and nodded. "Sophie's friend?"

She'd seen us dancing at Jasper's party last weekend and

had pestered me for days until I'd told her about Abbie. "Yeah. She was up there with me, talking." I shifted from foot to foot and jammed my hands in my pockets. "There might have been snogging."

Gemma's eyes widened, and she grinned. Then, as if dawning slowly crept in, her smile fell and she muttered. "Did he get a picture?"

I pinched the bridge of my nose. "I don't fucking know. Soon as I saw the camera, I got her out of there as quickly as possible."

"Damn it."

I exhaled as ice settled in my gut. "Yeah. I don't know when, but it's going to blow up in our faces. She doesn't look anything like you, Gems. It's going to get all kinds of ugly." Of all the stupid moves. All because I'd wanted something real just for a minute, I'd put Gemma and her life up for exposure.

"Any chance she called them herself?"

I shook my head. "Unlikely. I don't think she has a clue who I am. I only just met her."

Gemma frowned, her ruby red lips pursing. "I don't know. Max or Sophie could have said something. She wouldn't be the first girl to use you to get herself some publicity."

Involuntarily, I glanced in Abbie's direction. She was leaning over the DJ booth saying something to Jasper, and the poor bloke looked enthralled. It made me want to hit something. "She's American. She has nothing to do with them. I'm sure of it." I hoped.

Gemma studied me. "If you're sure. But we should probably make a point to leave together."

The weight that had been temporarily lifted while I was up

on the roof shifted and slithered back onto my shoulders again. I'd never minded Gemma's cover before. But now it felt like a tightening noose around my neck.

I woke to the smell of fried eggs. My nostrils flared just as my stomach rolled. From somewhere in the distance, I heard a voice talking to me, and it was getting closer. "You're a dark horse. You'd better get up and tell me all about it."

I rolled over and covered my head with a pillow. The only thing about the morning that I was at all thankful for was the grey and dreary weather outside. Perfect light to shoot in, if I could lift my head out of bed. "Faith, please I'm begging you to go away."

"I can't, love. What's that old black and white sitcom? 'You've got some 'splainin to do.'"

"Faith, my head feels like I've swallowed an entire herd of elephants whole and they're running around playing polo in my skull." I rubbed my tongue against the roof of my mouth. "Tastes like it too."

Faith just laughed. "That, my dear, is your first London hangover. It's to be celebrated. C'mon. Get up. I made breakfast. You'll feel better once you eat and have a Guinness."

I peeked out from under the pillow and duvet. "Guinness? You really think it's a good idea for me to drink again?"

"Well, I'm not asking you to get wasted again. You're a lightweight. I mean, you only had what, the two shots of sake?"

"Don't forget the stupid absinthe. I switched to water after that."

Faith's brow furrowed. "Yeah. Lightweight."

"God, what are you? Part Irish?" I grumbled.

"Now that you mention it, my mum is half Irish. Now get up. I know you want to sleep all day. But you told me yesterday you have work to do. Besides, I'm dying to hear about you and that smoking guy you were talking to at the bar. Sophie already filled me in. I can't believe I missed such a great party."

Eventually, I sat up and took the mug from Faith. I took a tentative sip. The bitter, fizzy liquid burned my tongue and throat, but the moment it hit my stomach, the rumbling and nausea quieted. I stared into the mug, surprised.

Faith just smirked. "Told you so. See, not all that bad."

"I can't believe that actually worked."

After dragging myself out of bed and a quick round in the bathroom with my toothbrush and mouthwash, I felt marginally better. Not to mention, I was starving. When I padded into the kitchen, the duvet clutched around me and my bunny slippers shuffling, I parked myself on one of the stools at the island. Faith placed a heaping plate of fried eggs, sausage and baked beans with toast in front of me. "Damn, Faith, you didn't have to make so much food. And you didn't have to cook for me."

"Well, I wanted to celebrate your first hangover morning. And I remembered your mushroom allergy. And don't get used to this. It's about the only thing I can cook."

"Thank you for remembering. And don't worry. I can handle cooking."

Faith grinned. "I remember from school. If it hadn't been for you, I might have starved in Uni."

I tucked into the feast and nearly moaned with pleasure as I chewed my sausage. "Faith, this is exactly what I needed."

"Glad to hear it. Now spill. I want all the details."

I had already made up my mind to keep things with Lex on the down low. At least for now. It was probably nothing anyway. Just a one-night kismet kind of thing. And to be frank, I was so not ready for it to be anything anyway. "Not much to tell. I had too much to drink." I pointed at my head with my fork. "Hung out on the rooftop for a bit. The guy at the bar was actually Xander Chase. He was there to photograph the party."

Faith scowled. "Xander Chase was there in person? And I missed it to stay home and plan for the new Calice product? Coffee-flavored Vodka, yuck. Please tell me there was snogging."

Oh God. "What? Between me and Xander? No!" I laughed.

"Bit of a shame though. From the pictures I've seen of him, he's well fit."

"There is that word again. I get the feeling I'm taking it in the wrong context."

Faith frowned. "What? Fit?"

"Yes. What the hell does it mean? Jasper told me I looked fit yesterday. I of course responded with 'Thanks, I've been working out.' And he just laughed at me like I was crazy."

Faith laughed, causing her dimples to appear. "It means you're hot."

"Oh. Okay. Well. Then of course Jasper thought I was nuts. He's a hell of a DJ, by the way."

Faith giggled. "And apparently that crush of his is the real deal. Sophie says he talks about you all the time."

I wrinkled my nose. "Oh, I think he's like that with all the girls. It has nothing to do with me, I promise you."

"Jasper is shameless and a bit of a tramp. But he's lovely outside of all his ridiculous flirting."

"I'll take your word for it." Then as subtly as I could, I added, "So what do you know about Alexi and Nick? They seem nice enough. And as you put it, they're both well fit." *Yeah, real smooth.*

"I don't know much about them. All I know is they're part of the R&B set."

I was going to have to play catch up on the British slang, otherwise I'd never be able to understand my friends. "R&B?"

"Well, depending on who you talk to, it's either the rich and beautiful set or the rich and bratty set."

I raised my eyebrows. I'd gotten the feel of wealth around him, but I didn't know it was a thing. "Come to mention it, last night was kind of a big baller night. It was like something out of Sophia Ritchie's diary or something."

"Welcome to rolling with Sophie." Faith laughed. "I don't go out too much with her friends, but every time we do, a celebrity sighting is nearly guaranteed. There are no lines, the men are beautiful, and the access is insane. I like to keep things a little more grounded though."

So, Faith wouldn't be able to help me with the scoop. Not like I needed the inside track to know Alexi wasn't interested in me really.

I shook my head and focused on my friend. "Enough about last night. How is Mr. Irishman doing?"

Faith's smile widened. "I get to see Liam in a couple of

weeks. So far, so good. We're just starting this long-distance thing. In fact, this visit will be our test run to see if it works. Right now, we're in the hazy long-distance-lust fog. You know when you have Skype sex all the time and you're in love."

I laughed. "No, I don't know about that, but I imagine I'll live every breathtaking moment with you... except for the Skype sex of course, because that would make for really awkward flatmate dinners later."

"So what's on the agenda today?" Faith asked as she started to clear her dishes.

"I want to get started on my photo assignment and explore the city a little. Want to come with and be my London guide?"

Faith looked out the window and studied the gloomy sky. "Sorry, love, I actually have to go into work today. I have a meeting with a client later this afternoon, which means I get to order coffee then stand around with my thumb up my arse as my boss takes credit for my work."

"Ooh, sorry. I'll try to have some fun for you too." I had an assignment to ace.

<hr>

Lex...

I couldn't explain it, but I was nervous.

It was now or never. It was officially my birthday. I was twenty-five years old. And about to be free of the old man.

My brain was still rattling from the party last night. But I hadn't had too much to drink. If it was possible, I'd had too much of Abbie. I felt punch drunk. Hung over on her taste. My lips were still buzzing from the kisses on the rooftop.

I hadn't slept. I tried to convince myself it was nerves over this morning's meeting, but I knew it wasn't. I'd been thinking about her. Unable to step back, walk away, not able to let any of her go. She'd been on my mind. And I was obsessed. Like an idiot.

Shit was too messed up with the whole Gemma situation. But today wasn't about that fucked up situation. I had bigger fish to fry. Today, today was about my freedom. And if I could gain some small piece of it back, I was going to.

I had already donated the birthday car. The one my father had given me like a clueless idiot. I'd called my assistant to have someone come and pick it up, and they'd done so last night.

I drove my own car into the garage and parked it in the family spot as always. The gates opened for me easily. After all, everyone assumed I belonged there. Well they were about to find out differently.

I took the elevators up to the office, along the way greeted by a myriad of assistants and VPs and mid-level managers, many of whom told me happy birthday. And I was grateful. A part of me was sad that I'd never feel this family atmosphere again. But the truth of it was it had been a long time since this place had felt like family to me.

And honestly it had only felt like family because my father had been too busy, and so a myriad of secretaries and assistants had looked after Xander and I and we'd run amok in these hallways. Boldly walking into people's offices as if we owned the joint. Which, as children, we had sort of felt like maybe we could someday. But Xander had already secured his freedom. Now it was time for me to secure mine.

I didn't even bother knocking on my father's office door, and instead I let myself right in. He looked up from his computer as if he'd been expecting me. "What took you so long?"

I closed the door and slipped my hands into my pockets as I made my way to the massive window overlooking the South Bank. "Let me guess, you've been watching me since I parked the car?"

"Of course. I expected you earlier."

"Did you?"

"I trust you didn't overindulge at your celebration last night?"

"Do you even know what it means to overindulge, Dad? It's ten in the morning. If I'd overindulged, you wouldn't see me until tomorrow."

He lifted a brow. "Do you have the same afflictions your brother does?"

I scowled at him. "Xander's fine now."

He rolled his eyes. "Yes, but he has a penchant for trouble."

"If you say so." He pushed to his feet. "Well since you're here, let's get you started. I already have the paperwork on its way down here from the lawyers. And your office is all set up. The contracts I want you to work on—"

I turned from the window to face him. "I think you misunderstood. I'm not here to accept. I'm here to tell you to your face that I decline."

He glowered at me. "I beg your pardon?"

I ground my teeth. "Sorry, Dad. I know you're disappointed."

I let the sarcasm and derision drip off of that last word. "Disappointed? You're bloody insane that's what you are. After everything I've offered you, you're turning your nose up at me? I see you had no problem accepting my birthday gift though. Well, I demand it back."

"Can't have it back. I gave it away to charity, in your name, of course."

His face had gone an alarming shade of raspberry now. "You drove in with the birthday gift I gave you."

I shook my head. "No, that's a gift I got *myself*. Yours was donated to a charity last night. You didn't notice I already had the car myself."

His face went beet red as he blustered. "What? Do you have any idea how expensive that car was?"

I laughed. "Do you?"

Cue the sputtering. "I don't know what has gotten into you, but if you do this, if you cut ties with me and the company, you're disinherited."

I nodded slowly. "Yeah, I figured that was coming. But the best part is that I don't need your money."

"You think I'm joking? No cars, no nothing."

"Dad, I don't want anything from you. There was one time in my life, *one time* that I wanted you. I wanted you to save us from that tosser Mum was going to marry. I remember begging you to come and pick us up. I begged you on the phone, I cried."

"What the hell is wrong with you? Why are you bringing up this nonsense?"

"Because it wasn't nonsense. The one time I needed something from you, you didn't come. You told me I was making too much of something. I tried to tell you, but you wouldn't listen. And then our lives were turned upside down. From that point forward I made it a point to never ask you for anything. I don't want anything you have to give me. I want none of it."

"Oh, and you'll have none of it. Your barge, your cars, how do you plan to pay for it? This lifestyle I've afforded you. The lifestyle your mother has."

"Oh, don't you start. You and I both know that she was richer than you when you married her. It's the illusion you let yourself believe, that somehow you made her and not the other way around. Oh sure, we all know you had some money. But Mum, she has the name, she has the title."

"You're just like her. She has a defunct title that doesn't matter."

"That may be true, but what do you have? Sure, your company's one of the best in the business. No one can begrudge you that. But what you don't have, is me. You certainly don't have Xander. But you haven't had him for years. He saw his way out a long time ago, and he took it. I wish I'd been that brave. Took me a while to get there, but here I am. I don't need you, and we all know Mum doesn't need you, so you're on your own. On your island with your piles of money. Enjoy."

He stepped into my space. I refused to back up. We stood nose to nose. And I could see the people outside the office curiously looking in on us. And they could hear every word. We weren't quiet. And I knew for a fact his office wasn't soundproofed enough. He wanted to make a scene, so he'd make a scene.

"Are you throwing this away for a woman? How's she going to feel about you when she knows you're broke?"

I grinned at him then. "That's just the thing, Dad, I don't need your money. I have money of my own now."

He scowled at me. "What? You think your mother's going to furnish your lifestyle?"

"That's the best part. I don't need Mum's money either. I'm finally free of you. Absolutely free. And God it feels amazing. So, Dad, you can take your job and shove it. It's a real shame too, because it didn't have to be like this."

I turned away from him then and started to stalk out, but he grabbed my elbow. "If you have another source, what have you done for it?"

The deal was done. He couldn't stop it. But I also didn't have to offer him any details. "Well, I guess you'll find out some-day, but you're too late to stop it. It's done. You and I, *we're* done."

"I will make you pay."

He grabbed me by the scruff and gave me a hard shake. I'd never seen him so angry.

But he was doing the exact wrong thing, putting his hands on me, threatening me. With a quick lift of my hands to where his held me, I made my hands form little Cs, stuck them out in front of me, snapped them back to where his thumbs held me tight, and plucked him off easily. "I promise you don't want to do that. I would never want to hit you. Because it's sad. It's a sad thing to hit an old man. But if you put your hands on me again, you'll find out just what happened that night long ago." He went pale and staggered backward. "Let me be clear with you Dad, you try and fuck with me, and I will end you. You try and fuck with Xander, and I will really end you. If you go anywhere near Mum, or try to put this in the papers and attempt to embarrass her, or if you try to take *anything* away from her, I will end you. Do you understand?"

The fear in his eyes told me that he did. He knew what I was capable of now. He finally understood. With that, I turned around and stalked out. I had my freedom. I never had to step foot in that place again.

I FIDDLED with my camera as I rode the tube. The energy on the train vibrated and shifted around me. The dark gray clouds of morning had dissipated and given way to lighter gray ones, but there was no hint of sunshine to be seen. It was official—my good weather run had come to an end.

The Brixton Market was exactly what I was looking for. Located in South London, it was home to immigrants from all over the world but primarily Jamaicans and Haitians. As I passed fruit and vegetable stands, I took occasional shots for my portfolio, focusing on the rich colors and the lively, animated faces of the people I passed. Navigating through the market, I finally paused when I heard the sounds of Jamaican dancehall music.

Following the thumping drum and bass tunes, I tugged the earphones out of my ears and smiled at the familiar Sean Paul song. Immediately, my mind went to the party the previous night. I flushed at the memory of Lex's hands on my ass, urging my body to fit against him as he stroked my tongue with his.

I had never been so reckless or stupid in my life. *Ever.* I didn't make out with random strangers, no matter how beautiful they were. All the dating magazines and articles I'd poured over with my friends since I was old enough to be interested in boys said to play it cool. Act unavailable.

Of course, then there were the *Cosmo* articles that taught women to take charge and go after what they wanted and how to seduce a man. I chuffed as I wove through the crowd. I was not the seduction type. I was the one who thought everything through. *I* was the cautious one.

Until Lex.

I couldn't help a little snort. It sounded like such a cheesy line. Except he hadn't delivered it like one. Though, I had a good idea of the kind of adventure he wanted to lead me on. The way his lips had slid over mine expertly, coaxing me into compliance. *That* was a man who had experience with *a lot* of women, certainly more than his fair share. It was like he made kissing a personal pastime.

Faith said he was part of the R&B crowd, and there was probably no shortage of women ready and willing to be with him. Heat flooded my cheeks, and the irrational flare of jealousy irritated me. Not to mention he was rich and probably had the feeling of entitlement to go with it. If something happened with us and it went bad, it would probably get ugly for me.

I finally found the source of the music and grinned. A group of young kids had taken over a corner of the market with an impromptu dance battle.

Grinning, I snapped several photographs. One by one, the kids came over after krumping their way to their friends and checked out the images I'd captured. With every click, I'd stopped time on a particular emotion or feeling. Their live energy. How they moved. How alive they were. I'd born witness to it all.

As the kids grinned and attempted to tug me into the dance battle circle, I laughed and shook my head. There was no way I was going to krump, but my new friends and fans didn't want to take no for an answer. They dragged me in and immediately surrounded me. I closed my eyes to let the sounds of Sean Paul and the voices fuel my movement as I enjoyed my moment in the middle of the dance circle.

With the music blaring, my body moving, the smell of fried plantains in the distance, and the sounds of laughter coming from my new friends, I knew I'd made the right decision. No matter how scary, no matter how stupid it seemed. No matter what everyone said, I'd made the right choice in leaving. My family didn't know or understand me. Easton certainly didn't understand me. All I had to do was let go and open myself to *every* new experience here.

The act of letting go was the hardest thing I'd have to do. My family was my family. I couldn't change who they were, and the sooner I accepted that, the happier I would be. But I could let go of Easton. I didn't ever *want* to go back.

With some distance, I could clearly see how our relationship had looked. On the outside, we were perfect. But on the inside, I'd completely vanished. Without him, I could be strong and take charge and have fun.

The music eventually transitioned to something else, and the kids howled and clapped for me. I waved goodbye to my new friends and took the slips of paper they handed me with their phone numbers so I could text them some pictures. I headed back out of the market, feeling lighter than I had been in days.

I headed for a part of town called Music Row. I'd heard that in the seventies it had been home to several music studios for young rhythm and blues singers trying to make it. Sort of Brixton's answer to Motown Records. My feet splashed in leftover puddles from the overnight rain.

Between two buildings in a not-quite alleyway, I caught sight of a section of puddles that looked like they formed a perfect circle. In the center of them lay a piece of chain and pipe. Getting down on my haunches I snapped away, lost in my camera and images for several minutes. The light from one of the buildings glinted in the broken glass window of another, and I lost several more minutes going for shots that were integral to my assignment.

Looking at my map, I rounded a corner, searching for the most famous studio of all. Brixton Gold. If I could get one good shot of it against the graying clouds, with maybe some people standing in front, I would have a good start for the assignment and could head back before the clouds opened up as they threatened to do.

"You know, I'm starting to think you're following me."

I whirled around, heart pounding. Leaning against one of the doors next to a youth center and record store stood Lex. With his dark jeans, tan sweater, and light gray pea coat, he looked distinctly out of place. If I'd shot a photo of him that moment, I would certainly have a juxtaposition shot. Or maybe I could use it to show how Brixton was becoming the new Harlem. With white urbanites moving in by the droves, taking advantage of the cheap rent and revitalization.

Or, I could just say hi. "Are you sure *you're* not the one following *me*?"

He shrugged. "I was here first. I thought that was you as you crossed the street. What are you doing in this neck of the woods?"

I held up my camera. "A girl's gotta eat."

"I would hate to see you starve."

Unable to help the sudden jubilant feeling, I giggled. "Well, it could still happen if I don't get the shots I need for this assignment."

"School. Right. You did mention that last night. I was a bit too preoccupied to ask you more about it."

I flushed and immediately looked down at my camera. *You will not think about the way his lips feel. You will not think about the way his hands feel. You will not think about how long it's been since you had a proper, honest to God, sheet-clawing orgasm.* "You probably know more about my school than I do, since your brother's my professor. We had a nice chat at your party."

Lex's smile faltered, and his lips thinned for a moment before he muttered, "London is entirely too small a world. He didn't mention you two had spoken."

I shrugged. *Maybe because he'd acted like an ass.* "Nothing to mention, really. Sort of inconsequential." Was I supposed to tell him that his brother told me to stay away from him? "Are you two close?"

Lex's gaze slid away from mine. "Sometimes a little too close for comfort." When his gray eyes met mine again, they were stormy.

My heartbeat slowed, each beat echoing between my ears. In the blink of an eye, I made my decision. "He said I should stay away from you."

His eyes went from a dark gray to cold, flinty silver. "What did you say in return?"

I shrugged. "That I barely knew you."

His loose shoulders and hands in his pockets would have had most people believing he was completely at ease, but I'd studied enough faces to know better. He was livid. Surreptitiously, I inched backward, looking to put some physical distance between us.

Alexi's voice was low and rough. "Did he say anything else?"

Oh no, I'd already stepped in it. There was no way I was going to roll around in it too. "No." I took another step back.

He studied me closely, his eyes roving over every inch of my face. Then as if sensing my unease, he stepped back. When he spoke again, his voice had lost its edge and was softer, coaxing, and seductive. "Do you plan on staying away from me?"

A small shiver stole through me as I debated the urge to flee. *Do not run. Not every man is Easton.* Besides, we were on a crowded street. "That would be a little difficult, since you're stalking me."

His grin was quick to surface, and I wondered how I hadn't seen the resemblance to Xander right away. *"I'm* stalking *you? You* wandered in to *my* hood."

I laughed as I took in the urban landscape of graffiti-sprayed walls, chip shops, and Ladbrokes gambling spots. "Right. Your hood."

Lex cocked his head as he continued to smile at me. "You're not buying it?"

I shook my head. "Nope. You're too fancy-pants posh. It's not even like you've got this rocker vibe to you so you can pull it off. You sort of stick out here."

He joined me in laughter. "Okay, so the sweater and pea coat are ruining the image. But, I assure you, I belong down here." He inclined his head toward the youth center. "I was kicking it with a few friends today."

"You were volunteering?" I'd assumed he spent his days sleeping till three, only to wake up and figure out where he was going that night. I'd never pictured him as the volunteering type. Not exactly a party boy. My mind conjured an image of him going through rural Africa digging wells. That image juxtaposed with one of him in a beautiful tuxedo, wooing donors for his latest cause. The image of dashing philanthropist worked better.

His grin faded a bit. "Don't let the swank parties fool you. I volunteer. I even have a job."

Shit. Had I insulted him? Immediately, images of him in a tux talking about the latest cause in the heart of Africa vanished and were replaced with images of some swank start-up, doing some cool music software or something. "Was that party swank?" I shrugged. "I couldn't tell by the chocolate fountain and chandeliers."

He tsked. "Uh-oh. Looks like someone's made a few assumptions about me." He added a teasing smile and wag of his finger to soften the words.

"Sorry. I guess I did. I can't really see you posting up here at the local Jamaican restaurant for rice and peas."

He sniffed. "I love Jamaican food. Rice and peas happen to be a favorite of mine."

"I stand corrected."

"So, you up for some company on your little jaunt?" He inclined his head.

He was so heartbreakingly handsome that I could only stare for a minute. Was he actually asking if he could tag along? With me?

My brain made a valiant effort at forming words. "Um, yeah. Ok." That had to count for a full sentence, right?

His voice was smooth as he asked, "So, did you have fun last night?"

"Yeah, I did. I was paying for it a little this morning. But Faith gave me a hangover cure, and I started to feel a lot better. Next time, I won't mix-and-match my liquor like that."

He nodded sagely. "What did she use for the hangover cure? Whiskey?"

"No. Guinness and a massive English fry up."

"Just as effective, I suppose."

He halted my movement by placing a hand on my elbow and I jumped. Would I ever find a way to get used to casual touches? Especially from him?

His brows drew down as he studied me. "Listen, about last night."

Heat flooded my face as I peered up at him sheepishly. "Um, yeah. Look it's no big deal. We got a little carried away."

Lex frowned and pressed his lips together. "I'm sorry I didn't get to talk to you again. It was a little crazy once we got back down to the party."

How was I supposed to play this? Why wasn't there a book for these kinds of awkward conversations? Boy says, "About last night..." You say...

And then have it filled in with the appropriate nonchalant, yet witty response.

I sighed. "Well, it was your birthday party. Lots of well-wishers." I sniffed. "It's no big deal."

His scowl deepened, and he shifted from foot to foot. "I had the impression that..."

I tipped my chin up. "I'm not sure exactly what I'm supposed to say."

"I just wanted you to know—"

"Alexi, look. I'm not good at this. It's not like me at all to make out with a guy that I've only met a few times. It really is against type. But you said it yourself. We're never going to kiss again." Shit, what the hell was wrong with me? Why did I keep opening my mouth and letting words spill free? *Shut up. Shut up now!*

"Abbie, I—" He shut his mouth and started again. "You're different. I—last night was intense." He sighed then scrubbed both hands over his face. "In all honesty, you freak me out a little. I spent most of this morning trying to figure out how to get your number then changing my mind as I reminded myself I needed to stay away from you."

"What did you decide?"

He laughed ruefully. "Well seeing as kismet has other plans, I'm thinking we should be friends."

Friends? "Friends. I can do that." Except after that kiss, I didn't exactly want to be friends.

"And maybe we'll give kismet a break, and I'll actually figure out a way to get your number." He smiled that lopsided grin of his, and I tried to remember what he'd said about being friends.

"Um, you're friends with Sophie, right? I promise you she has my number."

He smiled sheepishly. "Yes, well. I also wanted to be a little discreet. I wasn't sure how much you'd told her."

Well, he had a point there. I didn't exactly want to broadcast our kiss from the speakers. "Well, then how fortuitous that you ran into me today. In a city of millions of people."

His grin was quick. "So, are you going to let me tag along?"

———

Lex...

Abbie bit her bottom lip then blinked up at me. "Why?"

I silently prayed she'd ask me something uncomplicated. "Why what?"

"Why do you want to join me? This will probably be boring for you."

"Not at all. I'm fascinated by what you see with your camera. Trailing after Xander has taught me to appreciate a photographer's viewpoint. It's interesting." I shoved my hands into my pockets and rocked back on my heels. "And believe it or not, I like you."

"Well I am pretty fun, what with my adventurous streak and all."

She laughed, and the sound warmed me from the inside.

"I should probably stay very far away from you, as just being near you makes me think about how you taste, but," I licked my bottom lip, "I like you."

Yeah, wow. Being friends with me was going to be complicated. Especially if I kept saying things like that to her.

A light flush stained her cheeks. "I'm honestly almost done. I just want some shots of Brixton Gold, and then I'm going to head out."

I grinned. "How would you like an insider's tour?"

"I wasn't aware they gave tours."

"Well, not for the public, but I have an inside source that can get you in, if you're interested."

Her dark eyes rounded. "If you can get me in, I'd love to see it and take a couple of shots."

Thirty minutes later, she was beaming as we left the studio. "Holy cow, I can't believe I got to sit in there and listen to some of the old tracks and talk with actual music producers. I mean, how cool is that?"

I couldn't help but grin. She looked so happy. The tiny voice in the back of my mind reminded me of Gemma and our arrangement. I owed it to Gemma to not get caught up in this girl. If I did, everything we'd worked together on would be shattered.

When we got to the tube station, Abbie turned to me and grinned. "Thank you so much. I could never have had that kind of access if it weren't for you. I mean this assignment is pretty crucial, and I think I've blown it out of the water, thanks to you." She ducked her head and fiddled with her camera in a gesture I'd now started to recognize as nerves. Over what? Over me? Could she sense what I was thinking about?

"You're welcome. It was well worth owing Charlie to see that smile on your face."

She shook her head. "Why are you bending over backward to help me?"

"Because in a different life, you would be someone I would want to get to know better."

She nodded as if understanding. "Same here."

I rocked back on my heels. "So, what now?"

She shrugged. "Friends, I guess. Like you said. We'll forget last night happened."

As if I could. "Right. Forgotten. So, as your friend, I'm going to need your number. I'm also going to send you details of a photography opportunity if you want it. It'll be a nice party at a friend's country estate. You should be able to get some good photos." I shrugged. I was hoping to project confidence, but my heart thundered.

"Thank you. But you don't have to do that."

"I want to. Besides, it makes it easier to stalk you if I tell you where to go."

She snagged my phone out of my palm and put her number in. When she handed my phone back to me, our fingers brushed. Slowly I tugged her into a hug. A friendly parting hug. Except, after she initially stilled, she sort of melted into me, giving herself over to my care for the next several seconds. And as I locked my arms around her, I knew there was no way I could stay just friends with her. She drew back, and I held my breath as she blinked up at me.

Don't do it, mate. Your life is way too complicated.

But I never was very good at following the rules. Instead of letting her go, I muttered, "Sod it." I drew her back into my arms and slid my lips over hers. She gasped softly before she moaned into my mouth. When my tongue slid in to tease hers, she wound her hands into my hair, giving herself over to the kiss.

Fire flooded my veins, overheating my synapses. There was something I was supposed to be doing. Something I had to remember, but all I could focus on was Abbie, her lips, her smell, her taste.

I deepened the kiss, demanding a response rather than coaxing one. My head spun as jolts and sparks of electricity lit my skin on fire from the inside out. My fingers tucked under her T-shirt and played with the skin at her lower back, just as I had while we danced at the party.

She swayed into me, pressing her body against me from breast to hip. I groaned again as my body went rigid as stone. I released her abruptly. "Shit. I'm sorry."

Hazy, unfocused eyes fluttered open and blinked up at me. "Wh-what's the matter?" She blinked rapidly as the lights flickered back on.

"You mean besides being so turned on I was giving serious consideration to pinning you up against the wall of the corner shop and finding out how sweet you tasted everywhere? Nothing." I raked both hands through my hair.

She dragged in several deep breaths, and I fixated on her lips. What the hell was my problem? I'd kissed lots of women. But kissing Abbie was like kissing a live wire. I wanted more of it. To grab hold and never let go. But I waited a beat too long.

She took a step back as she adjusted the strap of her camera again, bringing it back in front of her like a shield. "I guess I'd better go."

I had no choice but to watch as she descended the stairs of the tube. Well, I'd screwed that one up. I should have just left her alone. I should have given her the tour then put her in a taxi. I should have left things as just friends with us. *Should should should.*

Instead, I'd kissed her—again. And not in that sweet way that said, 'I think I could care about you.' But in that desperate way that said, 'I won't be able to think about anything else until I'm with you.' Trouble had just landed on my doorstep.

AFTER ANOTHER SLEEPLESS night filled with dreams of Alexi, I strolled into the living room to find Faith surrounded by stacks of books. "What's all this?"

Faith looked up absently from the piles before turning her attention back to a hardback with a bare male ass on the cover. "New client. An author. I have to plan their PR package. Boss man has me getting familiar with her work before I start working on it."

"Let me guess, your boss is going to take credit for all this work too?"

"Probably." Faith sighed. "So, Mr. Lover has been calling the house line, looking for you nonstop. What do you want me to tell him?"

To fuck off, maybe?

I groaned as I slung my camera bag over my shoulder. Sooner or later, Faith would ask why I wouldn't at least talk to Easton. And then what the hell would I say? "Shit, I'm sorry, Faith. I hate to put you in this position, but I'm just not ready to talk to him yet. Mom must have given him your number. I know

I have to deal with him eventually. But my brain just gets clouded."

Faith nodded. "I completely understand. I was mostly just telling you to find out if we can turn the ringer off permanently, or if there is someone you anticipate calling the house phone."

I blinked. "You'd do that for me?"

"What are friends for? Besides, no one ever uses the land line. Most everyone calls my mobile, unless it's the council tax people or something. We don't need it."

"I appreciate it. I'll deal with him eventually, just not quite yet."

Faith eyed my bag. "You headed to campus?"

"Yeah. I'm just going to grab the bus. I want to use their fancy computers for my photo manipulation and printing on large canvases. I think they'll give the images I took on Saturday more pop if I go large scale."

"Well, from what I saw, they were fantastic. I mean, how did you ever get into Brixton Gold? That place is legendary. You must have some serious blagging skills like Sophie to simply talk yourself in there."

"Erm," I hedged, "I probably just got lucky. I need to drop off some job applications too." It felt like I'd applied for every possible job. My bad luck for arriving late. *Fucking Easton.*

My phone buzzed in my pocket, and I snuck a look at the incoming text message. A UK number I didn't recognize. It could only be Lex. The muscles in my belly fluttered. *Calm yourself. He's probably only calling to remind you that he is emotionally unavailable.*

Meet me a block north from your flat.

How the hell did he know where I lived? Muttering a quick goodbye to Faith, I took the stairs two at a time, nearly falling out of the front door. More sedately, I headed down Grove Park Gardens, barely even noticing the lush greenery and stately mansions. I didn't want him thinking I'd run to meet him.

My good judgment meter was clearly on the fritz. Everything about this guy said emotionally unavailable, and I'd just come off a relationship with someone who didn't know the meaning of love. I needed another guy like I needed another hole in my head. Rather, I needed another handsome, wealthy guy like I needed a lobotomy. But still, my breathing grew shallow at the thought of seeing him again.

But logic wasn't on my side. I knew how I felt when I was near Lex. Safe, but also edgy and tingly. I rounded the corner toward the row houses that hugged the Thames and slowed when I noticed a shiny black BMW sports car idling on the side of the road. When I got within ten feet, Lex climbed out, grin flashing.

"I was starting to worry that you wouldn't come out to meet me."

"Well, I didn't really have a choice. This is my way to school."

"Oh, is it now? Fancy that."

I raised an eyebrow. "How did you know where I live?"

"Easy. I asked Jasper where Faith lived. Told him a friend of mine was asking about her."

I wrinkled my nose. Now, thanks to the grapevine of our group of friends, Faith would think some guy was crushing on her. "What happens when Faith finds out there is no guy?"

"Who said there's no guy? My friend Nick was quite taken with her, as he is with many women. He just didn't ask where she lived, so I did it for him. If it happened to get me access to you too, then anything in service of a friend." His smile was infectious, crooked, and so sexy. "Why don't you hop in? I'll give you a ride."

I eyed the sleek, black sports car. I didn't know a ton about cars, but I knew a BMW was all kinds of expensive. Lex leaned against the car, confidence oozing off of him. He fit. The car, the setting, he belonged to a world I didn't understand. Everything about him oozed privilege. I shouldn't want him, but my body hummed with anticipation when I thought about his kisses. I cleared my throat. "I don't want you to go out of your way. School is in Ealing. I'll catch the bus."

He scrunched his face. "Come on, Abbie. Why ride with a bunch of tosser rude boys heading back to their council flats when you can ride in style? I promise I won't bite. Besides, we're friends, right? Get in."

I wavered for another second, but eventually folded myself into the sleek leather of the passenger seat. I was careful not to touch anything. "Um, thanks. It's University of West London in Ealing, right next to the high street."

He chuckled. "I know where it is, remember?"

"Right. I keep forgetting Xander's your brother. I appreciate the ride. So what did you want to see me about?"

He cleared his throat and shifted in his seat as he pulled into the road. "Well, mostly I wanted to see you. You know, see how your photos came out."

I breathed deeply then exhaled, unsure what to say or how to deal with him, so I said nothing.

"Okay, bullshit. I just wanted to see you. When you left yesterday, I got the impression I'd freaked you out... again. I wanted to make sure you—we—were okay."

My throat strangled my last intake of air, refusing to let it be expelled. Slowly, I forced my muscles to relax. "Honestly, I'm fine. I guess. Confused, frustrated. Did I mention confused? Every time we touch, it just seems to get pretty intense, you know? Then you turn around and tell me you don't want to be with me. Then you kiss me again. I haven't got a clue if we're okay or not."

He exhaled, and the tense silence stretched between us like sticky taffy for several minutes. "Shouldn't. That I *shouldn't* be with you, not that I don't *want* to be with you. Obviously, I'm doing a shit poor job of staying away. I swear to God, I'm not trying to confuse you." He laughed. "Hell, I'm confused myself. I know what I should do. Unfortunately, it's very different than what I want to do." He shook his head and changed the subject abruptly. "Why don't you tell me about the pictures you took."

Unsure of what to say, I told him what he wanted to hear. "The photos came out great, actually. I'm headed to campus to do some light touching up with Photoshop and grab some large prints."

Lex zoomed up to the stoplight on the Key Bridge, and I learned very quickly not to watch the road if we were moving. He drove like a maniac. If I had a car like his, I'd never drive it. And if I dared, it would be at a snail's pace.

"You know, your eyes light up when you talk about your work."

His intense focus on me made me want to squirm. No one had ever looked at me like that, like he really saw me, like he was dissecting my soul. Back to awkward and uncomfortable. "You have a way of making me edgy."

His voice pitched lower, and he started the car forward again. "Edgy bad or edgy good?"

"Honestly? I'm not sure. I don't really know what to do with you."

He grinned. "So you know, the feeling's mutual."

The hell it was. There was no way I made him edgy. "Yeah, right, says the guy who probably has women dropping at his feet all the time."

"You'd be surprised. I don't date much."

Now *that* was curious. "Why not? You're certainly good-looking enough. Smart, engaging. What deep dark secret are you hiding?"

I might have imagined the shadow that crossed his face, it was so brief. But the tension surrounding us thickened.

"It's complicated, but I guess no one's ever made me want to share my secrets." He frowned. "On Friday, you were talking about things you'd left behind. I'm curious. Did that include a boyfriend?"

Heat suffused my face. I wanted to open the window for some air but couldn't figure out which of the tiny buttons it was. "It's complicated."

"Ah, I see. A little tit for tat."

I rushed to explain. "No. No, it's not like that. I just— It was sort of messy. Basically, he kept my dream from me. I'd spent the last five years with someone who made me feel like I wasn't good enough." *Not to mention being an abusive asshole.*

His voice was calm, modulated, and he stared directly ahead. "Five years is a long time. A lot to let go of."

I winced as the memories swirled on the edges of my consciousness. "Tell me about it." I didn't want to go into it, but I wanted to talk to someone. I was exhausted from holding it all in, so I told him what I could. "Turned out I had him pegged all wrong. Once I figured out my mistake, I sent him packing."

"So when did he figure out that you weren't going to take him back?"

"Probably when I changed the locks. I left a note letting him know he couldn't get back into our place."

Lex coughed. "Oh, shit. What did the note say?"

A smile pulled at the corners of my lips. "You have a week to move out. Call my sister for a key."

"That's it?"

I shrugged. "Yep. He knew I was excited about the program. He hid my acceptance letter." I used the back of my knuckles to rub at my jaw. "I hate liars."

Lex frowned as he swerved around a garbage truck. "I wasn't sure if I should believe you when you said you'd just packed up your things and showed up here. And pardon me for saying so, but he was a total wanker."

I shrugged. "Don't I know it?"

He slid a glance toward me as he pulled the car into traffic again. "How do you know it was the right thing to do? Coming here?"

"I feel it. In my bones. For the first time, I'm really following my dreams." My heart skipped faster as I spoke. "I'm making it happen on my own terms, and it feels fantastic. I've never been happier." And that was the truth. For once, I didn't feel like I was shutting away who I really was.

"Your parents haven't called, begging you to reconsider?"

I chuckled. "Oh, they've called. Mom has called so often I'm wondering what London's stalking laws are. My sisters have called too. Dad sent an email or two, but he's more worried about my schoolwork than anything."

Lex smirked. "Let me guess, they can't believe you're making such a rash decision. And they're convinced you haven't thought all of this through."

Laughter bubbled out of my chest. "It's like you have our

place bugged or something. Hell, have you been speaking to them directly?"

His grin was quick and made his gray eyes crinkle at the corner. "No. I'm not James Bond after all. Don't let the accent fool you. I'm just dealing with my own rendition of the same song. I'm likely about to be disowned if I do what I want to do and not what my father demands. Problem is I couldn't really give a shit."

"Well, you need to have a plan. I have plans going all the way to Plan F—which I call failure."

He raised his brows. "That's a lot of planning. Tell me what Plan B is?"

"Finish the program and get a regular job here in London. Even if I'm not doing my dream job, I'll still have a master's degree. That should be enough to keep me going for a while."

"Going home isn't an option?" he asked.

My jaw smarted again. I wasn't going anywhere there was a chance I'd run into Easton again. I shook my head. "You know, I've probably been holding on to it as a possibility, but the longer I'm here, the more I realize that I don't want to give up my dream for anyone."

"A woman determined to find her own path. I like it."

"And what about you? What's your path?"

"How do you mean?" He hedged.

"Well, I realize I don't actually know *anything* about you. Except you volunteer and you have a job. But you're somehow privy to all my deep dark shit."

His lips curved into a tight smile. "How about you play hooky with me today, and I'll tell you."

My heart thumped faster. I wanted more of that feeling of time standing still that I'd experienced with him on the roof and in Brixton. With him, I could spend hours and have them feel like minutes. But *he* wasn't part of the plan. And he made me uneasy. He seemed nice enough, but then so had Easton. "I wish I could, Lex, but I have work to do. Lots of work."

"Well, do you have an actual class tonight?"

"No, but..." My voice trailed as he deftly pulled in to a parking space. "What are you doing? I really do have to work today."

He grinned. "Then let me help. I'm good with my hands, and I've always been curious about photography. You can show me the ropes."

He wanted to hang out with me? A rush of blood heated my skin. *You've just escaped domineering and smothering, is that really what you want again?* I shook my head to dissipate the errant thought.

Lex was *not* Easton. He was someone completely new. I didn't have much dating experience, but even I knew I couldn't let my past dictate my future. It didn't matter that the two men had that same air of sophistication. They were *not* the same.

Still, me and Lex in a confined space wasn't a good call. The way the energy crackled around us both tempted and scared me. "Are you serious? It's pretty boring."

"I'm serious. Besides, I like spending time with you."

Oh, great. How was I supposed to say no to that?

Before I answered, I needed to know something first. "Can I ask you a question?" I licked my lips nervously.

His lips tipped into a lopsided smile, and I couldn't help but smile back at him. "Depends on the question, but go on."

"What deep dark secret are you hiding?"

FOR SEVERAL HARD-FOUGHT BREATHS, I wondered if Abbie had seen past my carefully constructed walls. Could she see the darkness locked inside?

I frowned. When I spoke, my voice was even. "What do you mean?" A layer of frost dusted each of my words.

Abbie cleared her throat, and her fingers played with the strap of her camera bag. "You're different than most of the guys I know. You're attentive and charming sure, but you're also really paying attention to what I say. And you seem deeper than some of the other guys I've met here so far. But you won't talk about yourself. And maybe it's my limited experience, but most guys I know would relish the chance to talk about themselves. Instead, you probe into my head."

She dragged in a deep breath and tucked one of her slim braids behind her ear. "And I'm sure you've seen yourself in the mirror, and you're not a total douche bag about it. Hell, you even played superhero for me. So, in light of all these things that make you seem pretty great, I'm looking for your fatal flaw." She smiled sheepishly at me.

I expelled the breath I'd been holding. That was what she meant? She hadn't guessed that she should probably stay miles away from me? Well, I certainly wasn't going to be the one to tell her. She thought I was too perfect? Too nice? It was certainly the last thing I'd been expecting her to say.

"I've got flaws. And most of them aren't too pretty. But for the most part, I just keep things close to the vest. Opening up is a little hard for me." Especially with secrets like I had.

She chewed her lip. "It is for everyone."

I didn't want to lie to her, but I couldn't tell her everything. She'd run from me if she knew what I was. *A killer.* There was no forgiving that. "I'm working on opening up. But my fatal flaws won't hurt you, I promise. I'm just a regular guy."

She climbed out of the car and laughed. "Says the guy in the fancy car."

I followed suit and reached for her bag to help her. "Okay, a regular guy with a few more toys." *And a fucking fake girlfriend.* I'd never been more desperate to tell anyone the truth before. But I knew what was at stake for Gemma, so I kept my mouth shut.

She eyed my outstretched hand. "You were serious about helping me?"

"Is it so hard to believe I would want to?"

"A little. Yes."

"Well, I'm full of surprises."

She slid her camera bag off her shoulder and handed it to me. Our fingers brushed, and immediately I snapped my gaze to hers. The electricity jolted my body into instant alertness.

She licked her lips and took a step away. "Surprises aren't necessarily a good thing."

I smirked. She'd felt it too, but she was trying to ignore it.

Well, if I couldn't ignore how I already felt about her, there was no way I was going to let her get away with it. I was going to take my slice of happiness. It might be a bad idea, but I wanted to spend some uncomplicated time with her. Before I had to expose all my secrets.

———

Abbie...

"So why photography?"

I glanced up and gave Lex a quick smile before returning my attention to the printer. Bit by bit, pixel by pixel, the image of a grinning krumper appeared. "I was pretty shy as a kid. One of my aunts gave me a camera for my seventh birthday, hoping it would help me cope with being around people and unfamiliar situations. I pretty much never put it down after that."

"From what I'm seeing so far, it paid off. You're extremely talented."

"You should see some of the photographs in Xander's class. All those guys are good. This one guy has landscapes to rival Ansel Adams. I mean they're just so vivid and rich. When Xander said his name in class, it sounded familiar, so I looked him up. He's had actual gallery openings. I'm a newbie in comparison."

"Well, I think you'll do great. Just remember it's about getting Xander to connect with the images, and you'll be fine. It's all about knowing what makes him tick."

I grinned. "And what? You're offering to give me the inside track on your brother? I bet there's a hefty price to pay for that."

His gaze flickered to my lips, and he cleared his throat.

"Understanding my brother is easy. Xan says what he means and means what he says. Just show him something honest."

Oh, was that all it took? I ignored the twinge of guilt. This wasn't cheating, it was learning how to reach my teacher. Besides, I was a photographer. My lens always told the truth.

"Can I ask you something?"

He sat on the edge of the light table and turned the full brilliance of his silver gaze on me.

Nervously, I tucked more loose braids behind my ears. "Why did Xander tell me to stay away from you?"

He stiffened, and immediately I wished I hadn't asked.

He ran a hand through his hair. "I don't know why. But it looks like you're not listening to him."

I wasn't, was I? Or rather, Alexi had given me no choice. "Well, you are stalking me."

"Back to that again. Yesterday, you wandered into my hood, and today, I was just in the neighbourhood."

I rolled my eyes then chewed on my bottom lip.

"What's bugging you?" he asked, a light frown causing his brows to pucker.

"I—Nothing."

"Liar. You always chew on your lip when something's bothering you."

I narrowed my eyes. It made me uneasy to think he might already know me so well. "You don't know me well enough to know that."

"Oh, really? I saw the same thing on the balcony when you talked about moving here. I saw it again yesterday when I hugged you goodbye. And now you're doing it again. I'm pretty good at reading patterns. So, what's bugging you?"

I sighed. He wasn't going to let it go. "What are you doing with me?"

His smile was quick. "Right now, I'm helping you mat a photo. Fascinating work, by the way. I'm hoping you'll let me take a turn at the printer next."

"Can you be serious for a minute?"

"Sure." He dropped his end of the mat board and tried to comport his features. "This good enough?"

I shook my head and laughed. He was incorrigible. "Why are you chasing me?"

His brows rose. "Is this chasing? I thought it was me spending time with a friend."

I crossed my arms. "You kiss all your friends like that?"

The frown was back. "Oh, Abbie. You have no idea. The truth is *I* have no idea what it is you're doing to me. This isn't me. I don't run around chasing anything in a skirt. You're... different. And you're bloody driving me insane."

I didn't believe him. "Uh-huh."

He sighed deeply. "Every now and again, I think I can still taste you. Or I catch a whiff of your perfume. It's... inconvenient." He ran a hand through his thick hair. "Look, on the roof, that was the first conversation I've had with someone in a long time. A *real* conversation, anyway. Not one that was all surface talk or about what someone wants from me. I haven't been that open with anyone besides my brother in a very long time... maybe ever."

My heart twirled in joy, but my brain was quick to bitch-slap it into submission. Easton had said things like that to me before, and where the hell had I ended up? Absently, I rubbed my cheek. "You don't even know me."

"Maybe not, but I recognize you. You're looking for something real. Looking for something to make you feel alive." He shrugged. "I'm looking for the same thing. Doesn't hurt that you're beautiful."

Oh, he was good. I hid a smile. "And yesterday, in Brixton?"

He pitched his voice lower. "I just wanted to see what it would be like to hold onto you for a minute."

I shook my head. "I'm not sure what to do when you say stuff like that to me." I put up a hand. "Wait, not like I'm insecure or anything." Even better, now I sounded arrogant. "I'm not over-confident either." I sighed. Now would be a really good time for a muzzle. "In some ways you're so like my ex. In other ways, so totally different."

"Different can be good."

He took a step toward me, and I automatically stepped back.

"Remember, Abbie, I'm a completely different person. Whatever fucked-up thing sent you out of his arms, I'm glad you're here. I'm not that bloke. I'm not going to hurt you."

I licked my lips nervously. "I thought you said you wanted me to stay away from you."

He took another step toward me, and I took another step back. "I'm tired of being on my best behavior. And I'm not sure I can physically stay away anymore."

"Alexi, I—"

He stepped directly in front of me, and I backed right into the bookcase.

"It's easy, all we have to do is let go."

Lex braced his hands on either side of my head. When he closed the short distance between our bodies, my heart hammered, and I held my breath. Just once, I wanted to be able to be free. To be able to let go and enjoy him. To be able to live just a little. No rules, no control.

"Look at me, Abbie."

I stubbornly kept my gaze pinned to his broad chest.

His voice was a whisper that caressed my skin. "Abbie. It's okay. Look at me."

The pleading in his voice broke my resolve. How was I supposed to resist gorgeous and seductive and pleading?

When my gaze met his, his eyes were soft.

"Can I kiss you?"

My legs trembled as Lex's scent wrapped me in a warm cocoon of mint and something woodsy. He smelled fresh and clean. Like the fresh start I needed. Like the man I *wanted*.

I swallowed hard then nodded. My body wanted him, yet my brain was hesitant. This wasn't how things were supposed to happen. I wasn't supposed to get distracted. But here in the darkened photo lab, with the whirring of the printer for company, I wanted to lose myself, forget who I was. I wanted to lose myself in him.

When his lips touched mine, they were firm and warm. Electricity tingled over my skin. His hands lifted to my face, and his touch was soft as he stroked my cheekbones with his thumbs.

Heat flooded my body and my mind, and I couldn't think about anything other than getting closer. I wound my arms around his shoulders, then looped them around his neck. When I slid a hand into his hair, he growled low. His chest vibrated against mine while he deepened the kiss. With every slide of his tongue, my body softened and molded against his.

Through my clothes, I could feel the stiff length of his erection nudging my belly, and I moaned. Need and desire flooded my body as Lex's hands slid from my face to my hips. His grip was firm but yielding, as if he was asking permission for something. Eager to be closer to his warmth, I pressed my body into his, and his hands flexed. My breath caught when his thumbs started to trace a path along the hem of my shirt where a strip of my belly showed.

Lex dragged his head back, and I mewled a protest. The answering uptick of his lips made my body contract.

When he spoke, his voice was barely recognizable. As if each word had to be forcibly ripped out of his throat. "Is this okay?" He used his thumbs to trace a path along my flesh again.

I swayed into him, unable to help myself. I couldn't find any words, could only nod numbly as he played the pads of his thumbs over my skin. Fire tripped over every nerve ending, and I felt like I might actually combust if he kept touching me. But if he stopped, I was pretty certain I'd die.

Lex's gaze was hot and intent. The silver-gray of his eyes had darkened to nearly black. He cleared his throat. "If I do something you don't like or aren't ready for, just tell me, okay?"

Again, I made a herculean effort to move my head up and down. Why was he talking so much? I needed him kissing me again. Needed to feel the zing of excitement, the need drowning out all other thought. The tingle and the pull of my body as it readied for him. I'd never felt anything like it in my life. And the good sense part of my brain tried to shout a warning, but I was in no mood to listen.

But he didn't resume kissing me. He just kept touching me with slow lazy strokes. "I need to hear the words, Abbie. Can you do that for me?"

Shit. What the hell was the question again? There'd been

kissing, then touching, then he'd pulled back and—Oh yeah, he'd asked me to tell him if he did something I wasn't cool with. "Y-yes, I'll tell you." My voice came out all breathy and light.

Lex's hold tightened before he muttered, "Good."

When he kissed me again, he wasn't as gentle. Instead of coaxing a response from me, he demanded one, and my body gave him what he wanted. His thigh wedged between my legs, bringing him in contact with my throbbing clit. Through my jeans, I could feel the heat and hardness of his leg muscles and the friction he applied to my sweet spot. My hips gave an involuntary jerk, and he gave me a satisfied grunt.

As his hand stole up my T-shirt, I arched my back into his caresses. He left a trail of buzzing nerve endings in his wake as he traveled up my belly then my ribs to my breast.

I held my breath, and my body stilled in anticipation. My breasts could be extremely sensitive. I craved his touch, but worried about what he'd think of me if I lost control.

He dragged his head back again. "You want me to stop?"

Fuck no! To avoid sounding over eager, I managed to stammer out, "N-no."

"I am so happy to hear you say that." His lips slid back over mine as his thumb skimmed the underside of my bra. The shot of lust hit me hard, and I rocked my hips on his thigh. When he did it again, I threw my head back.

He trailed kisses along my jawline then dipped his head farther to my neck. "You taste so bloody sweet. And you feel even better than you taste. All I'll be able to think about from now on is how soft you are."

He traced a thumb over my nipple, and I cried out. Moisture and heat rushed to my center, and the building need tripped me so close to the edge of ecstasy. It wouldn't take much. Just one more stroke from his deft fingers, maybe two.

"Fuck, you are so beautiful," he whispered.

"Alexi...."

———

Lex...

The way Abbie said my name made my heart thunder. Like in that moment I was the center of her universe. It fired every protective instinct I had. I *wanted* her to be mine.

But she's not yours. When she finds out she'll run.

Or I would find a way to keep her because I wasn't sure if I could let her get away.

As I nuzzled her neck, I blinked, trying to ward off the intruding thought. She could be mine. I could let myself have something I wanted. Just this once, I might not have to hide. *She's not yours.* I wanted to surround myself with her softness and forget, but I couldn't. I should let her go.

Yet the lure of her soft skin and her open response was too much to ignore. I brushed my thumb over her nipple again. Her hoarse cry and the flexing of her hands in my hair told me she was already so close to letting go for me. There was something so pure in her response that it made me ache. She was so open.

My dick throbbed, once again begging me to sink deep inside her and forget all the nonsense about her not being mine. I could *make* her mine. Stamp her and make her forget that bullshit ex. I could make it so good for her right here. Just open her legs, plant my mouth on her sex and own her.

Easy Casanova, public shagging is off the table for this one.

Besides, you need to take your time. If I rushed this, I could lose her.

But when her hips rocked on my leg once more, I almost lost the battle with myself about taking her in the photo lab. My imagination conjured up all kinds of positioning with the machines and furniture at hand. It would be so good just bending her over, filling her hands with my flesh.

Through the foggy haze of my brain, I heard footsteps down the hall. My brain tried to focus on the sound, but Abbie scratched her nails through my hair, and a wave of lust drowned out rational thinking. I cupped her breast and groaned as the soft plump globe filled my hand. *God.*

When Abbie dragged my head back up and melded her lips back to mine, I forgot all about the phantom footsteps and where we were. I forgot all about why I couldn't be with her. I forgot everything. All that mattered was that moment with her, in my arms. It didn't even matter that I couldn't breathe.

It was Abbie that brought me out of the fog when her head snapped around. "What was that?"

My brain tried to shake of the blanket of lust enough to focus. "What?"

Abbie's dark gaze flickered to mine. "Muffled beeping. Do you hear that?"

The word beeping brought my brain into better focus. Beeping. Xander's ringtone. Right, my damn phone. Xander must have seen my car in the parking lot. "Shit." I swiftly removed my hand from Abbie's breast before stepping back and adjusting her T-shirt.

With an ease I didn't feel and hard-fought nonchalance, I slowly stepped away from her and dug in my pocket for my phone.

The display said Xander, and I muffled another curse before picking up. "Hey, Xan. What's up, big brother?" What I wanted to say was *what's up you wanker?* But my anger was better served up face to face.

"I saw your car. Are you on campus?"

I hesitated a minute before answering. I wanted to go back to touching Abbie, but something about the stiff set of her shoulders told me that wasn't going to happen now.

Her body eventually sagged against the bookcase, and she dragged in several long, deep breaths before she moved back to the printer. She didn't look at me, and a slice of pain stabbed at my heart.

Anybody could have walked in on us. I needed to be better aware of the risks, not just for me, but for her. It wasn't exactly a good idea to get caught making out with a professor's brother.

"Yeah, I'm on campus, just headed to come and see you. Wanted to ask you about something actually."

I hung up with Xander and turned my attention to Abbie. Her back was still to me. "Did I push you too far?"

She whirled to face me, and though her face was flush, her eyes were clear and vibrant. "No. It was..." Her voice trailed as she blinked rapidly. "No. I just—I think I lost my head for a minute—*again*."

"And that's a bad thing?"

She sighed. "It's a *confusing* thing. Clearly we, um, have some chemistry."

My body jerked as if she'd caressed me. Ready for action, dying to touch her again. "You can say that again."

"I'm just not in a good place at all. But every time I see you, it's hard to remember that I'm supposed to be more careful."

I wasn't sure what she meant by that, but I liked her open and vulnerable, not shuttered. "I won't hurt you."

Her smile was weak. "I've heard that before. You should go."

Damn it. I didn't want to leave things like this. "Look. I need to deal with Xander. I should have known he'd see my car. I'll call you as soon as I'm done with him."

She didn't respond.

Stepping up behind her, I gently brushed her braids off the back of her neck and planted a soft kiss at her nape. "I'm sorry I have to go, but can I call you?" I kissed her softly.

She hesitated. "Alexi...I..." Her voice trailed and something cold settled in my gut.

Shit. She was going to say no. Fuck that. I was keeping her. Even if she didn't know it yet. *Don't be an asshole. Give her space and she'll be yours.*

And if that didn't work, I wasn't above using every dirty trick in the world. Her body wanted me even if her headspace wasn't ready. I could be patient.

I cleared my throat and forced out the words that were the antithesis of what I wanted. If I was too much too soon, I'd only scare her, and that wasn't my intention. I wanted her willingly, wanted her to feel the inevitability of this as much as I did.

"Look, I want to see you again. I want to talk to you. I want to know what makes your eyes so sad." I took her hand and stroked the knuckles to serve as a reminder of what I could do to her body. "But, take all the time you need. You call me when you're ready. I know you have my number." That sounded cool and relaxed right? But really my brain was trying to think of all the ways I could make a call happen.

She nodded slowly. "Okay. I can do that."

Those words were enough to make my heart do flips. "And, Abbie?"

She shifted her head to glance at me. "Yes, Alexi?"

"I had fun today. I'll be tasting you on my lips until I go to sleep." *Yeah, way to be subtle.*

Fuck subtle. She was going to be mine.

Lex...

"Do you want to tell me why the fuck you're butting into my business you wanker?" I asked my brother through clenched teeth as I stalked into his office.

"Hello to you too, little brother. How's the post birthday hangover?"

"Cut the shit, Xander. You want to tell me where you get off telling girls to stay away from me?" Not that I expected a straight answer. I'd learned years ago that Xander wouldn't tell me anything, but I wasn't in the mood to beat around the bush. Direct questions were always the fastest.

Xander leaned back in his chair and watched me warily between narrowly slit eyes. "It's funny, she didn't seem like a rebel to me, but I guess she is if you're in here shouting at me."

Tension and anger swirled around us, sparking like a charged electrical storm. Growing up, we'd both learned to fight, to defend ourselves to the death if need be. We'd both been taught to never feel helpless again. A fight would, at the very least, leave us both hurt if not worse. But I'd be damned if I was backing down. "Answer the question, Xander. Why would you tell her that?"

"The better question is why do you care? You can have any girl you want. Like Gemma. Stop messing with my students."

I ignored him. "It's none of your business."

"Hate to break it to you, mate, but it is starting to be my business. You forget my fate is tied inexorably with yours. You start making new friends, and that starts getting very ugly for the brothers Chase."

Anger and annoyance made for a volatile cocktail. I glared at Xander. "In sixteen years, I haven't told a bloody soul what happened that night. I'm not going to start now. I've been with Gemma since we were kids, and I've never told her. This isn't about that night, Xander."

He sat forward with a *thunk* of his chair. "I saw you Friday night, Lex. I watched you dance with her. Hell, you're lucky I was the *only* one who saw you. Did you tell her about Gemma?"

The heat of shame pricked. I needed to tell her, but I needed to figure out what we were to each other first. "No need to. It was just a dance. She's a friend, and that's all. I'm not going to stay away from her just because you tell me to."

Xander stood with his hands planted on his desk. "I've never seen you look like that. I caught the whole damn sex-dance on film, and I felt like I was intruding on a couple in love."

Xander had it on film? It took sheer force of will not to ask to see the pictures from that night. "She's a friend. That's it."

"You can't have friends like that. You can't have *her* as a friend."

I stiffened. "What happened to grabbing my slice of happiness?"

"That was before I knew you were screwing one of my students."

"What does it matter to you? I'm not backing off, and I would appreciate it if you'd fucking butt out of my life."

Xander set his lips in a firm line. His eyes, a near mirror of my own, narrowed. The air around us crackled and vibrated with hostility. Then the obvious struck me. "You *want* her."

Weary dread knotted in my belly as Xander folded his arms over his chest. "I'm not an idiot. I don't date my students."

"That wasn't what I asked you."

Xander shrugged. "I recall it was more of a statement."

I wasn't going to play games. I loved Xander, but I also wasn't going to give up Abbie, or worse, if she didn't want me, let Xander have her. "Xan, I don't want to fight you over a girl."

"Easy, then don't. Stop seeing her."

Could I really walk away from her? Just a brief taste, and I was already reeling. "I'm sorry. I can't. I care about her. She won't say what it is, but something haunts her."

Xander was silent for a minute before he responded, "You can tell that from the photos she takes."

"I can be her friend if that's what she needs, Xander. Can you even offer her that?"

I TAPPED my foot up and down rapidly. Eventually Ilani reached over, put a hand on my knee, and mouthed. "Would you stop?"

I shrugged and whispered, "I'm sorry. I'm just nervous."

After Alexi had left me in the lab the day before, I'd managed to finish what I wanted to do, but every other thought had been consumed with him. He'd texted to apologize for running off, but other than that, I hadn't heard from him.

And now, I was a jumbled pile of raw nerves. What if Xander figured out who Lex had been with? Would he be pissed? He had told me to stay away from his brother after all.

And no matter what I tried, I couldn't focus on my classmates as they prepared their presentations and talked about their photos. My mind kept drifting back to Alexi. His lips on mine, the way he'd asked permission before kissing me. The reverent way he'd touched me. I shifted in my seat.

Ilani flicked a paperclip at my head. "Honestly, Abbie. If you don't stop, I'll sever your legs. It will be a real shame watching you wheel around London trying to take photos, but I'll do it."

"Shit. I'm sorry. I just want this whole thing over with."

Ilani nodded in understanding. "The reason I'm so calm is I medicated with a Xanax before coming today."

I couldn't help a silent snort of laughter, and I whispered, "You what?"

"I know. Seems stupid now as I'm buzzing just the slightest bit. I'm praying I get through my presentation without showing the whole class my knickers."

I shook my head and giggled. "You know, you're just outrageous enough that I can see it happening."

Ilani winked at me. "It's happened before."

At that moment, Xander walked in, and the room went silent, everyone nearly sitting on the edges of their chairs, waiting to see who the first victim would be. Everyone hoped it wouldn't be them, but simultaneously prayed it would be so they could just get it over with.

Xander stood in front of the class. "Good afternoon, my intrepid photographers. Today is a great day to tell stories with our art." He was clearly jazzed, but so far, he was the only one feeling that energy. Everyone else had that wrinkled brow, teeth-gnawing-on-lip look.

"So, have I got a volunteer?"

Nobody moved, as if terrified that even the slightest movement or a scratched nose would symbolize a desire to get flambéed by Xander first. Surreptitiously, my classmates slid glances at each other. Still, nobody dared move.

Xander jumped up and down twice, but his gaze never met mine. "C'mon, gang. There has to be someone brave enough. I promise it's not that bad. I've obviously taken a cursory look at these. Some were quite good. Others not so much. But we'll get to that. Remember, this is so you can learn."

My foot began its tapping routine again, and next to me Ilani groaned.

I held my breath. If I went first, I could spend the rest of the class lamenting my situation instead of pretending to look at my classmates' pieces but not really seeing them because my brain was too filled with Alexi.

My hand moved almost of its own volition as it slowly rose into the air. I cleared my throat. "I'll go first."

Xander nodded happily. "That's the ticket. I really would have been cross to have to select the first of you. And I don't think anybody likes me in a cross mood."

On wooden legs, I went to the laptop and the projector. The actual physical works were already in the student gallery hall. The university liked to open the building every Friday evening for exhibitions. They charged five pounds at the door. It also helped young, unknown artists get discovered.

I turned to face my classmates, and Ilani gave me an encouraging smile with a thumbs-up signal. My stomach rolled. Now would be a hell of a time to throw up. I was pretty sure that would piss Xander off more than having to select someone else to go first. Then I thought of something Alexi had said. He thought I was brave. He said he didn't know anyone who'd uprooted their life without a safety net. Maybe he was right.

I drew in a deep breath and stepped to the side with the remote. Xander hit the lights, and the image of the kids dancing in the market filled the screen. One in a lime green jumpsuit hung suspended in air, his knees bent and his arms back, his face a mask of both aggression and joy. That was, in its essence, krumping. Working out aggression and expressing emotion. I walked the class through where the photos had been taken and the scenario for the next few market shots. Then I let the photo speak for itself. I repeated the process for all twelve of the works I'd selected.

Yesterday, Alexi had wanted far more in-depth knowledge of every single photo. He'd been sucked in by each one.

When I got to the last four photos, I bit back a secret smile. The Brixton Gold shots. "I'd selected Brixton as a destination for these gritty, urban life photos in particular because I have a small obsession with the soul music that came out of England in the sixties and seventies. It's the music I grew up on. I wanted to see music row and see some of the old studios." When I showed the exterior of Brixton Gold, my classmates murmured appreciation. "I also got the opportunity to go inside and shoot some photos while they were recording." I flicked to the first image of the rapper Lady Jane in the booth. Then I changed the image to one of the sound engineer as he'd been rocking out to the song. The joy was obvious in his expression.

When I was done, Xander turned the lights back on, and I headed back to my seat. He stared at me for several long moments, and I shifted under his scrutiny.

When he spoke, his voice was quiet. "Can anybody tell me what Abbie's images made you feel?"

Immediately, people around me called out emotions like joy, energy, enthusiasm. Someone else just said, 'wow.' I flushed. I'd never had this kind of response to my work. Hell, I'd never even shown many people my work aside from doing what it took to get offered a program like this. Xander gave me a little bow. "Miss Nartey, your work is exemplary. Even I'm impressed, and I'm not impressed by anything."

Holy cow. Had I actually pulled this off? Was I a real-life photographer? Stunned into silence, all I could do was nod and try desperately not to cry.

As soon as the attention turned from me, I breathed a sigh of relief. The first person I thought of to call was Alexi. Of course, that would have to wait until I got home.

For the rest of class, I tried desperately to pay attention to the work of my classmates, but my mind kept wandering. The only person who's work I did make it a point to focus on was Ilani's. She'd become a friend, and I would at least give her that much respect. Though Ilani's critique wasn't nearly as positive as mine, neither had it been scathing.

When she returned to her seat, she slouched and threw her head back. "Was that as awful as it felt?"

I aimed for something that would make her feel better. "You're exaggerating. You did fine."

"I eeked out of that one by the skin of my teeth. The next assignment has to go better. I wonder what it will be."

Xander turned the light on after the last critique. "As Miss Bruce is asking in the back..."

Ilani slunk down further in her seat.

"Your next assignment is to photograph love in any form or all of its forms. I want to see it. And while nudes are an important part of photography and art, for this particular assignment, please leave the nudie shots out. I want to make sure you can capture the raw emotion properly before we start going into risqué territory."

Ilani leaned in and whispered, "I'd like to get into his risqué territory, if you catch my meaning." She winked.

I couldn't help a giggle. "You're terrible. Besides, you heard him. He's not looking to be seduced by any of his students."

Ilani shook her head. "I think he doth protest too much. I heard the rule was set by the administration."

I eyed her. "You're trouble."

Ilani grinned just as Xander clapped his hands together. "Okay, so who's up for a drink? My treat. You've all survived your first critique. You've lived to be critiqued another day."

I checked the time. Class had gone long, and it was already nearing ten. But I didn't want to miss out on the opportunity to get to know my classmates better.

"Got somewhere you'd rather be?" Ilani prompted.

"No. Just have to deal with some things back home." Easton had left five messages and even called Sophie trying to get a hold of me. And considering he and Sophie didn't get along, that was saying something. I would kill my mother for giving him a way to contact me. Next time I ran away from home, I wouldn't be leaving a forwarding address or phone number. "But you know what? It can wait until tomorrow."

Abbie...

An hour later, I smiled to myself as I watched the revelry around me. This was what I'd imagined when I'd wanted to come to school in London. Sitting in the pub with friends, my new classmates, having a Guinness. I couldn't believe my life now. The mild pang through my heart jolted me. I wasn't going to think about it or the reason I was here. I'd just enjoy it.

Xander sauntered back to the table, carrying another pitcher for the small group. Ilani sat next to me, and Milo a lanky, blond Swede sat across from me, Andrew next to him. He was British like Ilani. Amy, the South African, had bounded over to the Karaoke stand and was picking out a song.

The five of us comprised the majority of the students who'd lived through Xander's critique that night with passable grades. I had a feeling that that was something rare enough to be celebrated.

When Xander sat, Ilani crowded him. Amy trod back to the table, looking disappointed. "They didn't have that new Beyoncé song, so I'm not in the mood anymore." Then she too, immediately sidled up to Xander.

I just shook my head. It was like they couldn't really help themselves. He'd made it clear he wasn't going to date a student, but still, they trotted out their wares, hoping for a bite. Amy insisted on dressing like a Kardashian with her too tight, too short, too cleavage-bearing clothes and pounds of makeup. I didn't have a problem with the clothes. Hell, some of them were even cute. But for school and class, where they'd most likely be hunched over light tables and viewers, it made no sense. And then there was Ilani. My friend had a more subtle approach. She'd toned down the clothes, but her make-up was still expertly done, and I noted that she wore perfume. It made me want to laugh.

This was Xander Chase they were talking about. He dated supermodels. Neither of them stood a chance. But I wasn't going to burst their bubbles.

Not that I was completely immune to Xander. I wasn't dead, and he *was* pretty to look at. Not to mention he had this lazy, casual, sex appeal to him that would make any sane woman stop and blink a few times. But that was it. For me, it was like watching a beautiful landscape that someone else photographed. All of the beauty without any of the connection. My mind was already consumed with the other Chase brother.

As I drank Guinness and chatted with Milo, I started to relax, the tension rolling out of my shoulders. Xander's low voice from directly behind me startled me so badly I jolted and spilled my Guinness on my hand.

He chuckled. "You'll have to be careful. To the Irish that's a punishable offense."

"Yeah, I'll remember that." Grabbing a handful of napkins, I wiped off my hand and the table.

"Did you have fun the other night at my brother's party?"

My shoulders stiffened as I turned to face him, unsure what to say. Last time we'd talked about his brother he'd warned me off. "Yeah, it was fun. Could have been better."

His slate gray eyes narrowed on mine. "Oh, yeah, why's that?"

My temper sparked. "Some asshat irritated me and told me to stay away from a friend of mine. He was a bit of a prick."

Xander's eyes narrowed, and the hairs on the back of my neck stood at attention. That kind of scrutiny from him was enough to put any woman in a stupor. I shifted uncomfortably. Looking around, I noted Ilani giving me a raised eyebrow and Amy throwing death darts with her eyes.

"That prick notwithstanding, I'm sure you enjoyed the velvet rope party."

I shrugged. "I'm not really the private party person. I'm a rule-follower by nature, so I think the line or the queue is there for a reason."

Xander's eyes crinkled, and his laugh was rich and low. "Well, we'll see if you still feel the same way after you've been here a while. You keep hanging with that crew and you'll start insisting you won't fly commercial."

I tried to remind myself he wasn't making a character assassination. He just didn't know me other than my photographs. "You don't know me." I sliced him a look. He was picking at me, and I didn't know why, but it was rude.

Another flare of righteous indignation had my tongue loosening again. "And what's your deal? Want to explain why you were telling me to stay away from your brother?"

Gone was the cocksure swagger in his expression. Instead, an impassive mask replaced it. "I'd like my students to stay focused, and Lex has a way of making girls lose focus on things."

I could see that it must run in the family. "Well, I'm not looking to lose focus. I'm here to work." The words tasted bitter on my tongue and sounded just as acerbic to my ear.

Xander scrutinized me again. "Who wounded our Little Bird?"

I ground my teeth. "Nobody. And I'm not a little bird."

"Whatever you say." He sipped his beer then said, "But I saw you come down from the roof together, and then I saw him dancing with you. Well, I should say more like slowly fucking you on the dance floor, so I assumed you two had a thing going. I'm a little protective."

Fury bubbled just under the surface of my skin. I considered throwing my Guinness into his face, but then he was a male, so that had probably been done before and wouldn't faze him. I also considered grabbing the pitcher and bashing it into his head like I'd seen done in movies. But it was unlikely it was breakaway glass, and I doubted Faith had that kind of bail money. Besides, I was way too cute for jail. Instead, I leveled a gaze at him. "He was the birthday boy, and he asked me to dance. So I did. Haven't you ever danced before?"

His gaze flickered to my lips and he leaned in an inch closer as if to whisper a secret to me. "Maybe you should dance with me and see if I've managed to pick up the skill."

Was that flirting? It sounded like flirting. He had the nerve to act like I wanted something from Alexi, and then asked me to dirty dance with him? Okay, maybe I *would* bash his head in with the pitcher, breakaway glass or not. "Maybe, except I don't engage in inappropriate relationships with my teachers. It's not how I roll."

He kept silent, and I promptly turned my attention back to Milo. Out of the corner of my eye, I saw Ilani fanning herself. She was sure to have some questions later.

For what felt like hours, I kept my back resolutely to Xander. I knew he was still there and knew he still watched me simply because the hairs on the back of my neck stayed at attention. Then suddenly, the razor-sharp attention was gone. I couldn't explain it, but I knew he'd stopped focusing on me. He didn't attempt to speak to me again until I grabbed my coat to catch the last bus heading toward Chiswick.

"Going home so soon?"

"Well, I do have this professor with a stick up his ass, so I have to wake up at the crack of dawn to get him some decent pictures."

He smirked. "This professor of yours sounds like a pompous dick. You should have him sacked immediately."

I shook my head. "Nah, it would just inflate his ego." What the hell was wrong with me? This was the man who could fuck up my grades. I shouldn't be bantering with him. "Goodnight,

Xander," I said politely, very well aware that the remaining stragglers of our party watched us with keen interest.

"Goodnight, Little Bird. Your work today was promising."

I quirked an eyebrow. "I thought you said it was better than promising."

"Somebody was paying attention in class."

"Well, I *am* here to learn."

Slate-gray eyes studied mine intently, and I squirmed under the scrutiny. A hot flush crept over my skin. How the hell did he do that? His look had a way of making me want very dirty things while at the same time feeling slightly ashamed of that. Or maybe shame wasn't the right emotion. Maybe it was regret? Because that's what the morning after with someone like Xander would feel like. Like I'd taken a million steps backward on my path to self-actualization. Because while the man looked like he promised the kind of orgasms women wrote poetry, or dirty fanfiction about, he also looked like the kind of man to put your heart through the meat grinder.

"My only concern is what else you're learning and who's teaching you those lessons."

I watched him with a narrowed gaze. I couldn't figure him out. He was flirting right? Or was my damn flirtation meter off? He'd made it clear he wasn't into dating his students.

Did you hear him say a thing about dating?

"I'll be sure to be careful who I let teach me things."

His lips tipped into a smirk that, I will admit, made my panties want to revolt and burn themselves to ash. But while my body responded to the packaging, there was something about him I couldn't trust.

"Fair enough. C'mon, let me walk you to your car."

I shook my head. "Don't have a car. I take the bus."

He frowned. "The bus stop is close to your flat I take it?"

I wasn't a great liar. It was maybe a half mile along the Thames, but it was walkable. "Uh, sure. Close."

"You need to learn to lie better. Let me put you in a taxi at least."

I laughed then. "A taxi? Have you forgotten what it's like to be a student? That is lavish spending."

The muscle in his jaw ticked. "My treat. Matter of fact, why don't I just drive you?"

"What, and leave the rest of the gang behind? What would everyone say?" I widened my eyes and clasped a hand to my chest in mock scandalization.

"I don't give a fuck what they say. You need to be safe. You've already had a hell of a scare."

Fuck. My brain had compartmentalized that he knew about that. Way to go brain. "Look, I appreciate it. But I'm good."

He shoved his hands in his pockets and fixed me with a steely gaze that was all too familiar now. I'd seen Alexi give me the same look before. "You might be right about leaving the others. But from now on, I'll drive you home after class."

"I appreciate the gesture, but you will do no such thing. I've had quite enough of people telling me where to go and be and do. I'll get around on my own steam."

He stepped into my personal space. "I can make you do as I say."

I didn't mean to laugh. I really didn't. And maybe it was more hysterics than anything. But like Alexi, there wasn't anything truly threatening about Xander. Yes, he was bigger.

Yes, he could crush me if he wanted. But I had known pain before. And he wasn't the type to administer it.

I lifted my chin. "The last man who tried that ended up with a knife in his gut. You want to take your chances?" Not entirely the truth, but I'd let him wonder about that.

He lifted a brow, and then to my chagrin, he grinned. "I knew I liked you, Little Bird. Now I know why." He rubbed the back of his neck. "Fine, I won't force you into my car like a dodgy kidnapper. But please let me walk you to the bus stop. I'll sleep better tonight."

I could live with that. "Fine." I started walking and didn't wait for him to follow.

As he walked beside me in companionable silence, I tried to figure out just what it was that Xander wanted from me.

FOR THE FIRST time in two weeks, it wasn't a night terror that woke me out of a sound sleep. It was thumping on my door.

"Lex, open up." More thumping.

I rubbed my eyes and staggered out of bed. What the hell was wrong with my brother?

When I shuffled to the front door, I was thankful for the small favor that Gemma hadn't stayed the night. I yanked the door open and glared at, from the smell of it, a very drunk Xander. "What the hell is going on? What are you doing here?"

"What, I can't see my little brother anytime I want?"

I stepped back to let him in. "Jesus, mate, you smell like a pub."

"That's because I've spent the better part of the evening in one."

I frowned. "I thought you had class tonight?"

"I did. First critique. It was brutal."

I put on the water for coffee and snagged a bottle of water from the fridge. I tossed the water at my brother, who caught it with more agility than his condition should have allowed for. "I think you have this all wrong, Xan. When you give a brutal crit, it's the student who's supposed to go get pissed at the pub and drink his sorrows away, not the teacher." I crossed my arms as I leaned back on the kitchen island. "Come to think of it, they didn't see you like this, did they?"

Xander wavered on his feet a little. "Don't be stupid. I waited till they all left then got proper pissed on the good stuff. I might like my students, but I wasn't going to buy them all sodding hundred-year-old scotch."

I eyed Xander's leaning frame and yanked a stool under him, shoving him into a sitting position. "Why the scotch, Xander?"

"Because I felt like it. Now piss off."

"You're the one who showed up on my doorstep, remember?" How the hell had the two of us gotten so screwed up?

You know how.

We were close, but the one thing we couldn't talk about was the one thing tearing each of us up on the inside.

The night I'd killed a man to save my brother. *A life for a life.*

"Where else would I go, but to my savior?" Xander pushed himself up off the stool, weaving into the living area before finally collapsing onto the couch.

I winced as I watched my brother fall. Nothing made me feel worse than when Xander referred to me as his savior. It reminded me of exactly the kind of human being I was. The kind of man who had let my brother take the blame for something I'd done.

There was a reason we never talked about that night.

"You can have the spare room, Xan. You don't have to sleep on the couch."

Xander rolled over and gave me a wicked smile. "I would hate to intrude on Gemma's space in case she comes over tonight." Xander grabbed a pillow and plastered it over his face. "You can't have them both, Lex." The pillow muffled his voice, but I felt every word like a blow. "I'll make you a deal. You take Gemma and leave Little Bird for me."

So that's what this was about? *Abbie.* Xander wanted Abbie. "Did something happen with Abbie tonight?" As much as I loved my brother, I wasn't above giving him a good going over.

"She's already half in love with you, you know?"

I stilled. The explosion of joy spread quickly making me slightly euphoric, but also possessive. "What are you on about, Xan?"

"I can see it all over her. She's caught up in *you.* I don't affect her like that. At least not yet. Maybe if I had more time. After all, I'm sure I saw her first." He pulled the pillow away from his face and met my gaze. "If I asked, *could* you walk away? For me?"

The dig of pain in my gut was only matched by the rush of jealousy. "I'm sorry Xander, but I can't do that."

Abbie...

Faith's cheery, "You all right, love?" greeting wasn't enough to perk up my mood. Granted, if I'd wanted cheery, I wouldn't have had that second mug of Guinness. My mind was still a little foggy, despite the long walk home from the bus stop.

"Hey, Faith."

Faith bounded from my bedroom through to the kitchen. "Wow, you look wretched. Are you okay?"

I wrinkled my nose. "Yeah, thanks for that."

"Sorry. But you do. What's the matter?"

"Well, given Easton's stalking, I need to give him a call, and I also need to give my sister Akos a call, because I have a feeling that Easton's calling about our apartment in DC, or rather, *my* apartment."

Faith had the good sense to wince. "Ouch. Sorry. Do you need moral support? I could stand by with vodka shots or something. You know for fortification."

"I've already had two Guinness tonight. When your professor is buying, you don't say no."

"Especially if he's sinfully hot." Faith wiggled her eyebrows.

I rolled my eyes. "You'd think with all your interest in Xander you didn't have a man. How is Liam anyway? You head to Dublin soon, right?"

"Just one more week, then it's an all weekend shagfest."

I scrunched up my face. "Okay then. Don't get pregnant, okay? That would sort of ruin our girl power vibe we have going on here."

"Noted. I think I'd rather die. Looking after Sophie is difficult enough. Imagine if I had to change nappies too."

"Rough." I then noticed the pile of manuscripts on the counter. "Still bringing work home, I see."

"I know, can you imagine? The horror." She sighed. "I'm convinced I'm actually being punished. I mean most of the other assistant coordinators get an ereader device, and the books that come in are loaded on there, and we go through them that way. But oh no. My client is published by Tristar Publishers, who prefer paperbacks. I mean how archaic is that?"

"At least be happy you're working for a client in a genre you like and read a lot of. It could be worse. They could have you coordinating a press tour or whatever for a new textbook or something."

"You're right. Glass half full, I suppose." Faith yawned. "Don't you have a phone call to make?"

I threw my head back. Who was I going to fall victim to first, Akos or Easton?

I chose to deal with the most difficult conversation first. I slogged to my room then tossed my laptop on the bed and immediately opened up Skype. My finger hovered over the *Start Call* button to my sister for several seconds before I hit it.

When Akos answered, she wasted no time. "Shit, Abbie, we have all been worried sick about you. Do you know how many messages we've left? Mom and Dad have been beside themselves."

And so it began. "I'm not sure why. I called and left Mom a message, and I tried to Skype Dad yesterday, but he didn't answer."

Akosua blew out an exasperated sigh. "Well, that's not the point. You know full well your taking off like this isn't good for them. I mean they're old, for Christ's sake." My sister gesticulated wildly, waving her arms about as she tried to make her point. "Abbie, you can't just take off on the family."

"Well, if you remember, I didn't exactly 'just take off.' I'm at school."

"Look, the point is that you said you would put it on hold for at least a year to wait for Easton, then you turn around and decide to suddenly go. With no word as to why. I mean, can you imagine how Easton feels?"

No, but I could imagine how it would feel to dole out some of the same bullshit he'd force fed me for years. I forced myself to take a breath. And they all wondered why I ran away and didn't call. I tried to get my sister back to her point. "Akos, you have been calling me urgently, and you've sent no less than four emails about my apartment, so what's the matter?"

"Well, we need to have paperwork signed for a new renter. But Easton says he wants to just stay there."

I frowned. "He cannot stay there." My stomach rolled. I couldn't tolerate the idea of him in that place.

"Look, okay, you guys broke up or whatever, but he's still a guaranteed renter, and I don't have time to play property landlord till you get back. What's so bad about him staying there for now? He's your boyfriend."

"Ex." I corrected automatically. I wondered how my sister would feel if she found out how Easton really was. How he'd treated me. What I'd put up with for far too long. But Akos had never been the one I could confide in. She was nearly ten years older and too similar to our mother.

"Whatever. I started interviewing renters, and out of the pool of ten, four were promising. I've pulled their credit checks. I need you to sign and scan one of the agreements back to me. I just think it would be better if—"

I didn't let my sister finish. "Not Easton. I'm done talking about him."

While she talked, I tried to work my brain around the fact that Easton thought I'd let him stay there. Was he that clueless? Had he not seen how close I was to snapping?

"Okay, sure. Fine, Akos, send over the agreements. I'll pick one and send it back to you. Listen, I have to go. I need to call Easton."

Akosua paused and studied me. "You look tired, Abbie. When are you going to give up this bullshit dream and just come home already where we can take care of you?"

"I don't need taking care of."

"Look, so you weren't happy. It's fine. We all need a change sometimes. But why not get that change in a new city here? Maybe you and Easton can—"

"Let it go." I had to get off with my sister before I lost the fight for civility and control. "Sorry, Akos. I hear Faith calling. Check you later." I hung up on her mid-stream.

Cracking my neck, I moaned. I'd need a whole lot more liquor if I was to have more conversations with my family.

Faith popped her head into my room, brandishing my cell phone. "It's rung twice since you've been in here."

"Who was it?"

"Just a number showed on the display. UK mobile, if that makes you feel any better."

I frowned, then realized it must be Lex. "Um, thanks. Maybe one of my classmates."

"Uh-huh." Faith raised an eyebrow and hovered in the doorway. "You sure about that? Because just now you had a look of elation about you. Is it a bloke?"

"Faith, when would I have had time for a guy?"

"You do spend quite a few hours at school and on your little jaunts about London. You could be having some secret tryst I don't know about. Are you dating Daniel Craig, and you didn't tell me? I mean, I can understand why you wouldn't tell me, because, let's face it, I might kill you for him, but honestly, Abena, you should learn to share." She grinned.

"I'm not having secret trysts. I've been too busy working and avoiding my family and Easton. No secret boys to speak of." I lied smoothly. It wasn't like I could claim Alexi as my boyfriend or anything.

"Come on. I've been man deprived for weeks. Just tell me

who it is. Is it Xander? I knew you were going to try to sleep with him. I just knew it. Now you two are carrying on some secret love affair."

I giggled. "You're crazy. I'm not shagging my teacher. I promise. I get my A's the old-fashioned way."

"Sure, sure. But can you do me a favor and bring him by one of these nights so I can ogle him?"

I threw a pillow at her. "I'm not stupid enough to do that. I mean, sleeping with my professor, no matter how spectacularly good-looking, is so not my style. Besides, I still have some unresolved Easton business. I'm not just going to sleep with some guy." No matter how much Lex tempted me.

Faith waggled her eyebrows. "So, you do think he's nice to look at."

"Yes, well, I'm not immune to the good looks, for the love of God. I mean he's very pretty. But honestly, he doesn't do it for me. Besides, I'm here to learn from him."

Faith leaned in conspiratorially. "Just what is he teaching you? Has he got some fabulous technique or something? Come on, give a lonely girl a thrill."

I giggled. "You're incorrigible, Faith."

She grinned. "Wait till I tell Sophie. She'll get to the truth of the matter."

Sophie. I hadn't thought about that. Sophie was friends with Alexi. What if she knew everything? *There's nothing to know.* Besides, Lex hadn't been so keen on everyone knowing his business either.

"You two are ridiculous." Then in an attempt to change the subject, I asked. "Are the three of us still meeting for lunch tomorrow?"

"Yeah, I think I'm open, and honestly, Sophie lives one of

those fabulous lifestyles where I can never seem to pin her down on what she's doing. So who knows if she'll be there. Abbie?"

I glanced up at my friend. "Yeah, Faith?"

"You know you're not doing anything wrong, right? If you were to start seeing someone. I know we tease you a little bit, but at the end of the day, you're a free agent."

I exhaled. "You're right. I know you're right. I just wish my past wasn't intruding on my present."

Faith chewed her bottom lip. "Well, you won't know until you talk to him, but don't let him push you into a corner that doesn't give you what you want. That's just my two pence."

I gave her a soft smile. "Thank you for looking out for me."

"What are mates for? Now I'll leave you to either deal with your boyfriend or your hot teacher. Maybe I'll call Liam. All this talk of you getting some has made me miss him even more."

After Faith left, I stared at my mobile, my fingers itching to call Lex back. Instead of placing the call I wanted to, I shifted back to my laptop and Skyped Easton as I braced myself.

His response was instant. "Jesus, Abbie. I've been trying to get a hold of you."

Instead of fear or anger when I looked at his almost too handsome features, numbness surrounded me. "Yeah, I heard. I've been a bit tied up with school."

His brows drew down, making his handsome face seem harsher. "You can't just vanish like that, Abbie. I was worried."

He was worried? Hadn't he been the one to make me run? How had I not seen it sooner? For years I'd been blind to who he was. "As you can see, I'm fine, Easton. What do you need?"

He rubbed the end of his nose. "Yeah, I can see you're fine.

Is something wrong with your phone? I tried calling it, but it just goes straight to voicemail."

"Yeah, I'm not really using that one right now. I only keep it on for emergencies. I have a local phone."

There was a beat of silence. "Oh, well, are you going to give me the number?"

"No, Easton, I'm not."

He sighed. "You're still mad about what happened?" He sighed. "Fuck, Abbie, I said I was sorry."

He was sorry? "Easton, do you remember the time I did that all-girls night with my sisters for the bachelorette party? Do you remember the lesson you taught me about not answering your calls quickly enough?" The numbness spread as I spoke. "It was the first time you put your hands on me. It should have been the last. Or what about the time I told you I didn't want your poker buddies at the house because I had to study? You broke my tooth. I was dumb enough to listen to your pathetic apologies then. I'm not interested in hearing them now."

His brows furrowed. "Okay, I have a temper. I know. Sometimes, I just... you just... I never meant for it to get out of hand. I'm sorry. We can go to couple's therapy. I'll even go to anger management classes. Anything you want. Just come home. I'm tired of us being separated."

I shook my head. "We're not separated, Easton. We're over. I'm not the same girl I was a couple of months ago. I know better. Not to mention, you seem to forget you lied to me."

Now he clasped his hands over his face. "Abbie, I'm serious. I'll do whatever it takes to show you I can change. Just don't give up on me. I'll... I'll come to London."

Time slowed as I registered what he'd just said. My skin grew clammy at the thought of him in my sanctuary. There was no way I was going to let that happen. "I don't want you here. I think I was pretty clear about never wanting to see you again."

He frowned. "What? You can't mean that. You just need some time to cool off."

In that moment, I saw the truth. I'd been lucky to escape with my life. "No, I don't. I meant what I said. We're over. I never want to see you again. Don't call me."

I hung up and immediately rolled onto my side, bringing my knees to my chest and wrapping my arms around them. Hot tears rolled down my cheeks as shudders wracked my body. I'd let this happen. The first time he'd touched me, I should have run fast and far and reported it. Instead, I'd been so desperate to be loved that I'd stayed.

Now I could see the desperation for what it had been. But I was a different person now. There was no way I was going to let him ruin everything. I didn't want him in the same country as me, let alone the same city.

SHE HADN'T CALLED me back. Nor had she texted. Not like I was keeping track or stalking her... exactly. Max had invited me to the monthly movie night in celebration of her arrival. I'd been coming to these things off and on for years, but that night it was going to be strictly American iconic movies. Since it was in Abbie's honor, I knew she would be here. Yeah, it was official... I was a stalker.

Jasper eyed me from across the kitchen. "What's the matter with you, Lex? You look jumpy."

"Nothing." I crossed my arms and tried for nonchalance. Abbie had wanted some time to figure everything out, and Lord knew I needed time to sort out Gemma before our friends clocked onto the fact that we couldn't keep our hands off each other.

Or rather that *I* couldn't keep my hands off *her*.

Jas narrowed his eyes, and I wondered if he could smell the anticipation on me. "Things okay with you and Gem?"

I gnashed my teeth. Sometimes I hated having such a close-knit group of friends. One of them couldn't sneeze without everyone knowing that person had a cold.

"Yeah, fine. Why do you ask?"

Jasper cocked his head with a slightly evil gleam in his eyes. "Oh, you know. Just that we don't normally see you around so often. I just assumed that with Gemma planning the annual Aids Foundation Benefit, you'd be helping her out."

And I *had* helped her out. But as we weren't really dating, I wasn't obligated to shadow her at every turn. "What can I say? I love *Top Gun.*"

"Yeah, mate. As if you're here for *Top Gun.* I have a feeling a certain blonde is the reason you're hanging around more. Let's face it. You weren't exactly undercover when you called and asked for her flat address."

Wait, what? Jasper thought I had a thing for Faith? Fine with me. Until Abbie and I figured things out, let Jasper believe whatever the hell he wanted.

When Max signaled us all to the screening room and Abbie still hadn't shown up, I started to worry she wasn't coming. I checked my phone, but still nothing. Just in case, I left the seat on my right open. Unfortunately, Jasper sat on the other side of that open seat.

The constant edginess was starting to drive me slowly mad. But when I heard the trudging of feet on the stairs and the feminine voices, I started to relax.

Sophie took the short stairs to join Max at the back, and I made a mental note not to look toward the back of the room for the rest of the movie. I wouldn't want to have to wash my eyes out with bleach.

Faith bounded up to the middle row to sit between one of Max's best friends and model buds, Angel, and the newest model staying in the house, Tony. Jasper leaned over and whispered, "Tough break, mate."

I reminded myself that hitting my friend would not be a good call. Since Nick sat on the other end of their row, that left the only vacant seat between me and Jasper.

Abbie's steps halted when she looked around, and her gaze met mine. Her tentative smile turned rueful when she spotted her other neighbor.

"Hi, Alexi." Her voice was low, seductive. "It's nice to see you again."

I almost groaned. Last time I'd heard that voice, she'd been standing on the precipice of an orgasm. To Jasper she said only, "I trust you can keep your hands to yourself."

Jasper's laugh was rich and mellow. "Now what fun would that be?"

I clenched and unclenched my hands. Maybe hitting Jasper wouldn't be a bad idea after all.

"Jasper, behave please, or I'll make Faith switch places with me."

He whispered back, "I bet that would make someone happy."

She glanced at me questioningly, but then sat between the two of us. Immediately, Jasper placed his hand on the arm rest palm up.

Amateur.

I had already shoved up the arm rest between our seats, so I had no need for conspicuous declarations. At the same time, it meant accidental touching was entirely possible. Sadly though, if I took her hand, Jasper would definitely see, and our little secret would be out.

It was the best I could do. I had no choice but to sit there with less than two inches separating us and *not* touch her. As the movie played, electricity crackled around between us. I almost worried that any shift in the air would light a spark that would incinerate us both.

Unable to do much else but will her to touch me, I sat perfectly still, breathing evenly, only occasionally sliding my glance toward her. The muscle over her jaw worked like she was grinding her teeth, and her body was tight and rigid.

I wasn't sure it could get worse until the love scene started. I had to shake off the wave of lust as Kelly McGillis hovered over Tom Cruise. Beside me, Abbie shifted in her seat, rubbing her legs together then angling her body toward me slightly.

Good. At least you're not suffering alone.

Even still, nothing compared to the moment when I shifted in my seat and knocked her knee with mine. The subtle motion had me holding my breath. And her soft sexy gasp was enough to make the blood rush in my skull.

If I'd been watching the movie and not her, I'd have missed her mouthing my name as the actors onscreen hit their climax.

———

Abbie...

Hell. I was in hell. I slid a glance at Jasper, who resolutely kept his hand on the arm rest. Then there was Lex. Not that he was doing anything to be precise. Hell, he'd barely even looked at me. But every cell in my body focused on him like he had an unseen gravitational pull.

And with the arm rest up between us, it took every ounce of self-control not to just touch him and beg him to touch me like he had the other day. I'd been so close to an orgasm. I'd almost been able to taste it. Then it had been ripped away from me so forcefully I still hadn't recovered.

Now I had to sit through the movie with him right next to me and everyone watching us. I'd hoped to get there on time so I might have a chance to talk to him before the movie started, but Faith had taken forever to get ready. Maybe after the movie. Faith and I were likely spending the night. Getting a night bus or cab back to Chiswick late at night could be a pain in the ass.

When the movie finally ended, I breathed a sigh of relief. "Thank God," I muttered to myself. At least I didn't have to endure another love scene in such close proximity to Lex.

Max trotted down from the back. "Okay, boys and girls, now that we've watched an oldie, I have two options for the second feature. One is that new zombie movie, and the other is the movie about the sex addict. Faith and Sophie immediately piped up with no zombies.

Shit. I'd heard about the other movie. It was an indie flick with immense critical acclaim, and the lead actor was totally hot and particularly well endowed. There was no way I could sit through another movie sandwiched between Jasper *and* Lex. I wasn't going to do that to myself. "I, um—"

Before I could expose myself, Jasper glanced at his watch. "Oh, hell. I'm supposed to be at a gig in the South Bank in a couple of hours."

Nick piped up. "Oh yeah? The one with Rebecca Slough, the model?"

Jasper grinned. "The very same."

"Mind if I tag along?" Nick asked.

My heart sank. If Nick was going, then that meant Lex was going with him, and I really wanted some time to talk to him.

Nick leaned between my seat and Lex's. "What do you say, mate? You coming?"

I held my breath.

Alexi's voice was smooth. "No. I'm actually pretty knackered. I wouldn't last the night."

"All right, then you're on your own for a ride home."

Alexi shrugged, and I could feel his eyes on my profile. "I'll figure it out. If push comes to shove, I'll just take the tube or spend the night and grab a taxi in the morning."

A heady cocktail of relief and anticipation flooded my veins. When all was said and done, it was only me, Faith, Lex, and Angel left in the screening room. Max and Sophie had eventually retired to take their loud make-out session somewhere more private. Faith eventually leaned forward. "I'm headed to bed. I think there are the two spare rooms and the couch. Which one do you want, Abbie?"

Oh wait, we were *all* staying? Alexi too? I'd just assumed he'd be going back to wherever he lived. Um, yeah, that was so not going to work for me. There was no way I could survive the night knowing Lex was somewhere in the house after everything that had happened with us. "I um..." I slid a glance to Lex.

"Not to worry, I'll take the couch."

I frowned. "Are you sure? It doesn't look that comfortable."

"Let the man take the couch, Abbie," Faith admonished. "I'm headed to bed. You coming?"

"Um, I think—"

Faith inclined her head sharply, widened her eyes, and then tapped her temple. I groaned inwardly. Faith had invoked our I-need-to-talk-to-you-right-now signal. Of all the times. No doubt she wanted to give a full deconstruction of everything Angel had said and done in the course of the night. There really was no graceful way to back out of going with her.

"Yep, right behind you."

When I stood, I only allowed myself a fleeting glance in Lex's general direction. If I let my gaze linger on his, there was a high likelihood I would spontaneously combust. "Goodnight, guys," I muttered to Angel and Alexi.

As it turned out Faith did need me. And I felt like a terrible friend because I couldn't give the Angel deconstruction my full attention.

"I mean, he's acting like he's into me. I know you couldn't turn around lest Jasper leaned in for a kiss or something, but our legs were touching the whole time. I think that means something."

I pulled my focus together. "Maybe. Did you feel like you had a cocoon of tension wrapped around you?"

"Yes. And I swear that love scene didn't help."

"Tell me about it," I muttered.

"So, what do I do?"

Faith was seriously asking for my advice? I had no clue what to do with my own life, let alone anyone else's. "I have no idea. You guys should maybe talk about it. First things first though—What about Liam?"

Faith's face fell. "I don't know. Liam's great, but Angel... I mean, look at the guy."

"Oh, trust me, I've seen him." I sighed. "Look. I think you need to figure out things with the boyfriend you have before you deal with a new one."

She sighed. "Maybe you're right. I won't know what I'm dealing with until I see Liam again."

Faith headed to her room and me to mine. Alexi's whispered goodnight still lingered over me like a caress. Even thirty minutes later, while I tossed and turned in my bed, my body felt the magnetic pull to Lex. I could only assume he was on the large sectional in the living room. Was he having a sleepless night too?

The light from the moon cast a silvery shadow on the guestroom I'd taken at the back of the house on the lower level. The clouds were so low I couldn't make out any stars, and it gave the night sky an eerie quality.

After tossing over for the hundredth time, I finally gave up. I might as well try some warm milk because lying there wasn't going to solve my problem. And if Alexi just happened to still be awake, maybe we would have the chance to talk. Yeah, as if talking was what my too aware, too horny body wanted to do.

What I wanted to do was find out if what he could deliver was as good as his kisses promised. What I really wanted to do was let go of the ghosts of my past and the bullshit of the last several years of my life. I wanted to be free. And Alexi tasted like freedom.

With a frustrated sigh, I tossed off the heavy duvet and shivered at the chill in the air. Careful of waking anyone, I slowly opened my door and traversed the darkened hallway by feeling my way along the wall. On tip toe, I jogged up the stairs into the kitchen, though when I opened the door, I realized someone had already beat me to it.

With only the light under the ventilation hood on, Alexi stood stirring something on the stove. When he turned and smiled at me, my stomach dropped.

"You can't sleep either, huh?"

Lex...

I tried to calm my lust-buzzed nerves and smiled at Abbie.

"Do you want some hot chocolate?" It helped if I didn't look directly at her in that threadbare tank and those tiny shorts. Through the thin fabric, I could see the outline of her nipples, and they made my mouth water.

She was silent for a moment. No doubt trying to determine if she should run back to her room or not. "Um, yeah. Sounds good. Thanks. I was having a hard time sleeping."

"Yeah me too."

Glancing up the stairs, she licked her lips nervously. "Did everyone head to bed?"

I nodded. "Yeah. Angel went to bed soon after you two did."

She cleared her throat. "Listen, I'm sorry I didn't get a chance to call you back the last couple of days. I got a little busy."

I slid her a glance and handed her a mug. She took it from me, careful not to let her fingers slide over mine. After a tentative sip, she moaned.

I took a sip of my own and watched her carefully. "You really want me to believe that you weren't running from me?"

She straightened her back, which only made those full breasts of hers jut out. I tried desperately to focus on her dark eyes.

Lift you tossers, lift. I could do this. Show her I was a good bloke who was interested in what she said. And I was. Just so happened I was *also* very much interested in her tits.

"I wasn't running, I just need—"

"Let me guess, space?"

She made a frustrated sound and put a hand on her hip. "Yes. Space. Look, it's a good thing that call from Xander interrupted us the other day."

I lifted a brow. "How do you reckon?"

"It stopped us both from doing something stupid. I mean, I barely know you. And you sure as hell don't know me. And you made it clear yourself that you think this is a bad idea. You said we shouldn't. I'm choosing to listen to you."

I took another long sip and let the warm chocolate ease down my throat before I spoke again. "And if I said I was tired of trying to be good? And remember... I only said I shouldn't. Not that I don't want to."

Her eyes turned wary, and she took a cautious step back. "See, that's what I mean. You keep telling me you're not a good guy, and frankly, I'm in need of a good guy. I spent the last several years of my life dealing with someone who pretended to be something he wasn't."

"Abbie, I'm being honest with you about who I am. Is it a good idea for you to stay away from me? Probably. But will I hurt you? No." I took a step toward her, and she didn't retreat. "I think you already know you can trust me. I think you feel it every time you're with me. It was why you let me touch you the day you took me to the lab." I placed my mug on the island before closing the distance between us.

She didn't move. "Alexi, I—"

"Unless, Jasper's who you want." I forced the pang of jealously down. I didn't have a right to be jealous. But even as I said the words, my hands involuntarily clenched.

Her eyes widened. "No. Alexi, it's not that. He's a harmless flirt."

"Yeah, he is. I'd rather he not flirt with you though."

One delicate brow arched. "Seriously? Are you jealous?"

Yes. "No." I sucked in a deep breath. Big mistake. Her ginger shampoo wreaked havoc with my senses. "Okay, if it's not Jasper, then tell me, what are you so afraid of?"

Her wide dark eyes shimmered in the dim light, and with shaky hands she placed her mug on the table. "Me. I'm afraid of myself. I'm afraid of wanting this and being wrong about you."

I was afraid she was wrong about me too. But in that moment, I wanted to be the guy she could count on. The guy she could want. Not the unworthy asshole. "I won't hurt you, Abbie." I stood close enough to feel her warm breath on my neck. "Just give me a chance to show you," I said as I gingerly pressed my lips to hers.

My breath lodged in my throat as Alexi took control of the kiss. I had no choice but to ride the wave of pleasure as my knees shook and need pulled at my womb. He slid his tongue over mine then teased it inside his mouth and sucked gently, muffling my cry of pleasure.

I slipped my hands over his torso, skimming over rippled abdominal muscles and the hard planes of his chest, eventually digging into his T-shirt.

He tore his lips from mine, dragging in ragged breaths. "Abbie, now is a good time to stop if you don't want to do this." His gaze briefly flickered to my lips, but then he held my steady gaze as he waited for my answer.

"I'm scared that I don't know how to do this. But I want you."

"Fair enough." He deftly lifted me into his arms as if I weighed nothing, urging me to wrap my legs around him.

The position brought the hot, hard length of him directly against my heat, and I hissed, already dangerously close to bliss.

He kissed me gently, savoring my taste. "Are you okay with going back to your room?"

"I—I'm right at the bottom of the stairs." I wanted this —wanted him.

He carried me down the stairs and through the back hallway easily, as if I weighed nothing. Once in my room, he gently laid me on the bed and slid in next to me. When he kissed me again, his fingers drummed on the nape of my neck, holding me in position while his thumb caressed my cheekbone.

To hold on and attempt some level of control, I slid my fingers into the thick soft curls at his nape and gently tugged. With a moan, he smoothed a hand down my back to the curve of my ass and tucked me closer to his body. I rolled my hips into his, and Alexi tore his mouth from mine with a harsh curse.

"Abbie, you're addictive. I can't stop."

I trembled in his arms. "Then don't."

"Christ. You can't say things like that to me. I could happily occupy myself kissing you for decades."

I shivered as he slid a hand up under my tank top and found the hardened tip of my nipple. My body remembered the feel of his gentle teasing in the lab and wanted more.

Breathing hard, he pulled back. "Is it okay if we take this off?" He tugged on the hem of my tank softly. Even though his eyes were clouded with lust, I knew he would stop if I asked.

I nodded. And catching the hem with sure fingers, Alexi lifted the thin fabric over my head and deposited it on the floor.

"Wow."

Self-conscious under his gaze, I fought the urge to cover myself. Alexi kissed me softly before shifting me so that my head was closer to the headboard. He then settled his body between my legs, tracing a path of kisses from my lips to my jaw, to the sensitive hollow between my neck and my ear. Slowly, he brushed kisses over the tops of my breasts, and I held my breath.

Leaning down, he breathed soft kisses on first one, then the other nipple, each responding to his caress by instantly budding into hard little peaks. Focusing his attention on one, he drew the dark bud into his mouth, taking greedy tugs, while his thumb teased the other.

I bucked, and my back bowed as pleasure reverberated through my body. Alexi took his time, paying close attention to how I responded to his tongue and to the gentle use of his teeth.

Too impatient to wait, I tugged at his T-shirt and half dragged it off his body. With a chuckle, he released my breast long enough to discard the shirt. When he resettled into position, I sucked in a sharp breath. The heat of his skin nearly set mine on fire.

I traced my palms over the skin of his arms to his wrists. Some of his bracelets shifted, and I could feel faint ridges over his arms. What were those?

My gaze searched his looking for answers. I found them in a kiss. "We all have scars," he whispered before his teeth nipped my bottom lip.

Tingling started in my spine. I couldn't form a single coherent thought. The only way I could communicate was to hold his head in place and to rock my hips into his body.

Lex took his time, with a little lick here, a little nibble there. All the while his thumb and forefinger gently tugged at my sensitive nipples, sending stabs of need to my core.

I could feel every inch of his hardness throbbing insistently between our bodies, begging for attention, but still, he didn't rush. Didn't make any move to remove the rest of our clothing, just kept on leisurely kissing me and teasing my nipples.

He skimmed the flesh of my belly and the curve of my hip. I held on tight to his shoulders when he paused at the waistband of my teeny tiny shorts.

He lifted his head, and I had to force open heavy-lidded eyes.

"Are you okay with this? I would really like to touch you if you'd let me."

I gave him a vigorous nod. After all, it would eventually be my turn, and I was dying to have unfettered access to his body. "Yes. It's okay."

With what sounded like a muttered exaltation, his hand tucked under the waistband of my shorts and my underwear and slid immediately to my slick folds. Suddenly unable to breathe, I could only grip his shoulders tighter.

Sure fingers slid through my lips, seeking my center. Alexi met my gaze as he found his quarry. Silver eyes, wild with lust, gazed at me, watching my reaction as his questing finger found the center of my torment.

I cried out as he gently sank into me. Alexi held perfectly still except for his questing finger, gently exploring and retreating. Occasionally detouring to swirl around my clit, but always returning to delve just a little deeper inside me. "Jesus, you are so tight. So hot..." He bit his bottom lip as he sank in with two fingers, and his thumb traced circles on my clit.

Molten heat spread through my body. I parted my legs to give him even better access to my folds. "Alexi..."

"Do you have any idea how fucking sexy it is to hear you say my name. Like I'm the only one who can make you feel like this."

My whole body coiled with tension. If I could just... "Alexi, I—"

He kissed my jaw, then whispered. "Tell me what you like. Help me make you come."

Distress chased away some of the burning need. I didn't know what to tell him. Didn't know how to let go. I shook my head. "I... I've never... I don't know how..."

He paused and studied me, brows drawn down. "Are you saying that you've never had an orgasm?"

I shook my head and sighed. "On my own yes. Just not *with* anyone. I'm sorry, I don't think I can. I should have told you. I —" I squeezed my eyes shut, too embarrassed to look at him.

"Abbie." He kissed me softly. "C'mon, look at me. In here, it's just you and me. Why don't you tell me if something feels good, and we'll start from there. What do you think? Can you do that for me?"

Slowly, I nodded. "Yeah, I think I can do that."

"How about this? Does this feel good?" He slid both fingers out of me and focused his attention on my clit, making small circles with his thumb.

"Yes."

"Good. That's an excellent start. Now, do you want me to go harder or softer?"

He started nuzzling my neck again driving me mad with his teasing. "Harder."

He immediately adjusted his pressure. "How's the speed?" His kisses trailed back down to my left breast.

My back bowed as his lips wrapped around the tip again. If he could just... "Faster, please faster."

Lifting his head slightly, he released my breast to ask, "What about if I add a finger. Do you like that?" He slid his middle finger back inside my depths, and he hissed. "Fuck, I will never get over touching you like this."

He began a rhythm of sucking on my nipples that he paired with the stroke, retreat, stroke, and retreat of his finger while he circled my clit just how I liked.

My legs trembled, and heat tapped up my spine. "Alexi?"

"Yeah. That's it sweetheart. Let go. I have you."

"Oh, God!" Stars danced on the edges of my vision, and my climax rocketed through me as I held on tight to Alexi.

Even as waves of pleasure pulsed through my body, he continued to stroke me gently until I lay limp in his arms. He tucked me against him and wound his arms around me tightly. "You are so fucking gorgeous."

As the hazy fog of sleep threatened to drag me under, my brain clamped onto the knowledge that I'd only taken pleasure, but not given any. *Damn.* I hadn't gotten to explore very much at all. He'd distracted me with his very skilled fingers. Leaning up, I placed an open-mouthed kiss on his jaw.

He groaned and held me still. "Sweetheart, I'm holding on by a thread here. You start kissing me again, and I'm going to explode."

"But you didn't..." I tried again. "I didn't get to..."

He caught on quick to my meaning. "That's not what this is about. You let me touch you. That alone felt like Christmas and my birthday wrapped into one. There's no rush."

"But—"

He kissed my forehead. "But nothing."

I sat up a little. "But I want to touch you." It was true. I was curious. I wanted to drive him crazy. Wanted to explore his body. Have fun playing. I'd never really reveled in someone's body before.

He squeezed his eyes shut and lay his head back on the

pillows. "And believe me when I say I *want* you to touch me. But I'd like to take some care with you. You matter to me. And I don't want to cock it up by moving too fast. Do you understand?"

I nodded slowly. Where the hell had he come from? "I understand."

"Good." He settled me back against him, tucking my head under his as he held me. "Now maybe you can go ahead and tell me what kind of twat your ex was that he never made you come."

Heat crept over my skin. I'd known I'd have to answer this question eventually. I had just planned on having more clothes on to do it. "I—uh, I've only had one serious boyfriend since I was sixteen."

His brows shot up. "Just the one?"

I sucked in my bottom lip and raked it with my teeth. "Yeah."

There was a beat of silence. "Were you ever with anybody before him?"

I shook my head. "No. I figured I was the problem. I even went to see a doctor about it. She told me it was perfectly normal, that lots of women couldn't. I guess it turns out that I can."

I could feel him nodding. "Yes. Yes, you can." I heard the smile in his voice, and I swatted his arm.

"Modest, aren't you?"

"Nope. Not even a little bit. And to be clear—I would very much like to see you come again and again... And—"

I giggled. "Yeah. I get the picture." My heart did a happy flip, even though my brain tried to quell it. No need to get ahead of myself. No matter how hot Alexi was, I still didn't know him very well. But know him or not, I knew how he made me feel. And I liked it.

"Good. As long as I'm clear." He was silent for several minutes before asking, "So, do you have any plans on Saturday?"

My heart went from slumberous thudding to galloping, in seconds. "Probably getting some shots. Why?"

"That photo op I mentioned in Brixton, it's on Saturday."

Like a date? "Photo op?" I couldn't make my brain work properly.

"Yeah it's a party for the rich and bored." He examined one of my braids closely. "C'mon. I want to see you. You need to work. We'll kill two birds with one stone. What do you say?"

Hell yes. But I hesitated. Could I really do a London society thing? It was one thing to flit about the nightlife. It was a whole other thing to stroll into a garden party as a guest. "I'm not sure. It's not really my kind of crowd. Pretty sure I'd stick out like an elephant in a herd of gazelles."

He kissed my nose. "You'll be *my* guest. Don't worry about everyone else."

I liked the idea of being his guest, but still. I'd never fit in with Easton's friends. I'd always felt like the imposter. *He is not Easton.* "Sure. I'll come."

"Brilliant. Then afterward we can go out to dinner. I can show you my London."

I tucked my head and kissed his chest. Was it bad that the only part of London I wanted to see was him? "Sounds like a plan." And because I couldn't help myself, I kissed him again.

"Woman, didn't I tell you that you're killing me."

I grinned. "Sorry." Was this me? Lying in bed with a man, enjoying myself and not praying for him to drop off so I could finally relax enough to sleep myself? I liked the new me. I could certainly get used to this.

Alexi spent the next hour kissing me and asking me questions about my childhood until the gray light of dawn broke through the shadows of the night. He groaned. "I really don't want to leave you."

I didn't want him to go either. "St—"

He interrupted me by kissing me. "Don't say it. You tell me to stay, and I will. And that would mean a whole bunch of nosy questions. And frankly, I would like to keep you to myself for a bit, if that's okay with you."

I sighed. "You're right. You should go."

Thanks to more kissing that nearly got out of hand, it took him another ten minutes to leave my room. But when he finally slipped from my bed, I wished I'd had the courage to tell him to stay.

I FIDGETED with my camera as I waited outside the estate. The home was set on a sprawling lush lawn, complete with a garden maze. This was the stuff fairytales were made of. *Right.* Fairytales for *other* people. This did not look like my kind of party at all.

You are here for work. To make actual money, so suck it up.

Xander wanted me to photograph love. Easier said than done.

I snapped a few pictures, but nothing depicting love. Though I might be able to use some for later assignments.

I'd spotted Alexi as soon as I'd arrived, but he'd been engaged in conversation with a striking brunette, and from the angle of both their heads, it looked like an intimate conversation. When Alexi's hand rested on the brunette's waist, my stomach knotted.

I was just about to turn around when he looked up and beamed at me. "There you are."

I plastered a smile on my face through gritted teeth as he

approached with the same gorgeous brunette. Though surprisingly, the brunette smiled at me warmly.

"So, you must be Abbie. I'm Gemma. Lex has been telling me all about you and your photography. It would be lovely to have some candid shots of the party."

I had to look away from her startling beauty, and I fought not to stare at my shoes. I tried hard to swallow the bitter bile of jealousy, but it still stung to see Alexi with another woman, considering how he'd made me feel two nights ago.

"Of course. I appreciate the opportunity." I hoped that didn't sound as wooden to them as it did to me. It must have, because Lex frowned. I ignored his downturned features. "So, where do I start?"

Gemma led the way. "We'll have you go in through the side entrance. Mother will have a cow if you go in through the front and aren't a guest who will get into OK magazine."

I ground my teeth. So I was expected to shuffle in through the back like the help. Why the fuck had I agreed to this? I didn't belong here.

Because at the time Lex asked, I'd been in a hazy stupor of lust that I hadn't understood. Now I realized I wasn't exactly here as Lex's date. Of course not. I only briefly met his impassive gaze.

Gemma led me through the side entrance, chattering the whole way about the accessible areas of the mansion, the kinds of photos she wanted, and who the most important guests were.

When Gemma excused herself, Lex drew me into the library. "What's the matter?"

I shook my head. "Nothing. Everything is fine." I'd misunderstood, and that was my mistake.

He frowned and studied me. "No, it's not fine. I can see by

how your shoulders have crept up near your ears. You're vibrating. Just look at me and tell me what's wrong."

What the hell was I supposed to say? That I was jealous? That I'd seen the way Gemma touched him like she was all too familiar with him and it was driving me nuts? Or that I knew we were miles apart in status? That he belonged here in the country estate and I, well, I did not. The bite of jealousy surprised me, and I didn't like it. "Please don't. I'm here to work. And like I said, I appreciate the oppor—"

"Don't do that," he muttered under his breath with a chaser of ice and heat. I inwardly recoiled and braced myself. But nothing happened. He was angry and still made no aggressive move toward me. "Don't do that prim and coolly pissed-off thing. It's not you. I thought we...." His voice trailed.

I ducked my head and fingered my camera lens. "Alexi, it's fine. You should go talk to Gemma. She looks like she needs you."

"I'm sure she can handle herself. Right now, I'm more concerned with you. I'm not sure what I did, but last time I saw you, we were good, right?" His voice pitched even lower. "Better than good, I recall."

Oh God, did he have to bring it up? I was acting like a jealous brat, and I knew it. He didn't deserve it. It wasn't his fault. I inhaled then let out a long slow breath. "I'm sorry. I'm just tense. I want this assignment to go well. And I saw... Never mind."

He frowned as he studied me. "Why won't you talk to me?"

"I have work to do," I whispered.

"Fine, but I'm not letting this go. You'll have to talk to me eventually."

Abbie...

For the next two hours, I snapped photos of revelers. Old men chasing around pretty young things. Old women doing the same. And all the while, my eyes were drawn to Alexi like a magnet. Every time he walked into the room, they would disobey the command to *not* look at him.

This was pathetic. I'd just decided to leave when I caught sight of him with an older gentleman who looked like Lex might in thirty years. Given his crossed arms, lack of expression, and the way his body leaned slightly away from the older man, it wasn't a pleasant conversation. On autopilot, I snapped the picture. Lex's beautiful face turned toward me, and in that moment, I saw pain and resentment and... longing.

Yeah okay. Time to go. He wasn't longing for me; that was for sure.

I fought the tide of people as we all headed into the center courtyard for an announcement. The lady of the house—who someone had pointed out as Gemma's mother—stood and addressed her guests. I only half-listened as I shoved a canapé in my mouth and took a quick sip of champagne. I was pretty sure it was frowned upon for the help to eat at this little soiree, but what the hell did I care? These were *not* my people.

Mrs. Eastmoore addressed the crowd, thanked them for attending the party, encouraged everyone to continue to enjoy the food, and announced that dancing would start shortly. Certainly not any kind of dancing that me or my friends would be into. I snorted and several guests turned to glare at me. Time to blow this pop stand.

Quickly, I checked the pictures I'd taken, praying some of

them would suffice. The majority were lackluster, but I could use some from last week in a pinch. I wasn't going to squeeze any love out of this crowd.

Of their own volition, my eyes scanned the grounds for Alexi, and once again found him talking animatedly with Gemma. Pain knotted my belly. I'd told him I didn't want to talk to him, but that didn't mean it didn't sting to see him obviously so comfortable with Gemma.

Turning a circle in the wide hallway, I decided it was probably best to go out the way I'd come in before I got lost and trapped in this cross between *Downton Abbey* and British Stepford hell.

With my camera bag slung over my shoulder, I shuffled out the side door without anyone seeing me. My mind had already turned to the long hot bath I needed when I heard the shouting.

"How could you be so stupid? Do you understand how you made me look?"

My skin prickled as a chill settled around me. A fear and anxiety cocktail made a roiling, boiling science project out of my stomach. "Mind your business, Abbie," I mumbled to myself.

But as I bypassed the side garden, my feet rooted to the grass. When I saw the contorted features of a hulking man as he screamed in the face of a barely five-foot-five redhead, adrenaline coursed through my veins.

Over the years, I'd never told anyone how Easton had treated me because I was too embarrassed that he'd hit me. I could have been one of those statistics if I hadn't finally had enough. But what if I'd had someone to step in when I needed it? He might never have hit me in the first place.

He's bigger than you, and this time you're not brandishing a weapon.

I shook off the doubt demon that climbed onto my back. This was the right thing to do. It didn't matter that fear and doubt were like two sets of chains holding me back, begging me to turn away and mind my own business.

When I spoke, my voice wobbled. "Hey, are you all right?"

The redhead didn't even look at me, just mutely nodded. The man though, he glared. With all his fury directed at me, my steps faltered. "Just remember, he's a coward at heart," I mumbled to myself. *Yeah, easier said than done.*

"What the fuck do you think you're doing? Aren't you the help? Mind your fucking business," he snarled.

Anger had me cocking my head. My voice was steadier now. "You see, I would love to mind my own fucking business, but you're out here bullying a woman half your size and screaming the house down, so you've made it my business." Without taking my eyes off the man, I asked the woman again, "Are you sure you're okay? You don't have to stay here with him. We can go to my car, and I can drop you anywhere you like."

I desperately hoped this douchebag wasn't the woman's husband or something. Even as beads of sweat ran rivulets down my back, still, I inched closer. "My friends are inside, and they'll take care of you too if you want." I prayed Alexi would fulfill that promise, I just knew I had to get this woman away from this man.

"N-no, it's okay. I'm okay. It was my fault really, I—"

Echoes of my own life flashed in my head.

I took another step until I stood next to the woman, close enough to shove her out of the way of a fist, if one came. The man backed up, but his face was beet red, and the vein in his forehead had started to throb.

I licked my lips. "Look, why don't you take a minute to think this through. In the meantime, we'll go in the house." *Call the cops.* "We'll have a drink." *Escape out the front door.* "Then you two can talk this out." *Yeah, with your sorry ass behind bars.*

His words came out clipped and extra crisp with his accent. "Who the fuck do you think you are? Do you have any idea who I am? I will ruin you. You have no business butting into an argument between me and my wife."

Oh hell. She was married to this douche? In that moment, I knew the woman wasn't going to run away or call the police or do anything that she should. She was going to go on pretending everything was okay. *Like I had.*

"Consider me a Good Samaritan, making sure she was okay. You're nothing more than a bully."

Tendrils of fear snaked out and wrapped themselves around my spine as the man snapped a meaty hand around my upper arm. I winced inwardly as he applied pressure. Outwardly, I schooled my features to read disdain.

"What the hell is going on here?"

Even though I couldn't see Alexi, hearing his voice was enough to put me at ease. "I saw this woman here needed some help getting away from her idiot of a husband. Now he thinks it's a good idea to manhandle me."

The man advanced a step, and Alexi was at my side like a flash. "Sir Richard, my friend was just leaving."

Whiskey Tango Foxtrot? Alexi knew this asshole? Anger made my voice waver, and I hated it. "He was going to hurt her. If I hadn't stepped in—"

Ice dripped off of each of Alexi's words. "Maybe you didn't hear me, Abbie, but it's time to go."

I tore my arm loose from the oaf's grip and glared at Alexi.

Why the hell was he so furious with me? Had I broken some rich elite code? "I didn't do anything wro—"

The woman beside me shook her head. "Oh, no. You must have misunderstood. We were just having an animated conversation. My husband would never hurt me."

I stared at the redhead incredulously. He'd been gripping her so tight I could see hints of bruising on the woman's arms. But she was going to back up this asshat? I turned to face Alexi, and I saw we weren't alone. Gemma and her mother had followed him.

The older woman stalked over to the red-headed woman. "Emily, Richard, you'll have to forgive Alexi and Gemma's guest. Obviously, she misunderstood and shouldn't have gotten involved. Emily, why don't I take you inside so you can freshen up?"

Alexi stood firm by my side, but I could feel the chasm between us widening. "I'm not lying, Alexi. He was going to hurt her."

"Gemma, do me a favor and make sure Abbie gets the fuck out of here."

The bottom fell out from my stomach. *He doesn't believe you. In his world, things like this are par for the course.* And he was clearly pissed that I'd embarrassed him.

"You know what? Forget it. I'm done here anyway." Hot tears spilled onto my cheeks as I stalked out of the garden.

I RELAXED ONLY MARGINALLY as Abbie retreated. Fury nearly blinded me when I'd rounded the corner of the garden and seen the prick's hands on her. My first instinct was to give in to the violent rage that simmered just below the surface. The rage that had saved my life all those years ago. The rage I'd promised to never lose control of again.

But if I'd done that, I would have scared the hell out of Abbie. She would never look at me with trust again, and I didn't want that. Getting her the hell away from the arse was the only solution. She'd sounded hurt, but that couldn't be helped right now.

I stepped in Sir Richard Wembly's path as he stared after Abbie. "I think we've all had enough disagreements for one day. Wouldn't you agree?" The idea of that piece of shit going after Abbie made me want to kill something. And with my jiu-jitsu training, I would probably do some serious damage.

Rage clouded the older man's eyes as he shifted his focus from her retreating form to me. "If you know what's good for you, you'll stay out of my way."

I forced my body into a relaxed pose, though I was anything but. I'd seen the bruises on Emily Wembly. I doubted that Sir Richard would attack me, but as the man had physically assaulted his wife and just tried to go after Abbie, I stayed alert.

My family had known the Wemblys all my life. Not once had I ever had any inclination that Sir Richard was anything other than the refined member of Parliament that he appeared to be. *Until now.*

The look he had given Abbie had said it all. The refined politician was the mask. This was the real man, and he was no better than a schoolyard bully. If I hadn't come when I had, Richard would have hurt Abbie, would have continued hurting his wife. The angry savage inside reminded me how good it would feel to give this fool his comeuppance.

"I'm not staying out of your way. You are clearly having a problem controlling your anger."

"Where do you get off, you little shit? Just because I've known your family for a long time doesn't give you the right to be so familiar with me."

I let icy menace slide into my voice as I spoke. "Sir Richard, if I were you, I would listen very closely. Just because you sit in Parliament doesn't mean you control the world." I stepped into the older man's physical space and squared my shoulders. "Nick Wexler is a very good friend of mine. I seem to recall him saying you lack a way with cards. I'm sure you would hate for that to become public knowledge. After all, news like that would endanger your political career. You know the public hates a scandal."

The older man blanched then backed up a step. "No one would believe a pissy little upstart like you. One word to your father, and you're done. Cut off."

I let all the menace I felt bubble to the surface. "I'm sure you've heard the rumors about me and my brother."

The older man went pale.

I continued, projecting a calm I didn't feel. "I'm sure you wouldn't want to find out if they were true or not." It cost me a sliver of my soul to bring those early memories to the forefront, but I needed to make a point. "If I see your wife looking a little worse for wear ever again, or if I find out you bothered my friend, you might meet the same fate as Silas McMahon."

I didn't bother to see how the older man reacted. Instead, I turned on my heel and went after Abbie.

━━━

Abbie...

After an hour and a half of driving Faith's car through the slogging rain, I let myself into the empty apartment. I tossed my keys on the kitchen counter and went straight for the wine. I knew Faith needed some time with her man, but I could really use my best friend.

After pouring myself a large glass with shaky hands, I quickly changed into sweats before sitting down with my laptop, camera and turning on a DVR'd episode of *Eastenders*. But I wasn't in the mood to attempt to look through any of the pictures I'd taken.

But Faith was in Dublin with Liam, and Sophie was off to Jersey with Max, so I was all alone for the first time since I'd come to London. It gave me too much time to think, and my brain replayed the scenario from the afternoon over and over and over again. Had I done the right thing? *Yes.* Should I have gone with some back up? *Probably.*

It had been foolish, but I was glad to have been able to get that poor woman away, even if it was just for the rest of the party. She'd have to make her own choices when she got home. Adrenaline still coursed through my body, making my hands shake, and I very deliberately took a big gulp of wine.

The front door buzzer sounded, and I dragged myself from the relative comfort of the couch. With wooden legs, I trudged over to the answer box and pressed the buzzer. "Who is it?"

"Abbie, it's Lex."

Shit. What the hell was he doing there? I didn't want to see that look on his face again. The fury and disbelief I wouldn't soon forget. "Now's not a good time."

"Abbie, I want to talk. Please let me up. I need to see that you're okay."

Oh, really? He hadn't been too concerned about my well-being a few hours ago. At that point, he'd been more interested in keeping secret the fact that his close family friend was a wife beater. I depressed the buzzer again. "It's okay, honestly. I'm fine."

Lex's smooth voice came over the speaker again. "Abbie, I'm begging you, just hear me out. Just for a minute? I'd rather not have this conversation out here for the whole world to hear."

I'd rather not have it at all. But the truth was I *wanted* to hear him out. Wanted to hear some explanation that would make up for what he'd done. Needed to hear that he believed me.

I buzzed him in and opened the door before taking back my post on the couch.

When he strode inside, the air left my lungs. Every time I left him, I literally forgot just how beautiful he was. And then, when I saw him again, it all came crashing into me. "What do you want, Alexi?" For the most part, I ignored him, only catching his exploration of my flat from the corner of my eye.

"I like your place. It's cozy and girly, but not in a bad way. You've got nice smelling stuff everywhere and actual grown up things. I bet your kitchen drawers are full of all kinds of cooking utensils I've never even heard about."

I wasn't in the mood for his teasing. "Can you say whatever the hell you have to say and get out? I have to do some work."

"Are you headed back to the library to print canvases? I could give you a ride and then—"

I cut him off with a look. "And then what? We'll nearly screw each other in the lab again? I'm not interested in being with someone who doesn't trust what I say."

He cursed as he sank down into the couch next to me. As he spoke, he ran a hand through his hair. "Is that what you think? You think I didn't believe you?"

"You were clearly pissed at me. Look, I know that's not how you people do things in the rich circles, but I saw someone who needed help, so I acted. You had no right to yell at me like that."

He scrubbed a hand over his face. "I fucked up. I wasn't yelling at you because I was angry with you. I just wanted you out of there so you wouldn't see me lose my shit and give the arsehole a proper beating. I didn't want you to see me like that."

He hadn't been angry with me? "But you looked furious. And the way you spoke to me. I—I thought..."

He shook his head. "I'm sorry that's what you thought. I didn't know if he would get violent, so I wanted you as far away from him as possible. When I saw his hands on you, it took every ounce of my control not to knock his teeth down his gullet. It made me want to lose control and hurt him. *Bad.* That man is a piece of work."

I clutched the blanket tighter, leaning back as far away as the couch would allow and sniffled deep. "I thought you didn't believe me." I swiped at my nose with the back of my hand. "I'm not a liar, Lex."

"I know. I swear I know that. I'm sorry. I wish I could explain. I saw him trying to hurt you, and it was like my whole body seized. I wanted him dead," he finished on a whisper.

Her body trembled.

"Abbie, why didn't you just come in and get me when you saw them?" Frown lines marred the skin on his forehead.

You seemed busy. I swallowed the flare of jealousy. "Well, I didn't really think. I just saw them and acted. He's twice her size. I was worried he'd hurt her. I thought if he knew someone else was there and watching, he'd stop. I guess I was wrong."

"That was dangerous. You can't do things like that. You could get seriously hurt."

He might have had a point, but I wasn't letting it go. I glared at him. "I know. But I literally couldn't stand by and watch and not do anything. I just kept thinking, what if—"

His voice lowered. "What if, what, Abbie?"

The tiny voice told me to shut the hell up. To not spill the nightmare that kept me up most nights. "Nothing."

He took my hand in his, but I pulled it back. "Tell me, please. I want to understand. What if, what?"

I shook my head, unable to put voice to the pain I carried around. "Nothing, Alexi. Let it go."

He shook his head. "No. If we're going to do this, I want to know what's scaring you. What aren't you telling me? Whatever it is, I can take it."

My lungs constricted, and I thought they would explode if I didn't just breathe and get it out. "I kept thinking what if someone had seen Easton with his hands on me. Could it have made a difference? Would it have stopped him from hurting me?" With the gates now open, I didn't dare look at Lex. Instead, I dropped my head into my hands.

His voice was icy but barely audible when he spoke. "He hit you?"

I could only nod as sobs constricted my vocal cords. I could feel him nearly vibrating next to me.

"Is that why you're so uncomfortable with touching?"

I wiped away the tears and forced myself to face him. If I could look at him now, maybe I was strong enough to face everything. "I—I don't like surprise touches. Don't really do hugging. I generally stay out of striking distance." I shook my head. "I've never told anyone but my mother before."

"And she didn't have him arrested?"

My chuckle was harsh and mirthless. "She pretty much told me to suck it up. Told me how lucky I was that someone like Easton Peters would want me. With his parents' money and connections, I'd be set for life if I could figure out how to keep him happy."

"Fuck," he muttered through clenched teeth. "I'm sorry, but I'm not a big fan of your mother." He rubbed his jaw. "Wait, does he know where you are or how to find you?"

I shrugged. "He knows I'm in London. Not even my family knows exactly where to find me. But they have my number, and my mom gave it to him. I don't know how the system works here. I'm more than a little worried he'll show up to drag me home."

Alexi hung his head. "Is the phone in Faith's name?"

"No. Sophie's. Why?"

"Well, most people port their numbers and take them with

them. The system is so backward that it likely will have Sophie's last known address attached to it. We can check on that."

I shook. I'd hadn't given any thought to Easton finding me. I should have taken more precautions. But then I reminded myself that the last time I'd seen him, he'd been on the business end of a knife. He wouldn't likely underestimate me again. "I'll need to check and change it if I can."

"And every time I've seen you, I've given you no reason to *not* be afraid of me. I've practically mauled you every chance I had."

No. He couldn't think that. "Alexi. Don't. You're the first man I haven't been afraid of in five years."

"Don't do that, Abbie. Don't gloss over how I've treated you. I knew something was up, but I pushed you too fast. Any time we've been alone, I've put my hands all over you. Jesus, I'm a prick."

I put a hand on his knee. "Stop, Alexi." The sound of his name on my lips must have calmed him a little because the tension ebbed out of his shoulders. "From the moment you pulled me off the street, I've felt safe with you. In the first thirty seconds I knew you, my instincts told me I was safe with you. I knew you wouldn't hurt me."

"God, Abbie, I wish I'd known. I've probably been freaking you out these last couple of weeks."

"No. You've been opening my eyes." And that was the truth. I didn't have to live in a constant state of fear with him. It was easier than it ever had been with Easton. Even though there was a hazy edge to Alexi, I'd known from the beginning he would never hurt me. Physically anyway.

"Can I ask you a question?" He gazed at me through lowered lashes.

Now that my deepest darkest secret was out, I didn't have anything left to hide. "Yeah, shoot."

"How did you get the courage to break up with him? Men like that are dangerous."

"Well, what I told you was the truth. When I found out he hid my acceptance letter from me, hid my dream from me, I snapped. It was like someone splashed ice water on me, and I finally woke up." I tipped my chin up. "He hit me for the last time that night. I pulled a knife on him and told him to get the hell out."

His eyes bugged. "You pulled a knife?"

A faint smile pulled at my lips. "Yeah, I can't believe it either. London was the dream I had been holding onto, and if he'd had his way, I would have never gotten to realize it. He made me feel like I wasn't deserving of it. That last time, as the pain ran through me and I could taste the blood in my mouth, I'd just had it. I knew if I stayed, he'd eventually really do some damage, so I turned on him with the knife I'd been using to cut the onions for lunch." A nervous giggle escaped. "You should have seen the look on his face."

"I can imagine. But that was so dangerous. He could have really hurt you."

Yes, he could have. But he'd already done enough to me. At the time I hadn't been thinking about that. I'd only been thinking about getting him the hell away from me. "I suppose so. At any rate, I had the locks changed that night and packed. Told my sister to get movers for his stuff then rent my place out. The plan was to run here for a fresh start. But, turns out he anticipated me trying to leave him. He'd shredded my passport and torn up my birth certificate, so I moved back home and had to wait a full month to get a new one. He used that time to try and weasel his way back in through my family."

Slowly, Lex scooted closer to me. He took care not to make any sudden moves but ever so slightly reached for my face, then stroked his thumb over my cheek. "Is it okay if I hold you for a minute? Your flatmates aren't due back any time soon, are they?"

I turned my face into the caress. "It's okay. Faith and Sophie are out of town for the weekend."

He still didn't move. "If I do anything to scare you, just tell me, okay?"

I nodded, and he gently drew me to him, tucking me against his chest. Together we lay there, and I let the sound of his heartbeat soothe me.

I wasn't sure how long he held me before I had the courage to say, "I'm sorry I freaked out on you at the beginning of the party. Just seeing you two together, it was like seeing the picture that should be. I knew I didn't belong."

His fingers stroked my arms gently. "What do you mean?"

"I mean, look at you two. You fit. Gemma's beautiful and intelligent. And you two clearly grew up in the same circles. And I am none of those things. I can just see the disaster that would be our two families meeting. My crazy African relatives with their wild gesticulations, your very British and very reserved relatives. In my head, it's total chaos. I know we don't make very much sense together."

He traced his knuckles over my cheek. "Gemma is my friend. Just a friend. I can't think of anyone else but you. The way you laugh, the way you look at things with wonder, the way you taste. And as far as crazy family goes, don't forget my Nomean side. That line is littered with coup de tats and assassination attempts. How's that for crazy? *We* fit, Abbie. I don't want you thinking that we don't."

His seductive voice rolled over me, and I tried to hold fast, but his hand had transitioned from my cheek to the back of my neck, and he was massaging the knotted muscles there. Coaxing me toward him. "Alexi, I—"

"Abbie, I want to be here with you. More than I want anything else. But I don't want to push too fast or too hard."

I shook my head. "You're not pushing me."

He pulled me up for a kiss. The brush of his lips against mine was soft and gentle. Completely undemanding. Just pleasant with a hint of electricity.

I drew back a little to meet his gaze, like the night he'd first kissed me. But unlike that night, I went back for more, and I melded my mouth to his. I wanted this, had wanted it since I'd met him. There were still some things to work out, but for once, I wasn't going to overthink things to death.

Lex slid his tongue into my mouth and stroked mine. The syncopated rhythm had my blood boiling in seconds. He dragged my leg over his lap so that I sat straddling him. The thick ridge of his erection melded against my hot core, and I moaned at the contact.

Oh, Jesus. Need and lust wove a heady blanket around us, leaving us completely oblivious to the surrounding world. The television became a distant memory as soon as his hands stole up my sweatshirt, closing around my breasts through my tank top. His thumb rolled over my nipple, and I shivered as I tried desperately to climb closer to him.

He dragged his lips from mine, and his breath came in ragged gulps. "Shit. Abbie. You are completely undoing me. I can't think straight."

Loving the heady feeling of making him lose control, I worked my hips again, and Alexi cursed against my lips. Leveraging us both off the couch, he secured my legs around his waist then muttered, "Where's your bedroom?"

I stiffened momentarily. I wanted this. with Lex, and he wasn't going to hurt me. "Um, down the hall at the end."

He nipped my lips playfully again. "You're safe with me."

I slid my hands into his hair and tugged gently. "I want this to happen. I want to know what it feels like to lose control with you."

He groaned and laid his forehead against mine. "You're killing me. You're not supposed to tell me that. Now I'm even less likely to behave myself."

"I don't think I want you to behave."

His eyes flared, and his hands flexed on my ass. "Are you sure?"

I nodded. "Just for once, I want to go after what I want. And you're what I want."

It took him seconds to get down to my room, and with a yank of my door, he had me deposited on my bed in even less time. He followed me down, leaning his body against mine. He nuzzled my neck first with his nose, then took quick, tiny, love bites. I clutched him to me.

Lex sat back and studied my face. He drank in the sight of me. "Do you have any idea how beautiful you are?"

I quickly averted my gaze, and he tipped a finger under my chin to bring my attention back to him.

"I mean it."

Lex traced the back of his fingertips against my cheek. My eyelids fluttered closed as I waited for a kiss. When none came, I opened my eyes to catch him watching me. "What?"

He shook his head. "I'm just looking at you. I want to freeze this moment in time."

When he kissed me, his mouth was soft, as if asking for permission. The tip of his tongue edged over my lips, and I parted them. In slow delicious licks, he explored my mouth, sliding his tongue against mine, comingling our breaths. Devouring me.

He tugged me up on the bed and smoothed his hands over my arms until I raised them over my head. Slowly, he tugged off my sweatshirt, then my tank top leaving me in just my bra and sweatpants. For a long second, he stared at me. He traced his fingertips over the overflowing lace cups of my bra just as I reached behind my back and unsnapped it. My breasts spilled forward, and Alexi groaned.

His eyes darkened from silvery gray to slate. "I have been dreaming of your breasts and how they taste since the other night."

Feeling a little self-conscious, I hesitated before sliding the garment off my arms.

The moment I was free from the satin, Alexi reached for me and kissed me again as he slowly set me back on the bed. His hands traversed the bared flesh from my waist to just beneath the soft flesh of my exposed breasts.

I wove my hands in his hair, luxuriating in the silky feel. His thumb traced the underside of my breast, and my breath caught. I lifted my hips off the bed, bringing my aching center in contact with his erection.

He groaned and squeezed his eyes shut. "I'm fairly certain that you're going to kill me if you keep moving like that."

Eager to test out his theory, I rocked my hips again, and Lex cursed under his breath. "Shit, Abbie, I'm trying to go slow here."

"How's that working for you?" I rocked again.

He molded his hand to my breast and rubbed his thumb in a circle over my nipple. "It's an exercise in control." Between his thumb and forefinger, he rolled the tight bud and pinched it softly. My hips bucked, and I cried out.

Lex nuzzled my breasts, kissing each one in turn. "How are you feeling? Still better than okay?"

I smoothed my hands over the hard ridges on his shoulders. "Y-yes. Just surprised."

"A good surprise or a bad surprise?"

"A good one," I responded softly. I'd never been this vocal in bed before. A small part of me worried I was doing it wrong. "A *very* good one."

"Excellent, let's see if I can't do that again." He latched his lips around my nipple and drew deep. The thick ridge of his erection aligned with my hot center, and he sent charged electric pulses to my core as he took long pulls from my breast.

My breathing was ragged as I called his name. "Alexi."

"Mmmm?" He turned his attention, and his expert tongue, to my other nipple.

"You're still dressed."

He pulled back and stared at my heaving chest, seemingly mesmerized. Sitting back on his heels, he yanked his sweater over his back and off his head. I sucked in a shuddering breath when I caught sight of the hard, muscled abs underneath. *Wow.* The other night, it had been too dark to get the full effect. He looked like he'd been chiseled out of stone. Surprisingly, he also had several tattoos. Something that looked like writing on his ribs and wrapping around his back. And a Gemini tattoo over his heart. But there wasn't much time to explore the beautiful man in front of me. Apparently, he had other plans.

He caught me staring at him and smiled. "Come to think of it, you're wearing too many clothes entirely." His hands tucked into the waistband of my sweatpants and my panties, and he tugged them down, smoothing them over my legs.

I jolted when I realized I was naked. The shocking vulnerability threatened to take hold, but I held it at bay by meeting his gaze directly. I could do this. I wanted this. He was so unbelievably sexy. And I'd already come to care about him more than I probably should, but I couldn't help that.

Mimicking him, I said, "You're still overdressed, Alexi."

He chuckled. "Okay, you might have a point there." Shifting off the bed, he yanked off his jeans and boxers and grabbed his wallet before discarding them. I tried to meet his gaze, but I couldn't. My eyes focused on his thick erection. I swallowed hard.

"Sweetheart, my eyes. They're up here."

Flushing, I dragged my gaze up to meet his. As if sensing my sudden hesitation, he kissed me again, slowly as if to tell me no pressure. What I'd wanted was a flash of heat and torn clothing. But he was giving me seduction. I was afraid of seduction. Afraid of wanting it. Afraid of needing it. "Alexi, I—"

He lifted his head. "You want me to stop?" His eyes pleaded with me to say no, but his set jaw told me he was prepared to.

"No. I just—I—" No matter what I tried I couldn't get the words out properly.

"Whatever it is, you can tell me."

I swallowed. "I don't have much experience. I haven't got a clue how to seduce or anything."

The smile that spread across his face was possessive. "You've been seducing me with your eyes, your smile, and your lips since the moment I met you. I'm about to die because I want you so bad, and you want to pretend you haven't got a clue how to seduce? Me thinks the lady wants to torture me some more." He nipped at my shoulder.

I giggled. "I'm serious. I need you to take the lead."

"And so I am. I want you so much I can't think straight. I can't focus. All I can think about most days is how you sound when you laugh. And how you taste. I can take the lead if you want, but don't worry about seducing me. I've been seduced since we fell into that puddle." He kissed me again. This time a little more demanding. Instead of teasing my tongue into mating with his, the kiss was authoritative. Skilled and insistent.

He shifted over me until he settled between my thighs, and I could feel the heat between us. His erection was mere inches from my slick core. One shift of my hips, and he'd be nudging my entrance.

Lex dragged his lips from mine and placed open-mouthed kisses along my jawline, the column of my throat, my collarbone. When he dipped to kiss my breasts again, I moaned just before his lips covered the pointed tip. With his hand, he teased the other nipple until I whimpered. Releasing my nipple, Alexi continued the path of hot kisses down my stomach, past my belly button. He nipped at my hip bone, and I squirmed. Was he going to—

Oh. God. Yes.

Alexi settled between my thighs and gave me a long leisurely lick to my heated center. I dug my hands into his hair. I felt him shiver, but he didn't stop the long expert strokes of his tongue, except to occasionally pause and suck on my flesh.

Electricity singed every nerve ending as he continued to lap at me. Quivers began deep inside my womb, spreading throughout my body until I thought I would crack under the pressure.

Lex's deft thumbs separated my flesh slowly. He slid a finger into me and murmured against my flesh. "C'mon sweetheart, come for me. I want you to come."

Perhaps his permission was all I needed. Maybe the sensations were too much. Maybe he was too skilled with his tongue. Maybe I knew he was the only man who could ever make me come. Whatever the reason, I broke apart in his hands, shattering into a million pieces as my orgasm rolled through me.

"Alexi."

He waited until I stopped shaking, then kissed the inside of my thighs and licked his way back up my body. He brushed his lips to mine briefly. "You are amazing. I'm dying to see that again." I flushed and looked away, but he turned me to face him. "You're beautiful, always."

Warmth bloomed in my chest and spread to my extremities. I was falling for him. There was no point in lying to myself. There was nowhere else in the world I would rather be.

I turned into him and kissed him, tasting myself on his tongue and pouring all the emotion I felt into it. He groaned into my mouth as I sucked on his tongue. Feeling emboldened, I trailed my hand down his chest. He drew in a ragged breath when I found what I sought.

"Oh, fuck, Abbie." His hips bucked, pushing his straining erection into my hand.

I trailed hot open-mouthed kisses along the column of his throat and relished in the feel of his stubble. When I found his nipple, his hips bucked again. With my thumb, I stroked the soft head of his length, spreading the moisture that had leaked.

Hovering my lips over his erect nipple, I whispered, "Is something wrong, Alexi?"

Something that sounded like a strangled moan tore from his chest, and he dug his hands into the sheets.

"I'll take that as a no." I brushed my lips over his taut nipple, and I felt the shudder that rolled through his body. Carefully, still milking his erection, I grazed his nipple with my teeth.

He bucked again, digging a hand into my braids, gently tugging my head back. "I swear to God, Abbie, you have to stop. Right now. If you don't, I'm not sure I'll be able to—"

I ignored him, instead grazing his nipple and pumping his erection again.

Before I knew what was happening, I lay flat on my back and he had my hands locked above my head, restrained with one of his. His hold was gentle, and if I'd wanted out of it, he would have let me go. And he kept most of his weight off of me, giving me space, showing me I could trust him with my body. "You're a very naughty girl."

Quickly, Alexi reached under the pillow and grabbed a condom. Rolling away, he sheathed himself before settling back between my thighs. He kissed me deep, and I widened my legs to accommodate him. His erection nudged me, and I moaned as he rocked inside.

"Wow." Alexi dropped his forehead to mine. He retreated an inch, then pressed forward again until he was fully seated inside me. "Abbie..." My name on his lips sounded reverent.

My gaze met his and immediately all my insecurities vanished. All my worries. None of it mattered anymore. In that moment, everything was perfect. I felt perfect.

The corners of his lips tipped into a lopsided smile as he retreated and sank back in. The need took my body again as he drove me higher and higher. I clamped my legs around his hips, and he muttered curses under his breath. When I pulled him to me for a kiss, he growled low in his throat.

I nipped his lower lip with my teeth, and he scooped his hands under my ass, lifting my hips to his. The new angle had him stroking a sensitive spot deep within, and I sobbed at the pleasure. My toes curled as I held onto him. Only when I murmured his name on a sigh did he stroke into me a final time, then cried out my name on his climax.

Lex...

Satiny heat slid across my body from chest to feet. I inhaled Abbie's ginger and pumpkin shampoo. She smelled so good, and she felt even better, warm and soft, tucked into my side. Cranking an eye open, I took in my surroundings. Everything in the room was white. From the curtains to the duvet to the wicker rocking chair in the corner. On the bureau were dozens of photos. And on the far wall, I recognized some of the photos I'd taken with Abbie.

Her deep, even breaths told me she was still out. I couldn't remember the last time I'd actually slept with someone. The few times I'd tried always ended up with a disastrous nightmare.

But with Abbie, I'd actually been able to escape my nightmares. More like I passed out after exhausting myself. I hadn't slept for more than two hours at a time in over a month. But with Abbie, all I'd dreamed about was her. Guilt pricked at my subconscious.

I had to deal with the Gemma situation. She'd encouraged me to go after Abbie at the party, but still, I had an obligation to her. But it was way past time for me to start living my life. Gemma would have to understand. And staying away from Abbie wasn't going to happen. It was almost as if she'd dragged me into her gravitational orbit with her wit, strength, and beautiful smile.

I picked up one of her slim braids and inspected the woven strands of black and lighter brown pieces as they shimmered in the soft morning light. She shifted in my arms, grinding her hips into my crotch, forcing a hiss from me as my semi-hard dick sprang to attention.

As if they were heat seeking missiles, her hips scooted back into mine, and I gnashed my teeth together, praying for control. She was so hot, so undeniably sexy without even trying.

What the hell had I gotten myself into? I wanted her more than I'd ever wanted anybody in my life. But if I wasn't careful, I'd lose her. I had too many balls to juggle. The safest thing for me to do was to leave her alone. But I knew I couldn't give her up. I wanted a thousand moments like this. Mostly because I was a selfish wanker.

She wiggled again. I continued to hold her and ignored the sweet agony. Fascinated by the contrast of my pale hand and her smooth, gleaming, dark skin, I stared as my thumb drew lazy patterns on her shoulder. I could ignore it, just for the pleasure of holding her.

Ah, who the hell was I kidding? I was moments away from waking her when she wiggled again. I wanted her. Again. Even though I'd had her three times in the middle of the night.

My hand rested on her hip and reflexively contracted when she scooted her ass further into my groin. I groaned. "Jesus, Abbie, I'm only so much of a gentleman. You do that again, and I'm not going to be responsible for what happens."

She giggled, and the sound was low and earthy, like she should do nothing but laugh all the time. "If you want to pretend later that I took advantage of you in your weakened and food-deprived state, then that's okay."

I grinned. "The authorities will eventually find me in here naked, half starved, tied to the bed, and horny, very horny."

She turned in my arms. "Now we're talking."

The shy looks and tentative touches she'd given me the other night were replaced by bolder, more confident caresses. She was no longer timid, but a woman completely aware of her sexual effect on me. Her delicate fingers wrapped around my erection, and she purred. My brain short-circuited, and I moaned as I pushed my hard length into her hand. She slid her soft palm over the tip of my dick, and I shuddered. I could come right now. With no effort, she'd reduced me to a pile of hormones. A pile of hormones with no brain that would have completely forgone the basics of survival for sex.

"Alexi," she whispered and kissed my chin.

Heavenly bliss radiated through my body, and all I could focus on was her voice and the way her soft hand worked me, bringing me closer and closer to the edge of oblivion. I'd wanted her for so long. Now that I had her, I couldn't control myself. That was a dangerous and heady combination.

"Do we have any more condoms?"

My eyes fluttered open as my brain had a panicked start. *Condoms.* Damn. We'd used three last night. I only brought a pack of four. If I was staying the weekend, we'd need more. *Lots* more. "I only have one left."

"Hmm, that is a problem. We can raid Faith's chest, but more than one, and she'd probably notice. We'll eventually have to go get some more."

I shuddered as her hand slid down to the root, then back to the tip again. The pressure she used was exquisite. Last night, between lovemaking sessions, we'd spent hours exploring each other's bodies. Touching, experimenting. In a few short hours she'd become an expert on how to drive me to the brink of madness.

Unable to take her teasing anymore, I snatched up my wallet, grabbed another condom and tore open the foil. I rolled away from her and quickly slid the condom on before rolling onto my back. "I see you like to tease me. You like the control."

She smiled at me. "A little."

"Then come here, love. Show me what it feels like to have you in complete control of my body."

She levered a bare thigh over my waist and positioned herself over me. As she slid down over the length of me, I knew how much danger I was in. I was falling in love.

I WOKE with a start to violent thrashing next to me. Quickly, I scrambled out of the way to avoid an arm.

"No, God, no, please stop. You're hurting me, please."

I shook as my heart thundered. What the hell was he dreaming about to provoke such a violent reaction? "Lex," I called out. "You're okay, you're having a bad dream." I watched him carefully, but he still tossed in the bed, with his legs tangled in the sheets. "Lex, I need you to wake up."

"Oh God, oh God, oh God, what did I do? What did I do? Everyone will know. What have I done?" His voice was tinny and raw, not like the man I knew, but more like a small child's. Shit, what was it they said about waking someone from a dream? Was I supposed to wake him or was I supposed to let it play out? Fuck me, I had no idea. But I sure as hell couldn't leave him like this. He might hurt himself.

Scooting marginally closer to him, I called out again, "Alexi. Alexi, it's me Abbie. I need you to wake up. It's okay. You're safe. I'm here, but you need to open your eyes now, okay?"

His head shook violently from side to side. "No, no, no, no, no. What have I done? What have I done?"

All right. That was enough. I had no idea what he was dreaming about, but I wasn't going to watch any longer. With a hand on his shoulder, I shoved him... hard. "Alexi, wake up!"

He sat up with a jolt, eyes wide and panicked. He stared at me, blinked several times, then sagged into the pillows.

I inched closer to him. "Are you okay?'

He cleared his throat. "Yeah. I'm fine."

"Fine? I hardly call that fine." I gestured to the tangled sheets around his legs along with sheen of sweat on his chest.

He scrubbed a hand over his face. "Sometimes I have nightmares. It's fine."

I frowned. That was no regular nightmare. "How long have you had them?"

He shrugged. "Since I was a kid. It's no big deal. I'm sorry you had to wake up to that. I usually sleep alone."

I tucked that bit of information away. Him sleeping alone was a very good thing. Although, that could also mean he kicked out his sexual conquests after the deed was done, which was bad, but I'd worry about that later. "I was really worried. How often do you have these nightmares?"

"It used to be only every once in a while when I was stressed, then in the last couple of months, they've been coming more frequently. A couple of times a week. Sometimes more than once a night."

"And you don't know what they're about or what's triggered them?"

His eyes shifted away. "No. I'm sorry I woke you. Let me make you breakfast."

I stiffened. I knew a dismissal when I heard one. He

seemed so relaxed now. No, scratch that, more like resigned. "Look, you don't have to talk about your nightmares with me, but don't act like I'm crazy, okay? I'm only trying to help, but I guess talking about you isn't part of the package."

He quirked a brow. "What's that supposed to mean?"

"I get it. You want me, but you don't actually want to have to talk to me."

"Shit, Abbie, it's not like that." He shifted in bed and the sheet slipped, showcasing his killer body.

I tried to focus on his eyes and his words, not his six-pack. "Then what is it like?"

"I don't know why I have them, and I mostly just deal with them. Don't be mad. Please. I'm not shutting you out. I'm not used to sleeping with anyone. So, I'm not used to anyone asking about them. If we're going to be sleeping together, I need to figure out what triggers them so I don't wake you or I can stop having as many, but perhaps that's something we can figure out later?"

I bit my lip. Maybe he wasn't ready to have this conversation, but we'd have to have it eventually. Just not today. "Okay. I can live with that."

He immediately changed gears. "So how about I make you breakfast?"

⌯▭▭⌯

Abbie...

An hour later, I smiled up at him. I could get used to this. Sexy, shirtless Alexi, making me breakfast. It really should be a crime to have him walk around like this. If I didn't have my camera in my hands, I'd be tempted to forget all about taking it slow with him.

He looked up from the sizzling sausage in the pan and gave me a devilish grin. "What are you staring at?"

"You." I snapped a photo, oblivious to the light or the surroundings or the composition. I only wanted to capture him as he was. I held up my camera. "Do you mind?"

Something flashed in his eyes, but then he shook his head. "Not as long as you're my photographer."

I giggled. "This could get very dangerous, very quickly. There's nothing sexier than a man cooking. Add to that he looks like you and he's running around shirtless, and..."

He raised a dark eyebrow. "And what?"

I grinned. "And you'd probably burn your sausage."

Laughter burst out of him, and he tossed a dishtowel in my direction. "You have a dirty mouth, Abena Nartey."

"You know, it's weird, you are *not* the first person to ever tell me that."

"Somehow, I had a feeling." He cracked eggs into a bowl one-handed, and I could only stare. Easton had never lifted a finger in the kitchen. Neither had my father, for that matter. My mother had forced me and my sisters to watch her cook from the moment we could sit in the highchair, so we would eventually be able to make okra stew, kenkey, and oxtail for our husbands.

He checked the fridge. "Do you have any mushrooms?"

"Oh, no. I'm allergic. EpiPen and everything."

He winced. "Got it. No mushrooms in your omelet then. I'll tuck that away for future reference. Is it bad? Like do you need the hospital or anything?"

"Not if I use my EpiPen right away. I usually just need to rest for a bit."

"That's pretty scary, Abbie."

I shrugged. "It's not so bad. Mushrooms are pretty easy to avoid."

I studied him intently and snapped another photograph.

"You keep staring at me like that, and I'm likely to forget I promised to nourish you."

"I can't help it. You're beautiful."

His skin flushed, and I snapped another photo. Was he embarrassed? "This can't be the first time someone has pointed out how good-looking you are."

He shook his head slowly. "No, not the first time. But it's the only time it's come from someone who mattered or didn't want anything from me."

I bit my lip. "Well, given last night, I want all kinds of things from you."

He groaned. "Jesus, Abbie, you're killing me. We actually have to leave the flat today, okay?"

"Why?"

He stalked toward me, then looped an arm around my waist and nearly crushed my camera between us as he kissed me. When he backed away, he ran his hands through his hair. "Because if I keep thinking about the fact that I have you here to myself, those pictures you're taking will get a whole lot naughtier."

"And that's a bad thing?" What was wrong with me? I was never this open with anyone. Sexual banter wasn't exactly something I did. With Lex, it came naturally, easily.

Alexi's smile sobered as he leaned forward on the kitchen counter. "So what are we doing here, exactly?"

I froze. "Wasn't that supposed to be my line?"

"When I want to know the answer to something, I ask."

I used my camera like a shield. This was not a conversation I'd mentally prepared for. "I'm not exactly sure."

He nodded. "Okay, then let me be blunt. I'm falling hard for you. I know it's soon. I know you are just coming off something, but I want you to be aware. You can take your time to figure things out. I'm not going anywhere."

He was falling for me? I shook my head, trying to right the fantasy. But all I saw was this half-naked, sexy, god of a man standing in my kitchen, making me breakfast. Everything inside me wanted to say yes. God, yes, that I wanted to be with him. But I didn't have a clue how.

"Alexi, I want you." I licked my lips nervously. "You're like this fantasy come to life for me. I'm having a hard time believing this is real. That you exist. That you want me. I—is it okay if I go a little slow? I've had crappy instincts for years. I want to be able to trust them again before I jump in with both feet."

Alexi turned down the stove then flipped the omelet. Slowly, he sauntered over to me with a smile. "Like I said, we'll take this as slow as you want. I can wait for you to figure out how to trust me."

"It's not that at all. I trust you. It's me I don't trust."

"Hush." He kissed my forehead. "It's okay. Just know that I care about you. We can figure out the rest as we go."

"You're sure about that? Our friends, at least Sophie and Faith, will start dissecting us with a microscope and very sharp scalpel. Can we just keep this between us for now?"

He studied me, his face inscrutable for a long moment. "As long as I get to see you, and I get to be with you, I don't care if you never tell them."

As man lotteries went, I'd won the freakin' jackpot. But I

didn't want him thinking I was trying to hide him. "I'll tell them. I just need to sort through everything first."

"Fair enough." He nodded. "Actually, I'm thinking, why don't we do something out of the ordinary?"

"Like what?"

"Have you been to Paris? We could catch the train, spend the night. Catch a flight back in the morning and I'd have you back before your class."

Paris? He was kidding right? "You're not serious."

He shrugged. "Why not? I could use a trip out of town for a bit. And it is the most romantic city in the world. And I'd love to show you some of my favorite spots. What do you say?"

This was his version of going slow? Except, Paris. The longing to live a fuller, more adventurous life pulled at me. But reality crashed in. I couldn't exactly afford Paris. If even for a night. "I wish I could, but funds are a little tight right now. I still don't have a job so it's not the best idea for me. But I would love to see Paris with you. I've never been."

He chuckled. "Silly, beautiful girl. I'm asking you to go to Paris as my guest. Think of it as our first date. How long will it take you to pack?"

As first date ideas went, okay, that was kind of baller. But a niggle of unease tickled the nape of my neck. "Alexi, I love the imagination, but that's too much. I can't let you pay my way to Paris."

"Why not?" His brow creased. "I owe you a proper first date. One where I take you out, and we eat and explore."

"And I don't object to that. Or ultimately to Paris. I just object to you paying for it."

"It's not a big deal. I want to."

And I wished that for once I could take the generosity and

not think about it, but I couldn't. "I'm sorry. It would make me feel funny. Like I'm being kept or something. I'd rather go somewhere on my own steam. Ya know?"

He nodded, but his frown remained. "It's only money, Abbie. I don't mind."

"But I do. Maybe we can have fun in this city instead. There's still so much I haven't seen or explored."

For a second it looked like he wanted to argue with me. But then his brow smoothed out and he kissed me softly. "Fine, have it your way. Now, go get a shower woman. Breakfast will be ready soon, then we're going to go out and have some fun."

"We could have fun—"

He laughed as he shook his head while waving a spatula in my direction. "We're going to have fun *outside*, so I don't lock you in this flat and torture both of us by taking my time with you over and over again until neither one of us can walk. Now go."

He swatted me on the ass before turning back to his cooking sausage. I could get used to these feelings. Freedom and excitement and longing.

***

Abbie...

This wasn't supposed to happen.

When I'd come to London, I'd been running. Running from myself, running from my past. Running from everyone. Running from *everything*.

I wasn't supposed to meet someone. Hell, I didn't even feel like a whole person or like I was capable of taking care of myself entirely. How the hell was I going to avoid making the same mistakes I'd already made before?

Already, I was too caught up. It was just too intense. He mattered to me too much. And it was terrifying because I was going to lose myself and there would be no coming back from this. If he broke me, or worse, hurt me, I wasn't going to recover. There was just no way. If I had been a shell of myself after Easton, I would be fractured and completely broken when Alexi hurt me.

Or, maybe he won't hurt you.

That was a nice thought, but a part of me knew better. Part of me knew that there were secrets he was hiding. Something he didn't want me to know. Part of me knew that he wasn't being transparent.

Or you're being paranoid. You think he's like Easton, so you're looking for reasons.

That was also true. As far as I was concerned, everyone was Easton. It was unfair. I saw Easton around the corner. I saw Easton in the face of every man that came within a foot of me. I saw Easton everywhere. Even when Ilani, or Sophie, or Faith made a quick movement, I saw Easton, preparing myself for the jolt of pain, the snap of surprise, the shiver of shame. I saw him everywhere. And that was on me. I had let him take over my life entirely. He'd been in charge of my emotions, my self-worth, and that was on me. Not on him. I had given up that much of myself and my power. And I wasn't going to do it again.

I was determined to do things I loved to do regardless of what that meant for someone else. Call me selfish. I didn't care. And being with Alexi felt selfish. It felt like the last thing I should be doing because it felt good, and it was fun, and he made me smile. So for that reason alone, I was going to keep doing it. The parts that scared me were the parts where I felt protected with him, because I wasn't giving up that kind of control ever again. And I didn't know how to separate the two.

That was probably something I needed to broach with Dr. Kaufman soon, but for the moment, it was fine. And I did feel safe with him, but there were a million ways to hurt me. There was something about him that told me my body was safe with him, that he would not bring physical harm to me. But that didn't mean he couldn't shatter my heart.

I wasn't going to think about it. I was going to enjoy what I had. And right now, that was orgasms.

I was a huge freaking fan of orgasms because I'd never had one with Easton. And knowing that I'd been missing out all this time made me want to kick my own ass for having lived with that for so long. Jesus! And my favorite part was that determined look Alexi would get on his face, eyes narrowed, determined, that oh-so-sexy smirk, knowing that he was going to have some fun playing.

That shit was just plain hot. And I got to enjoy orgasms just for the sake of orgasms. Not having to reciprocate. Not having to worry that I wasn't pleasing him. He just wanted to please me for pleasure's sake, and that was incredible.

Over the last two days, we had been entwined in each other. Emotionally. Mentally. Physically. We'd gone incognito wearing hoodies and sunglasses as we meandered around the South Bank, then headed west to the Notting Hill Festival. The whole day, my hand had been firmly tucked in his.

When I'd finally sort of kicked him out of my flat that morning, he'd grumbled, but also complained that he had work to do and that I was too enticing a distraction. I'd taken the opportunity to pick up my camera. It had been a few days since I'd taken any shots, and I wanted to get back at it. After all, that was why I was there. Falling in love wasn't part of that.

Who said anything about love?

No, not love. Falling in *like*. That was the thing, right?

The point was, I was there to study. And Alexi, while beautiful and enticing and fun, was not really at the top of the agenda. So, I needed to get back to it.

I headed toward Kingston Upon Thames in the morning, taking my usual stroll up to the 65 bus stop, traversing along the Thames and humming to myself as I walked. It wasn't raining, thank God, but I had an umbrella packed, just in case. The sky was gray, but that was London, though it wasn't bad in terms of temperature. Cool enough for a jacket, but I didn't need all the accoutrement of hat, gloves, and scarf. None of that. As I marched, I smiled. When I made it to the bus stop, I perched on the seat and turned back toward the river, shooting the rowers as they passed. When the bus arrived, I climbed on the second level. It was my favorite spot with a vantage point. I hadn't planned on getting off until Kingston, but the park we passed had some kind of kid's fair going on, so I hopped off there. They had some entertainers I could probably capture with my old striker, hopping on and off the bus as I pleased.

There were still some puddles around the bus stop, which I narrowly avoided by hopping. I bumped into a man dressed in all black and gave him a brief smile of apology. When his gaze pinned on me, icy blue, dead, flat, cold, I shivered. "Sorry," I mumbled and then scampered away from him as quickly as possible. The chill of the way he looked at me went bone deep. I made a mental note to avoid him again.

There was a funny thing that happened when people saw you with a camera. Immediately, they ran up to you with their cell phone. "Oh, would you mind taking a photo of us?" I didn't mind. I wasn't in a rush. And truth be told, I was happy. Not in that way of wide-eyed exploration, but in a way that sort of settled in the bones.

There were musicians and clowns in the park, and children laughed with delight while adults shook their heads in disbelief at the street magicians. Laughter was everywhere when the street magician guessed a card and then pulled it out of some girl's hair. It was as if everyone else could feel my joy and elation too.

I glanced over at the women's bathroom and I frowned. God, of course, there was a line. Could I hold it until I got to Kingston and find another bathroom?

No.

I trudged over as the first hint of drizzle permeated air. Ugh! Fantastic.

As I stood in the line, I shifted on my feet. The chill I'd experienced when I first stepped off the bus hit me again. I frowned and turned around, but I didn't catch any glimpse of the man with the icy blue eyes. A woman with a baby squalling in a stroller came up behind me, and she reached in to stroke the little baby's hand. It was a toddler about age three, doing the universal pain-in-the-ass cry.

"You can go ahead in front of me."

The mother fed me a grateful smile and so did the little boy. All full of baby teeth and something blue sticking on his lips.

The woman in front of me saw what I had done, and she rolled her eyes before stepping aside and saying, "Yeah, go on you two."

In a tick, the woman was up to the front, the toddler boy saved by the kindness of strangers.

I watched as two teenagers holding hands giggled and ran by to the side of the building.

I looked ahead of me, and at least six women stood in line outside, which told me at least two more were inside as we waited. I could step around and catch a picture of the young teenagers in love then come right back and still be in the same spot. I skipped around the corner.

But I couldn't find the couple. "Hello?"

I was going to sneak up on them and just photograph them in the moment. I hoped I could get a photo of them at least hugging or something.

The hairs on the back of my neck stood at attention again. Something told me, *run*.

But like all those times when I'd made Easton angry, the way that little voice had screamed inside me, *Run. Run away. Don't come back. Run.* I didn't listen.

Instead, I whipped around, ready to confront whoever it was giving me the heebie-jeebies because I refused to be afraid anymore. And there was the man with the ice-blue eyes. "Boy, you are a tough one to get a hold of."

"Why are you following—"

I couldn't finish my question. Something was shoved over my head and blackness surrounded me. *Jesus Christ...*

He was going to kill me.

To be continued in London Soul...

Thank you for reading LONDON ROYAL I hope you enjoyed the beginning of the London Royal Duet.

Before her, I was: Rich. Entitled. A possessive pain in the ass.

I thought love wasn't for me. And then I met her.

To save the woman I love, all I need to do is expose my secrets. Secrets that will have consequences for her and my crown.

Order London Soul now so you don't miss it!

And you can read Zia and Theo's story in Bodyguard to the Billionaire right now! Three words, Royal, Billionaire, Twins! A bodyguard who knows how to handle her weapons and Royal intrigue that will have you wondering who the killer is! Find out what happens when a filthy, rich billionaire hires a body double, but the simple plan goes awry. **One-click Bodyguard to the Billionaire now!**

> "... *Sinfully sexy. ...A nail-chewing heart-pumping suspense. It was a complete entertainment package."* --***PP's Bookshelf Blog***

Meet a cocky, billionaire prince that goes undercover in Cheeky Royal! He's a prince with a secret to protect. The last distraction he can afford is his gorgeous as sin new neighbor. His secrets could get them killed, but still, he can't stay away...

Read Cheeky Royal for FREE now!

Turn the page for an excerpt from Cheeky Royal...

UPCOMING BOOKS

London Soul
Royal Playboy
Playboy's Heart
Big Ben
The Benefactor
For Her Benefit

"You make a really good model. I'm sure dozens of artists have volunteered to paint you before."
He shook his head. "Not that I can recall. Why? Are you offering?"

I grinned. "I usually do nudes." Why did I say that? It wasn't true. Because you're hoping he'll volunteer as tribute.

He shrugged then reached behind his back and pulled his shirt up, tugged it free, and tossed it aside. "How is this for nude?"

Fuck. Me. I stared for a moment, mouth open and looking like an idiot. Then, well, I snapped a picture. Okay fine, I snapped several. "Uh, that's a start."

He ran a hand through his hair and tussled it, so I snapped several of that. These were romance-cover gold. Getting into it, he started posing for me, making silly faces. I got closer to him, snapping more close-ups of his face. That incredible face.

Then suddenly he went deadly serious again, the intensity in his eyes going harder somehow, sharper. Like a razor. "You look nervous. I thought you said you were used to nudes."

I swallowed around the lump in my throat. "Yeah, at school whenever we had a model, they were always nude. I got used to it."

He narrowed his gaze. "Are you sure about that?"
Shit. He could tell. "Yeah, I am. It's just a human form. Male. Female. No big deal."

His lopsided grin flashed, and my stomach flipped. Stupid traitorous body...and damn him for being so damn good looking. I tried to keep the lens centered on his face, but I had to get several of his abs, for you know...research.
But when his hand rubbed over his stomach and then slid to the button on his jeans, I gasped, "What are you doing?"
"Well, you said you were used doing nudes. Will that make you more comfortable as a photographer?"

I swallowed again, unable to answer, wanting to know what he was doing, how far he would go. And how far would I go?

The button popped, and I swallowed the sawdust in my mouth. I snapped a picture of his hands.

Well yeah, and his abs. So sue me. He popped another button, giving me a hint of the forbidden thing I couldn't have. I kept snapping away. We were locked in this odd, intimate game of chicken. I swung the lens up to capture his face. His gaze was slightly hooded. His lips parted...turned on. I stepped back a step to capture all of him. His jeans loose, his feet bare. Sitting on the stool, leaning back slightly and giving me the sex face, because that's what it was—God's honest truth—the sex face. And I was a total goner.

"You're not taking pictures, Len." His voice was barely above a whisper.

"Oh, sorry." I snapped several in succession. Full body shots, face shots, torso shots. There were several torso shots. I wanted to fully capture what was happening.
He unbuttoned another button, taunting me, tantalizing me. Then he reached into his jeans, and my gaze snapped to meet his. I wanted to say something. Intervene in some way...help maybe... ask him what he was doing. But I couldn't. We were locked in a game that I couldn't break free from. Now I wanted more. I wanted to know just how far he would go.

Would he go nude? Or would he stay in this half-undressed state, teasing me, tempting me to do the thing that I shouldn't do?

I snapped more photos, but this time I was close. I was looking down on him with the camera, angling so I could see his perfectly sculpted abs as they flexed. His hand was inside his jeans. From the bulge, I knew he was touching himself. And then I snapped my gaze up to his face.
Sebastian licked his lip, and I captured the moment that tongue met flesh.

Heat flooded my body, and I pressed my thighs together to abate the ache. At that point, I was just snapping photos, completely in the zone, wanting to see what he might do next.

"Len..."
"Sebastian." My voice was so breathy I could barely get it past my lips.
"Do you want to come closer?"
"I--I think maybe I'm close enough?"
His teeth grazed his bottom lip. "Are you sure about that? I have another question for you."

I snapped several more images, ranging from face shots to shoulders, to torso. Yeah, I also went back to the hand-around-his-dick thing because...wow. "Yeah? Go ahead."
"Why didn't you tell me about your boyfriend 'til now?"
Oh shit. "I—I'm not sure. I didn't think it mattered. It sort of feels like we're supposed to be friends." Lies all lies.
He stood, his big body crowding me. "Yeah, friends..."
I swallowed hard. I couldn't bloody think with him so close. His scent assaulted me, sandalwood and something that was pure Sebastian wrapped around me, making me weak. Making me tingle as I inhaled his scent. Heat throbbed between my thighs, even as my knees went weak. "Sebastian, wh—what are you doing?"
"
Proving to you that we're not friends. Will you let me?"
He was asking my permission. I knew what I wanted to say. I understood what was at stake. But then he raised his hand and traced his knuckles over my cheek, and a whimper escaped.

His voice went softer, so low when he spoke, his words were more *like a rumble than anything intelligible. "Is that you telling me to stop?"*

Seriously, there were supposed to be words. There were. But somehow I couldn't manage them, so like an idiot I shook my head.

His hand slid into my curls as he gently angled my head. When he leaned down, his lips a whisper from mine, he whispered, "This is all I've been thinking about."

Read Cheeky Royal now!

Royals United
Royal Tease
Teasing the Princess

Royal Elite

The Heiress Duet
Protecting the Heiress
Tempting the Heiress

The Prince Duet
Return of the Prince
To Love a Prince

The Bodyguard Duet
Billionaire to the Bodyguard
The Billionaire's Secret

London Royals

London Royal Duet
London Royal
London Soul

Playboy Royal Duet
Royal Playboy
Playboy's Heart

London Billionaires Standalones
Mr. Trouble (Jarred & Kinsley)

Mr. Big (Zach & Emma)
Mr. Dirty(Nathan & Sophie)

The Player
Bryce

Dax

Echo

Fox

Ransom

Gage

The Donovans Series
Come Home Again (Nate & Delilah)

Love Reality (Ryan & Mia)

Race For Love (Derek & Kisima)

Love in Plain Sight (Dylan and Serafina)

Eye of the Beholder – (Logan & Jezzie)

Love Struck (Zephyr & Malia)

The In Stilettos Series
Sexy in Stilettos (Alec & Jaya)

Sultry in Stilettos (Beckett & Ricca)

Sassy in Stilettos (Caleb & Micha)

Strollers & Stilettos (Alec & Jaya & Alexa)

Seductive in Stilettos (Shane & Tristia)

Stunning in Stilettos (Bryan & Kyra)

~~~

In Stilettos Spin off
Tempting in Stilettos (Serena & Tyson)

Teasing in Stilettos (Cara & Tate)

Tantalizing in Stilettos (Jaggar & Griffin)

The Shameless World

Shameless

Shameless
Shameful
Unashamed

Force
Enforce

Deep
Deeper

Before Sin
Sin
Sinful

Brazen
Still Brazen

Love Match Series
*Game Set Match (Jason & Izzy)
Mismatch (Eli & Jessica)

DON'T WANT to miss a single release? Click here!

USA Today Best Seller, Nana Malone's love of all things romance and adventure started with a tattered romantic suspense she "borrowed" from her cousin.

It was a sultry summer afternoon in Ghana, and Nana was a precocious thirteen. She's been in love with kick butt heroines ever since. With her overactive imagination, and channeling her inner Buffy, it was only a matter a time before she started creating her own characters.

Now she writes about sexy royals and smokin' hot bodyguards when she's not hiding her tiara from Kidlet, chasing a puppy who refuses to shake without a treat, or begging her husband to listen to her latest hairbrained idea.

Made in the USA
Middletown, DE
17 January 2021